NICK GAITANO

SPECIAL VICTIMS

A NOVEL

SIMON & SCHUSTER

NEW YORK

LONDON

TORONTO

SYDNEY

TOKYO

SINGAPORE

SIMON & SCHUSTER
Rockefeller Center
1230 Avenue of the Americas
New York, New York 10020

SIMON & SCHUSTER and colophon are registered trademarks
of Simon & Schuster Inc.

Designed by Hyun Joo Kim
Manufactured in the United States of America

10 9 8 7 6 5 4 3 2 1

Library of Congress Cataloging-in-Publication Data
Gaitano, Nick.
Special victims: a novel/Nick Gaitano
p.   cm.
1. Art —Collectors and collecting—Illinois—Chicago—Fiction. 2. Murderers—Illinois—Chicago—Fiction. 3. Police—Illinois—Chicago—Fiction. 4. Chicago (Ill.)—Fiction. I. Title.
PS3557.A3586S64   1994
813'.54—dc20
93–27253
CIP

ISBN 0-671-87014-9

In memory of Sparky: dearly missed,
forever remembered.

SPECIAL
VICTIMS

CHAPTER 1

T HE YOUNG WOMAN LAY DYING ON THE FRESHLY CHANGED, STERILE sheets of the hospital bed, and Arturo Alleo's wife was visibly upset because it didn't look anything like the way it always did in the movies. That would be her only frame of reference to a young person's death. But this was no movie, this was the real thing.

Mr. Alleo had done everything in his power to protect her from life's ugliness; had protected his wife and his darling daughter, Sophia. But he hadn't been able to protect either of them from one of the few powers on this earth that was even greater than himself: disease.

Mr. Alleo had watched this young woman and her mother, both of whom he loved as much as he was capable of loving anyone, sitting in front of the television, sobbing as a gorgeous Ali McGraw passed away in some stupid movie. Sophia didn't look like that, not this woman on the bed. She looked terrible, a battered angel who might not make it through the weekend. Dying, Mr. Alleo knew, was an ugly, brutal business.

Sophia didn't know that she was dying, no one had yet come right out and spoken the dreaded words. If she suspected she was, she didn't seem afraid. He'd seen men die, more times than he liked to remember, and it was never like this, they never took it so calmly.

Then again there was a difference between dying of liver failure and being shot three times in the head at close range. Sophia's face seemed drained of blood, lined far beyond her twenty-three years. Her once shapely body was now skeletal; the nightgown her mother had dressed her in sagged over bone, no longer filled out in any way at all. If the tubes were removed, she would appear to belong more in a casket than in an expensive and exclusive Chicago Gold Coast hospital suite.

Mr. Alleo had to look away, the sight was breaking his heart.

In his lifetime he had done terrible things, and, later, after his acquisition of power, he had ordered terrible things to be done to others in his name. He'd fought brutally for survival in his childhood home, first with his brothers, and then, later, when he was finally old enough, he had done vicious battle with the man who was his father. Later, he'd fought in Korea, and after surviving what they'd had to offer over there he'd come home, and Mr. Alleo had found his calling: violence. As a younger man violence had been almost like a drug to him, his aphrodisiac, arousing him, but those days were long in the past. Today he used his power reluctantly, and violence only when necessary. Today he wanted nothing more than to spend his golden years in peace.

But even when he was a man of violence, he'd never brought any of it home with him, his family had never been touched by it. Until now, until this illness had come into their lives and broken the heart that he'd thought had been burned out of his chest many decades ago.

He wished that he could trade places with her; he was sixty now, and had lived a full life. He'd seen more than most ten men would ever see in long lifetimes, done more than a hundred average men could ever dream of achieving. From a West Side slum to an Oak Park mansion, Mr. Alleo had risen, crawling over the broken backs of those who'd had the temerity to try and stand in his way. He'd carved his own royal flush out of the grotesque hand of cards that fate had dealt him, and he had no fear of death, thought that the devil himself trembled in terror at the thought of Arturo Alleo's arrival in hell. Why couldn't it have been him who had caught the disease, why did it have to be his daughter, his beloved Sophia?

He was feared, held in awe, from New York down to Miami. Italian villagers he'd never met spoke his name in whispers. He was welcomed into the homes of kings, and had twice dined with a president, but now his daughter lay dying, and he was powerless to keep her alive.

He fought the urge to smash his fist through the glass of the hospital room window. It would disturb his dying daughter, and would further upset his wife. Worse, it would show his impotence, would let the whole world know of his weakness. So he would fight the urge, he would have to. No man had ever seen him show even a trace of human frailty.

There was one slim hope, and he was waiting to hear about it now. A rumor had circulated last winter, when one of Mr. Alleo's more vicious colleagues had fallen deathly ill. The man—a savage killer who commanded his own crime family, second in power in the Midwest only to Mr. Alleo's own—had received a compatible heart for a transplant. It had been somehow delivered straight to the hospital, the red tape had been cut, all waiting lists waived. The reasoning had been that if he didn't immediately get a compatible heart, his minions would go out and find one on their own.

The thought had crossed Mr. Alleo's mind, but it was an impossibility, at least in his daughter's case. She had a rare blood type, which made her special, and that specialness now seemed to spell her doom.

What could Mr. Alleo do? For the first time in his life he was defenseless against an enemy. How could he mobilize the army at his disposal in a way that would save his daughter? He had no access to blood bank records, and even if he did, what would he be able to do with them? Find out where some other young girl was, a girl who had the same blood type? Then go and tear her liver from her body? He could rip it from her body without hesitation or guilt, to save his daughter it would be a pleasure. But even if could find such a woman, what would he do after that? The thing, a liver, couldn't last long, once it was out of the other young woman's body. How would he get it back here in one piece? Would he have to freeze it? Were there tubes that you connected to it in order to keep it alive until he could get it to the hospital?

And who would he send out to get it? The people who worked for him were loyal, to a degree, but you didn't have to show high intelligence to get into his line of work, and many of them were lazy by nature, always looking for shortcuts.

His hope lay in the family of the man who'd sought similar help last winter. He would owe them, and they were brutal peasants who would not hesitate to collect someday. But he would do anything they asked of him, if only they could help him save his daughter's life.

He walked out of the room and went down to the nurses' station, nodded at the woman behind the desk, then reached over and pulled the phone onto the counter without bothering to ask permission. He dialed a number, waited three rings, then nodded to himself when the surliness in the voice of the man who answered on the other end quickly turned to obsequiousness the second that he heard Mr. Alleo's voice.

13

"Did my message get through?"

"Yes sir," the man said. "I gave it to the man myself."

"I'm still here, waiting. You get the number right?"

The man told Alleo the number of the phone that was assigned to his daughter's room.

"Time's running out," Mr. Alleo said.

"Mr. A, the boss was happy to help. I took care of it, I put Lenny on it right away."

"Lenny? What's his last name?"

"Roman, he's called now, it *was* Romano." The guy was making conversation, acting like an equal. That might be the way the Eagle liked to act these days, but Alleo had no use for such nonsense. Listen to this idiot, still going on.

"He used to be a figher, a lightheavy, Mr. A, you might have seen him fight years ago."

"I don't have time to watch fights," Alleo said. He was trying to make a point here, to a man too dense to understand: If his daughter died, then this Lenny character would die. This man hadn't gotten the message. It wasn't like the old days, when what you *didn't* say was more important than what you did. This newer breed of soldier was stupid. You had to hit them over the head with a sledgehammer.

"What's *your* name?" Mr. Alleo asked.

"Thomas, Mr. A." The man did not sound very confident at all now. "Thomas Gerardi. Come on, we met a lot of times . . ." Were this man's *feelings* hurt? What was the Eagle surrounding himself with, prima donnas? Alleo remembered meeting the man, but decided to pretend that he didn't know who Gerardi was.

"Thomas Gerardi. I won't forget it. I won't be calling again." He hung up the phone. Let this over-familiar barbarian think about *that*.

He walked back into his daughter's room and his wife looked up, with hope. She was waiting for her miracle, for her *God* to intervene. And when Sophia died she would blame herself, as if their daughter's death would be punishment for her very own most terrible sins. Worse yet, Alleo knew his wife would blame him as well.

Alleo leaned over Sophia's bed and wiped, then kissed, her brow. He pushed her stringy, damp hair back, staring down at her with love.

"God help us," his wife said, tearfully. He hoped that Sophia did not see his grimace.

He sat down next to his wife and took her hand in both of his own. He did not tell her that if help came their way, it would be in the form of a ruthless killer, sent by the devil, not by God.

As the night deepened, Paul Harris began to worry. It was his girlfriend's—*girlfriend*, there, it was out—birthday, and they were supposed to celebrate it together tonight. But he hadn't heard from her. She hadn't called all day. Which wasn't like Marian; they usually talked several times every day, even on the days when they were planning to see each other.

The problem, Harris knew, was with Marian's other boyfriend. The man had suffered a tragedy some time back, and she felt sorry for him, that was all. She'd told Paul that she'd stopped sleeping with him last spring, which would have made it several months ago now, couldn't the guy take a hint? She would have to tell him, sooner or later, that she was cutting him out of her life.

Her problem was that she was too generous, too loving. He hadn't known that about her at first, hadn't really even cared. But she'd grown on him, had somehow gotten past the high walls that he'd long ago built around his heart.

She'd torn those walls down, to the point where Paul even suspected that he might be in love with her. It was a strange concept for him, the thought of being in love. He'd never told a woman that he'd loved her in his life. Many had spoken those words to him, and when they had, he'd taken his leave. Love wasn't in his plans. Making money had been.

But suddenly money wasn't all that important. He needed it, to be sure, to maintain his lifestyle and to eat and pay his bills. It certainly wasn't a commodity he'd ever belittle. But for the first time in his life, he'd met a woman he cared about even more than he loved money. He'd have to think about that, before he went any further with her. There were things about his past life that he might someday have to tell her. Did she love him enough to understand? She would have to. Especially once he'd told her that he'd given all that action up because of his love for her.

He didn't have to think about that tonight. He didn't want to worry about what might happen in the future. What he wanted to do was get Marian over here, get her over here just to look at her beauty. He loved her. Yeah! You're damn right, he did. And tonight, he might even tell her. If she ever got her ass over here.

He wanted to call her, but he didn't know if that was right. One of the things she couldn't stand about her old boyfriend was his posses-siveness. The man always wanted to know where she'd been, who she'd seen, what she'd done. She would be sensitive to over-possessiveness right now, so he wouldn't call her, at least not just yet. In a little while, maybe. In a little while, for sure.

CHAPTER 2

The Collector stood in front of a full-length mirror on the evening of his fortieth birthday, admiring what he saw reflected back at him in the semi-darkness of his bedroom. He liked it dark; the night-time was all that he truly trusted.

He did his best work in the dark, when nobody could see him.

Staring back at him from the glass was an unsmiling face, haughty, arrogant, full lips twisted into a snarl of unrelenting scorn. There was a full head of wavy, jet black hair, hair that he had dyed every other week. The face was unlined, unscarred, uncaring. A Roman sculpture with a few slight flaws—the nose had been broken several times, and by the time he could afford plastic surgery, it still hadn't been able to make the nose seem normal, and there was slight scar tissue around both eyes, from the years he'd spent in the ring. But none of it, neither the beauty nor the scars, lent the face even a modicum of humanity.

The head was supported by a strong neck, with prominent veins that stood out, even in full repose. A neck that curved down into shoulders that were wide, but which were not the shoulders of a man who lifted weights; the Collector was built more like a ballet dancer than a football player. When fully dressed he had often been mistaken for being skinny. It had been fun, when he'd been a young man, to see the look on the faces of women when they saw him naked for the first time.

Slim-hipped with prominent abdominal muscles and pecs, there was no fat apparent to him as he critically studied his frame. Not on the sides, nor on the waist, either in front or around in back. His body had been honed into the weapon that he needed it to be.

Nobody would ever hurt him again; nor would they dare make fun of him. Neither his father nor any other man would ever again come into his room at night, and do things to him that made him hurt.

His legs were the most heavily muscled part of his form, thighs like small slim tree trunks that he'd built by pushing junk cars uphill in his youth. Later, as a boxer in his late teens and early twenties, he'd jog three miles at a time carrying half a railroad tie on his shoulders. Duckwalk with that damn thing on his shoulders, for blocks at a crack. He would do silly things like that years ago, when all he cared about was soothing his rage by hitting another human being. Back before he'd found something to love that couldn't hurt him; before he'd discovered art.

Today he didn't use such primitive methods to stay in shape.

Today he ran on a treadmill that was inclined up as far as it would go, and he worked out on a Nautilus machine that stood in the center of one of his condo's three immense bedrooms. He would put the weight pin down on the lowest plate, and do hundreds of reps, never counting how many he did. He'd lift, push, strain and struggle until he couldn't do a single repetition more. Then he would stop, wait, catch his breath, and start all over again.

The Collector lived alone, in an apartment often surrounded by clouds. The walls of his vast living room were made of glass, from ceiling to carpet, on three full sides. He could stare out at the endlessness of Lake Michigan, or he could turn his head on a whim and look out at billions of lights shining up at him from the other two windows' borders. Craning his neck, he could see the Sears Tower to his right and over to the west; looking to his left, the radio masts of the Hancock Building appeared as two tall insect antennae, often twitching in the Chicago wind. Below him, people were less than ant size, and huge trucks were reduced to Tonka toys. A snap of a switch closed the view off to him, as heavy velvet drapes were motored closed with a muted hum.

Here in the master bedroom, the Collector had no windows. He kept his own hours, and he often had no wish to know what time of day it was.

The nighttime was his best friend, his lover, so much so that if he had a choice in the matter he would never venture out of his home during the hours when the sun was shining. But he had to. Every day. No one ever knew how uncomfortable he was in the daylight hours, though. In fact, oceans of people parted at his passing, he could feel them watching him, admiring or resenting his presence.

There were no clocks in this bedroom, no phones or answering machines, and when the door was closed and locked there was complete and utter silence. The walls, floor and ceiling had been expertly and heavily soundproofed. The door was heavy oak, trimmed right to the cut of the thick shag carpet. In here the Collector could sleep or he could think, weaving dreams or conceiving plots. He did all of these, and often, with the single exception of sleeping. His survial instincts stopped sleep from overtaking him for too long a period of time, although he sometimes wished that he could sleep longer, just once throughout an entire night. The dreams always haunted him, though, forced him into wakening.

Now he tightened his muscles and admired the jumping biceps, the blood-gorged veins. His legs looked lacquered, hairless and smooth. Clumps of tiny veins criss-crossed his chest, a small second bicep seemed to emerge from atop the first. He relaxed and stood calm, his posture exact, his breathing normal. He had spent three hours of this Sunday night in exercise, building his power, slowly erecting the exact musculature that he needed to do his work.

Although it was his birthday, there would be no calls or visits. No cards stood open on his mantel; he'd neither expected nor received any gifts.

But he'd bought himself one, and in a little while he'd enjoy it. His gift to himself was hanging on the fourth wall of his living room, the one that wasn't glass. Out there, the curtains were closed, and a small soft light with a tiny brass shade was right now shining down on his new acquisition. It was waiting for him, patiently. He would shower, then pour a glass of wine, sit down and enjoy his present.

The bedroom door was open, and from somewhere out in the apartment he heard the soft burring of one of his telephone lines. He couldn't make out which number it was that was ringing, but he wasn't particularly curious; he didn't make a dash to the phone. Whoever it was would be calling a number that was registered to one of four phones far from here, numbers that were registered to a bank of phones that sat on a desk in a filthy rented office down at the end of the South Loop. The numbers were bounced over here, to one of four different lines, given out in specific order of importance to the very few people who could reach him.

They were all attached to machines, and the Collector would return the calls he felt like returning, which would most likely be the ones he believed would bring him profit. Sometimes, though, he'd take calls on his personal line. The one of the four that he gave out to women. He had needs, and he was sometimes prone to overindulging himself with women.

For now, though, he let the phone ring, and he turned away from the mirror.

He felt strong. Powerful. He had the feeling that he was special, that nothing or no one could stop him.

He was not a man to dwell with angst upon his impending middle age, nor one who felt that his skills had eroded with the passing of the years. Forty was but a number to him, a four and a zero and then nothing more.

The further away he got from his childhood, the happier he'd be. He looked good, he felt good, and he made more money in a single year than all of his ancestors had managed to put together in their lifetimes. So to hell with them, with all of them. He'd gotten even with the ones who had hurt him, and he'd done his best to forget the names of the ones who might still be alive.

Now the Collector flipped on the bathroom switch, and the room was flooded with light from the dozens of bulbs that surrounded his steam-proof bathroom mirror. He took three steps down into a marble bathtub that was as large as his childhood bathroom, closed the smoked glass doors behind him, and twisted the double handles that turned on the dozen shower jets. He was immediately hit with needle sharp sprays from the front and the back and the sides, the water as hot as it could get, the handles turned all the way to the right, and he stood there stoically, gritting his teeth, testing himself against a power, the force of nature. When at last he could move without inordinate pain he stood under the spray and soaped himself, his face now a mask of indifference, the challenge having been met. Then he let the water tear the soap away from his body, as he prepared to challenge himself anew.

He reached out and flipped both handles hard to the left, and felt the icy water attack him, then stood back and smiled, his arms held out wide as the cold water shot out at him, easing the pain, the Collector shivering, tingling, his penis and scrotal sac shriveled. The Collector stood there as the icy water struck him, then put his hands on the wall and his face right into the spray.

CHAPTER 3

THE DEAD MAN'S SHOTGUNNED BODY LAY SPRAWLED ACROSS THE bloody car seat, the right hand draped across an expensive cellular phone. The skin of the man's hand was far lighter on the ring finger, where the finger met the hand, than it was on the rest of the hand, and a large circle of white seemed painted onto the otherwise well-tanned wrist.

It appeared to Jake Phillips's training officer that a large ring and a good watch had been removed from the body. It wasn't something that Phillips had particularly needed to be told. He might be young and new, but he wasn't dumb. Nevertheless, he didn't comment. It was too damned hot to argue. Even after dark, it was still hotter than hell.

Phillips felt the sweat dripping down his back, under his sport coat, knew that the sweat was darkening his shirt. He should have worn a T-shirt instead of an undershirt. He was starting to be able to smell himself. This crazy, rotten weather. For eleven days in a row the temperature had risen above ninety degrees. Some days it hit one hundred. Some days it even went over. A record-breaking summer heatwave, with no relief in sight. Jake put a solemn, competent, professional expression on his face, then looked over at the car.

The car was idling, in Park. The driver had for some reason taken the time to stop and put the gear shift in Park before his killer had shot him; was that some kind of a clue? The corpse was being kept from slumping over by its seatbelt, its head up against the steering wheel, most of its chest and belly splashed against the opposite door.

It was exactly the sort of thing that Jake Phillips had been dying to see. His first day in Homicide, and here he was, catching a bad one.

His father—dead three years now—had told him when he'd first joined the force: "Forget about Homicide, stay in uniform; there's more money to be made, and nobody blames you for nothin'." Which was the way the old man had served his thirty years: in uniform, making money hand over fist, with nobody blaming him for nothin'. Even the few who tried to blame him never got past the desk sergeant.

Which was not quite the way Jake wanted to spend his career.

He had been devastated to discover that his father had been a rogue cop. As a child he'd believed that *all* cops made enough money to live in a large house in Beverly, with a summer home in Michigan. His father had always had two cars, and their mother, forget about it; in the winter her minks were envied and in the summer she wore the best linen. The only thing filthy about the entire Phillips family was the money that their patriarch would deposit with a flourish when the church basket was passed around on a long thin pole by the volunteer Knights of Columbus usher.

His father, the crook. But he'd always provided well. A man who'd seen that his eldest son was left with a lot more than money after the old man retired.

There were very few old-timers around who didn't know who Jake's father was. The only coppers his father had shunned, those he'd refused to help, had been those who trafficked in what he'd considered to be dirty money: drugs and Mafia payoffs. And there were even fewer "honest" cops who weren't somehow in the old man's debt. He'd looked at favors for what they were, the true coin of the realm of the Chicago Police Department. These old-timers were the bosses now, and had smiled down at Jake since the day he'd been sworn in, men with lots of gold braid on their uniform caps, taking Phillips under their wings and helping him along.

Which was why he was in Homicide tonight, just four years into his career.

Phillips knew that there would now be plenty of good and hard-working detectives who would be angry at him, some who would actually hate him. Because they'd been passed over for promotion. For the first time in his career, though, Phillips didn't give a shit about what anyone thought of him. He'd spent the past four years trying to live up to a dead man's image, but it didn't matter any longer; he'd realized his dream. He'd wanted to be a Homicide cop since he'd been a little boy.

And now here he was, twenty-seven years old and working his first murder. He walked around the dead man's car and tried to act like he knew what he was doing.

There were seven digits punched into the dead man's car phone, they floated there on the digital readout: 5-1-2-5-8-0-0. Where was the 5-1-2 exchange? Phillips didn't know.

He did know that the dead man had been shot through the driver's side window, that much was clearly obvious; the window was missing, destroyed by the power of the gunshot blast. Glass was embedded in the dead man's face, in his hands; it was scattered all over his bloody torso. He'd taken most of the buckshot in the chest and in his gut, the killer shooting through the glass, probably holding the barrel down with one hand so he wouldn't miss the kill. A white guy on the near South Side, shot dead in his Cadillac on a desolate street.

It seemed open and shut to Jake's FTO—Field Training Officer— Jerry Moore. The dead man had been pushing or selling drugs.

Moore and Phillips had been the first detectives on the scene, and Moore had preserved the integrity of the kill to the extent that he was capable. He'd had some tired, sweaty uniformed officers tape off the area for a site of twenty feet in either direction, and now he had them manning the blue wooden police barricades, keeping out the curious.

Phillips paid strict attention to everything going on around him, taking it all in, socking it away for later. He intended to have another partner soon, one he could impress with his knowledge, with how quickly he learned the ropes. He didn't plan to be working with Moore any longer than he had to; the guy was a bigot and a low-class pig.

The two of them had shaken hands and hit the street two hours ago, and Moore hadn't mentioned Jake's father one time. For the moment, however, he could learn from the man, and that was all this so-called partnership was about, as far as Jake was concerned.

Inside the taped-off square, people who made their living from human misery were milling about, indifferently. They'd seen it all before. Except for him. He was trying to act nonchalant about it, but although Jake could hide his nervousness, there was nothing he could do about his sweat. He watched the lardass slob who was training him, looking for hints as to how a hardcore Homicide cop should act.

He also was stuck watching Moore do things that he had no desire to be taught. Moore the bigot entertaining the mostly white uniformed cops, kidding around so that they'd think he was one of the guys. Moore looking at the crowd of black faces outside the tape and making fun of them.

"Welcome to Baboon Island," Moore said, and made his voice high and feminine, mimicking his stereotypical view of a black woman. "'Don't you *touch* me, motherfucker, I know my cons-tipa-tion-al *raats*.' Look at 'em. Dirty no-bath-takin' hot-water-hatin' motherfuckers, you can smell 'em all the way over here."

Phillips turned away from him, trying to keep his face straight. He did not want the man to know that he disgusted him. The black uniformed cops pretended that they didn't hear what the idiot was saying.

Moore was a big man, as dumb as he was tall. His waist had expanded as his hairline had receded. He was sweating heavily in the night's heat, had pulled the knot of his wide paisley tie down a couple of inches, and had unbuttoned the top button of his white short-sleeve shirt. His .44 Magnum hung under his left arm, from a soft leather holster which he polished carefully and often.

"Who do you think he was trying to call?" Moore heard the words and turned slowly toward the speaker. He was training this kid, Phillips. Obviously not well enough. The kid still hadn't learned not to interrupt when Jerry Moore was holding court.

"I don't give a fat rat's ass *who* he was trying to call. Maybe he was calling your old lady, Philly, did you ever think about that?" Moore spoke the words and turned his back on the kid, thinking that that would teach him, that he'd humiliated the bastard. But it didn't appear to be what he'd done, 'cause here he was, looking for more.

"I figure his wife, if he was married." The kid didn't sound humiliated in the least. He was speaking as if he hadn't even heard Moore's insult. "That's who *I'd* call if I knew that I was dying. Or his girlfriend if he was single."

Moore sighed. "He probably tried calling the cops, or an ambulance or some fucking thing. That romantic notion shit, you got to get it out of your head, Phillips." Moore took a deep breath. He had to teach the new guy a lesson.

"Here's a white guy in a brand-new Cadillac, caught a shotgun blast in the belly in the middle of a shine 'hood. He got the presence of mind to pull over to the curb, he got the sense to reach for his phone, what do you think he's gonna do, call his sweetums up and tell her how much he loves her before he croaks? Forget about that shit, this is Chicago, not Hollywood. He looks to be in his mid-thirties, a yuppie facing mortality. He was calling for help, not to say goodbye to anybody. At worst he was calling a priest." Moore shrugged.

"This guy, he probably thought that he'd live forever. Somebody taught him different."

"He's from Evanston, his sticker says."

"The doctor'll give us his name and address, if he's still carrying his wallet. If it's gone, we'll run his plates, if somebody ain't already."

Moore, filled with his own self-importance, looked at the young man in front of him. He'd teach the kid something here, show him how a detective works.

"The ring's gone, his watch, too. The guy comes in from the suburbs, to buy or sell dope. Probably selling, from the looks of the car. The deal went bad, the shooter grabbed the dope, the ring and the watch. Case closed, Philly, it's simple."

Moore smiled. "Don't worry, kid. They won't all be like this, you'll get a chance to be a detective, if not tonight then tomorrow. In this heat, we'll get forty to sixty shootings a day, and some of them got to die. Won't all be white like this guy, neither. Usually, it's about ten to one, in favor of dead baboons."

Moore looked over at the assistant medical examiner, who was carefully inspecting the inside of the car. The doctor was dressed in what looked like a white plastic suit, with a face mask and everything, taking no chances with all that blood. Moore could only imagine what his dress suit looked like under the shiny, white, blood-stained material, how hard the guy must be sweating. The AME did not like Moore, he knew. The feeling was mutual. Moore did not have much use for men who had a lot of education.

"Where's that fucking Tulio? He gets here, we go home."

"This isn't ours?" Phillips said, and there was no mistaking the disappointment in his voice.

Moore looked over at him, lips twisted downward, not even trying to hide his disgust.

A slight kid, had to have connections to have come so far so fast. What could he be, twenty-five, twenty-six? Too young to make the death squad without having some important clout, which was why Moore had taken it pretty easy on the boy so far. A couple of shots here and there was all, no one could bitch about that. When you were new on the squad, the bulls were supposed to break your balls a little, it was the way that it had been done since Moore's grandfather had walked a beat.

He dressed well, which meant he either came from money or he was working a little something extra on the side. Moore would keep an eye on him, check him out very carefully before he showed him what he himself had going. He'd learned way back when he'd been a rookie that it went better for you if you shared the wealth. It not only made your partner grateful, but it clove the two of you closer together, made you both a part of the same conspiracy.

Mindful that the kid more than likely had weight backing him up, Moore spoke to him now with exaggerated patience.

"No, Philly, this ain't ours. This one belongs to *Special Victims*." He waited until the revulsion settled in his belly before he continued speaking.

"Was a time once, when I first came on, when the bulls got everything, rapes, murders, burglaries, muggings, whatever happened on your watch. Then they went to a special Homicide division, then they created a section just for violent crimes. Now you got gang experts and community relations coppers, rape counselors and grief specialists, all carrying badges. Finally, we got Homicide away from violent crimes." Moore cleared his throat and spat on the ground. "We even got broads in charge of some of the departments, too. This department, shit, what it's becoming, it's enough to turn your fuckin' stomach."

"What's Special Victims?"

"It's a bullshit section they created for dead people who got money." Moore looked over the heads of the crowd outside the tape and grunted. "Here comes one of their hotshots, you can ask him what he does for yourself."

CHAPTER 4

LIEUTENANT TONY TULIO WALKED THROUGH THE GROWING CROWD with his badge hanging from a chain around his neck. He wouldn't have needed it to identify himself; his bearing, his looks, all shouted out what he did. To the passive observer he was one of two things: a cop or a killer, either one to be avoided. Tulio had eyes that his father used to say were the color of the grapes that his own father had once stomped into wine; very dark, nearly black, with just the barest hint of red when he became angry or was overly tired.

Both of which he was on this sticky mid-summer Sunday night. He was on call for Special Victims, the boss taking his turn just like everybody else, out on his second call of the night already, looking at standard homicides that some lazy bull had decided were special.

Tulio was wearing a patterned blue short-sleeve shirt, worn out of his pants to cover the gun attached to his belt in the back. The pants were dark green, with deep Velcroed pockets positioned right above both knees. The lower pockets were filled with things that jiggled when Tulio walked. Lockpicks, notebook, various other equipment. There were comfortable gym shoes on his feet. His hair was moderately short, barely long enough to comb; his hair was brown, and under the soft glare of the streetlight, a couple of lines of gray could be seen. The street lights did not show the small lines at the mouth, or those around his eyes, none of which had come from laughing.

Tulio nodded to a couple of the uniformed cops, one of whom held the tape up so that he could pass underneath. He ignored the insults shouted out by some of the spectators who yelled them when they'd figured out that he was a cop. They felt safe hollering at cops, cops were held to a higher standard of behavior. Throughout the crowd were those who would know him, and these people would never dare shout out an insult. Some of the others would learn, sooner or later, that Tulio was not a man who would take a lot of their bullshit.

He felt Moore glaring at him as he walked toward the death car, and he sighed inwardly, warned himself to be calm. There was bad blood between them, going way back.

Suddenly, Tulio shouted.

"Get the hell away from there!"

A uniformed cop had been leaning into the driver's side window of the death car, thinking he had a right to do so now that the medical examiner had backed out of the vehicle. The cop pulled back at the sharp reprimand and looked around him, angrily, saving face with indignation.

"You talking to me?" the cop said, and Tulio heard Moore grunt loudly.

"You're goddamn right I'm talking to you! Get the *hell* away from that car!"

"Oh, jeepers, you better do as he says, kid, he's a tough one," Moore said, sarcastically.

"You the senior man here?" Tulio was in no mood to be polite. "What did you do, stumble into detectives, Moore? You were gonna let this guy shut the goddamn car off?"

Moore shrugged. "What's the difference? The vic ain't going nowheres." Moore smiled. "When we first pulled up? I had a half-a-orgasm when I saw the car, Tony. It looks just like yours; I thought you'd been whacked out by one of them shvoogies you're always shootin' at."

"When I shoot 'em," Tulio said, feeling a need to show off, "they don't come back for revenge." He regretted the words the moment he'd spoken them.

There was a slender young man now stepping toward Tulio, his hand held out respectfully. Tulio walked past him, past Moore and over to the car, stood looking at it closely. The medical examiner joined him.

"Tony."

"Doctor."

Tulio leaned into the car, saw the number on the phone, came back out, and wrote the number down in a small black vinyl looseleaf notebook.

"What do we got?" Tulio asked, almost absently, as he carefully studied the number.

The doctor produced a pack of cigarettes and offered one to Tulio. Tulio shook his head. The doctor lit a cigarette and blew a stream of smoke into the air. Tulio knew what was coming next; the doctor said it every time. He stuck his head back into the car, carefully looked around.

"I'm the only doctor in the city whose clients never complain when I light up during an exam. Surprised to see you twice in one night. Did you finish up over on the West Side already?"

Tulio spoke into the dead man's face, raising his voice so the doctor could hear him.

"Those markings on her chest? It was what I thought, gang signs. Some junior auxiliary hotshot, wanting to break into the big time, impress the elders with his daring-do. I went over and talked to the leader of the Nation, Calhoun, for a few minutes."

"I'd have liked to have been there for *that*."

"No you wouldn't have," Tulio said, and pulled his head back out of the car. "Got an extra pair of gloves?"

"Sure." The doctor handed Tulio a pair of see-through light plastic gloves. He worked them onto his hands, walked around to the passenger's side and opened the door, leaned in without kneeling or letting his clothing touch the seat. Using one hand to prop himself up, Tulio quickly searched the body.

"Pictures taken?"

"All shot, integrity's preserved," the doctor said.

Tulio took out a wallet and looked at it closely, holding it in one hand. The other hand, the one holding him up, was beginning to ache.

"Calhoun was packing. I made him a deal. Told him to give up the slasher, or I'd take two years off his life, federal, then be waiting on the penitentiary steps with state charges the day he walked."

"And he *talked*?" The doctor seemed surprised. "*Calhoun*?"

Tulio shrugged in response. There was now a small pile of the dead man's effects lying on the seat next to Tulio's straining arm. A wad of large-denomination bills, some change, a copy of an invoice, and a St. Jude medal that had been around the dead man's neck. Tulio reached over and shut off the car's engine, took the keys out of the ignition and pushed himself out of the car. He shook his arm, made a fist and relaxed it. He walked over to the back of the car and used the keys to open the trunk, made a quick inspection, then slammed the trunk shut. He left the keys in the trunk lock. He stripped off the gloves and let them fall to the pavement.

"Still," the doctor said, not wanting to let it go. "*Calhoun?* The leader of the Insane Unknown Zulus, ratting out a member to the law?"

Tulio looked at the doctor, to make sure that he wasn't being played. His face was blank, and when he spoke he spoke simply, his voice flat and without emotion.

"We were alone," Tulio said, and heard soft laughter come from Moore.

"That's right, hey, Philly, pay attention to the man. He been out here so long, he's turned into one of them. Ask him how many jigs he's shot, go ahead, ask him." Moore grunted. "Ask him how many B&Es he's pulled." Moore laughed. "The son of a bitch, he can bust any lock, he's a regular fuckin' Pink Panther."

Tulio was looking at Moore when he spoke to the doctor.

"He gave up one kid, and that kid will give up the others. There were three of them, the witnesses gave up that much. I'll be talking to the kid in a little while. I'm going to deal with it personally, I won't lose this one, not after what they did to that girl." He raised his voice now, still looking at the doctor, his words meant for Moore.

"The problem is, Doctor, it's these lazy slob bulls. Every call they get, they beep Special Victims. They're too lazy to work the cases themselves, these Homicide guys. If there's even one thing distinctive about the killing, *bam*, they call us in. It's laziness is all. I'll take care of it the next time I meet with the captain."

"Hey, tough guy," Moore called over, "I ain't no street gang leader, don't try and lean on *me*."

Tulio could feel the tension coming from the other officers. This was the sort of thing they loved to brag about in bars after they got off duty. He knew he should let it go, forget about this slob. Moore wasn't important enough to get upset over: he was just another fat cop who took money he didn't earn, looking to be a big shot in front of a bunch of uniformed coppers. Still, Tulio couldn't help himself.

Looking casually at Moore, he continued.

"There should be dancing in the street when some of these pigs retire. You got your incompetents, you got your malcontents just looking to put in their twenty . . ."

Tulio paused and went over to a uniformed officer, scribbled something in his notebook with his back turned to Moore, then said something to the officer that even the doctor couldn't hear. He came back to the car and leaned against it, put his notebook back into one of the large lower pants pockets, pushed the Velcro down onto its tab on the pocket, then continued as if he hadn't ever walked away.

"Then, Doctor, you got your guys working both sides. You know what else Calhoun told me? You know who he's paying off?"

"Bullshit!" Moore was livid now, walking rapidly toward Tulio. Tulio waited for him, leaning casually against the car. Behind Moore, the young kid who was obviously new to street clothes was slowly, warily following him, not knowing what was going on.

Moore came within a couple of steps of Tulio and stopped.

"You don't ever accuse me of being on the take!"

"I say any names, Doctor? Did I accuse anyone of anything?"

"You got something to say, you say it to me, to my face!" Moore shouted.

"You know, Doctor," Tulio said, with just a hint of a smile, "all day long, I got to deal with assholes. I make a habit now of only talking to them when they have something I want to know." He looked over at Moore. "I already know how to cuss, and I have no desire to learn how to take bribes from the mob or from some geechy street pusher. So what the hell have I got to say to you, Moore?" Tulio say, and Moore charged.

Tulio was ready. He stepped to the side as Moore's weight carried him into the car, and he grabbed the back of the man's rumpled shirt. This close up he could smell Moore's stale summer sweat. Tulio slammed him against the car, pulled him back and pushed him into the car again, then grabbed him by the hair and shoved his head through the shattered window.

"You see this guy, you son of a bitch! Take a good look, Jerry!" Tulio pulled him out and turned him around, shoved him up against the car and stepped back. There was a lump of the victim's blood in Moore's hair. Tulio's lips were twisted into a very slight smile. Moore brought his hand up, had his fingers on the butt of his pistol.

"Go ahead, Jerry," Tulio said, softly. "You pull that on me and I can kill you right here. You drew down on me in front of witnesses. I'll do it and get away with it, too. Take it out, Jerry, come on, I want you to. Please."

Slowly, Moore took his hand off the pistol grip. Moore's partner was standing next to Moore now, not knowing what to do. He reached a tentative hand out as if to help, but Moore pushed it roughly away.

Tulio stepped back, defusing the situation. Somewhere far behind him he could hear the crowd cheering him on, enjoying the free and unexpected action, cops at each other's throats. Then the uniformed cop he had spoken to minutes earlier came back. The cop handed him back his scrap of paper, and Tulio looked at it, nodding his thanks.

He looked up.

"Come here," he said to the young kid near Moore. The kid looked at him, frightened, not knowing what to do. "Look, you want to solve your first homicide, or what?" Phillips slowly walked toward him.

"The dead man made a night delivery of artist's etchings to a curator three blocks away. The receipt was in his pocket, and there're other etchings in his trunk. Listen. Let me teach you a little something. Take a look at him before they haul him off, you'll see a guy who never worked a day in his life. There're no callouses on his hands, his fingernails are manicured. I'd say he came from money, didn't believe that anyone could hurt him. He was always so safe, so protected, secure in who and what he was. He saw these folks around here as life's victims." Tulio looked hard at the young man, then handed him the paper.

"This was a crime of opportunity, unplanned. Look at the front of the car, there's a fresh dent in the fender, a little paint around the dent. It's the only mark on the entire car, and the vehicle only has a couple of thousand miles on it."

Moore had gotten himself somewhat together, was standing slightly away from the car now, his hands balled into fists, breathing hard and glaring at Tulio, but not saying a word. He knew what Tulio was doing, how he was saving his own ass and would make it look as if he was doing the kid—and Moore—a favor. Tulio knew that there wasn't a thing that Moore could do about it. Now that he had it all in the palm of his hand, Tulio was no longer smiling. He spoke in a low, professional voice, showing off a little, he knew, for the benefit of the kid and the surrounding uniformed cops.

"Here's what happened," Tulio said with confidence. "The shooters, they saw this guy come out of the curator's. They followed him, figuring he was holding. Got in front of him over here in front of the light and slammed on the brakes. The vic slams on the brakes, but still, he bumps the car a little, gets paint on his fender, so the other car was small, the fenders didn't match up. The shooter gets out as if to inspect the damage, and when he sees that there's no bank bag or whatever on the front seat, he lets the guy have it, then grabs his ring and watch."

"Wait a minute, wait a minute," the kid said to Tulio. "Where you getting this from?"

"He shoots the guy, grabs the jewelry, then he panics. Maybe some cars came by, maybe the gunshot was louder than he thought, maybe there was more blood than he expected, who knows? But he leaves the wallet, doesn't even check the pockets, the victim was carrying at least a grand in his right front pocket, but these geniuses, they got a Rolex, a diamond ring, they think they've scored big. The shooter gets back in the car and takes off." Tulio paused for effect, then handed the kid the slip of paper.

"What's this?"

"It's your shooter. His name's Merronius Heugely, he's got a record going back to the seventies. He's done this sort of thing before, trust me."

"How do you know?"

"Anyone looking for it could have figured it out in a minute." Tulio shot a withering glance at Moore, who looked away. "Most of it's right there for everyone to see, and the rest was on the car phone."

"He was calling the guy who *shot* him?" The kid fell silent, realizing how stupid he sounded.

"He punched in the license number of the car of the guy who shot him. Probably dialed it as soon as he saw the shooter getting out of the car with a shotgun. Nine-one-one's no good on cellular phones, he'd'a wound up getting whatever department was nearest to the closest cellular relay station. Look. E-A-Y eight-hundred. The Y is the twenty-fifth letter of the alphabet, which is the reason for the two and the five. Heugely only lives a few blocks away from here. You go over there with your *partner*, and he'll be watching television, eating a late supper, and he'll act all surprised that the po-lice is at his door. Lie to him, tell him you have a witness. He'll fold, he has before. These guys, they aren't wired right, they're not only stupid, see, they're unimaginative. If you can't get a confession out of him, just look around. The murder weapon's probably under the bed."

His work done, Tulio turned and began to walk away.

"Hey, Tulio?" the new guy said, and Tulio turned around, walking backward, and lifted his eyebrows at the young man.

"Uh, thanks," the kid said. Tulio saw the look of hatred that Moore was giving the young man. He stopped.

"What's your name?"

"Phillips, Jake Phillips."

Tulio was surprised.

"You Jack Phillips's kid?"

The young kid nodded his head, embarrassed. Tulio walked over to him and shook his hand warmly, holding it in both of his own, smiling at the young detective.

"Your father, he was good to me," Tony Tulio said. He lowered his voice so only Phillips could hear "He went to bat for me more times than I can count."

"Uh—he spoke highly of you . . ."

"He was a second father to me. No offense."

The kid seemed more than embarrassed now, he seemed shy. He had hunted for words and was probably mad at himself for saying something stupid like "He spoke highly of you." Tulio patted him on the shoulder.

"What do they got you with *that* asshole for?" When the guy seemed too afraid to answer, Tulio continued.

"You ever need anything, you give me a call. I'm at Special Victims, two floors up from you guys."

"Thanks, thanks a lot," Phillips said. He seemed about to lick Tulio's hand. Tulio wondered if Jack had ever told the kid how much he had really done for Tulio, how many times he'd saved his ass. Tulio nodded and began to walk away, then turned, wanting to get one last shot in at Moore.

"You want some advice, Jake?" Phillips just stood there. "At the end of your shift, go right to the commander and request a new training officer. The guy you're with's an idiot." Tulio spun on his heel, turning his back on the man he'd just insulted, knowing damn well that there was nothing Moore would do, giving him his back so Moore would know that he knew.

And now so did every other cop at the crime scene, and cops, they loved to talk.

C H A P T E R 5

It was closing in on midnight, and Paul Harris was starting to feel fear. Christ, another first for him. Had something happened? Had Marian been hurt? In her work, he knew, she often had to be on call, her beeper had taken her away from his apartment more than once since he'd known her. At first, he hadn't minded. Then later, after his feelings for her had grown, he'd begun to resent the intrusion into their time.

But what was he to do? Tell her to quit her job? It's what her other boyfriend was always badgering her to do. Harris couldn't bring himself to behave in the manner that *he* did.

Screw it. He reached for the phone, dialed the number that he knew by heart. Shit, he got a machine. He waited for the tone.

"Marian, it's me, Paul." He put concern into his voice. "Look, I'm sorry to bother you, but did you forget we had a date? I won't beep you, you might be busy, but I *am* getting worried. Call me as soon as you check your machine. I won't go to sleep until I hear from you, okay?"

Harris hung up the phone and sat looking down at it, deep in thought. If that other guy had hurt her, he would kill him with his bare hands. It would drive Marian away from him forever, but even that wouldn't stop him, it wasn't something he could ever let happen, allowing anyone to hurt Marian Hannerty.

And he knew that the man was capable of it, that he was mean and vicious and cruel. Harris himself had some familiarity with such feelings. But soon, that would be a thing of the past. His anger went away whenever he was with her. She always made him feel so alive, so happy, so free!

He got up and walked away from the phone; it would never ring if he stared at it. He would force himself to tell her tonight, about how all this waiting had made him feel. Tell her and see what she said, she was smart enough to explain it to him. If she ever called.

Should he call her again? No, not tonight. She would see that as being pushy, and he had never been aggressive toward her.

So he'd wait and he'd suffer. Maybe find some work to do. He punched his fist into his other hand and wondered where the hell she was.

Lenny Roman had once been a fighter, and a good one too, for a time. It was all he'd ever wanted to be, for as long as he could remember. He had reason for wanting to be a fighter, going back to when he was a young kid, when he was still in St. Columba's.

He'd watch the Pabst Blue Ribbon or Gillette Friday night fights with his father back in the fifties, in their rooms above the tavern that Lenny's grandfather owned. Those nights were the only time Lenny could remember that his father ever spent with him, unless he was beating his ass. On some level Lenny knew, even then, that the truth of the matter was that on those nights the two of them just happened to be in the same room at the same time. Still, it made him feel that they were close; that there was a bond there that was important, that he was like his friends at school who went fishing and shit with their dads.

They'd watch Randy Turpin; Johnny Bratton: "The Cuban Hawk," Kid Gavilan, Sandy Sadler; BoBo Olson and Carmine Bassilio. And they'd watched, together, Mormon Gene Fulmer get the shit kicked out of him by Sugar Ray Robinson in their second fight. Eddie Macon, Sonny Liston, Cleveland "Big Cat" Williams, the two of them had seen them all.

On some Friday nights, his father would even speak to him.

"You see that punch? Jesus fuckin' *Christ* that Robinson can throw a fuckin' punch."

They'd watched, on their little black-and-white television set, some of the best fights that had ever been staged in the history of boxing. Later, when Lenny was regularly on television himself, he once told an interviewer the story of that time, embellishing it for the audience.

"My old man and me," Lenny had said, "would sit around the living room, him with his beer, me with an ice cream he'd buy me, and we'd watch them Friday night fights." He shrugged, as if it was a normal thing, one of the many special moments they had shared. "It kept me off the streets, kept me on the straight and narrow."

Back then, you could get away with lying like that to reporters; today they'd punch a button, and the story of your life would appear on their computers.

He'd wink to his father after every televised victory, once he was sure that the fight was his, then say hello to his dad after the decision was confirmed, when the announcer stuck the microphone in his face, wanting to know how he'd done it. Lenny believed his dad was truly proud of him, now that he'd amounted to something important. It was a belief that lasted until his old man had come to him, with a sly look in his eye, and told him that to save his father's life, Lenny had to go into the tank.

The old man had a problem with the cards. With dice and horses, too. He was usually in the hole, they were almost always broke, but sometimes the old man would hit it really big. When he did he'd disappear for days, return with stories he would tell down in the tavern, with the white apron around his waist, Lenny sweeping the floor and listening and pretending that he wasn't, while Grampa looked on silently with undisguised contempt. The old man would be talking about this great place, Las Vegas, about the things that went on there, around the clock, and of the important people he knew, how he'd met them at the tables.

There was a framed picture of his father behind the bar, sitting at a table with a bunch of dark-haired men wearing sunglasses in the darkness of a cocktail lounge, brown drinks in fancy cocktail glasses in front of them, with a sign in back that told people they were entering the door to Dino's Den at the Fabulous Riviera. His father would point to the picture and tell anyone who would listen the names of those guys sitting at the table with him, and sometimes he'd change the names; he'd mixed them up a lot.

The decline and fall of Lenny Roman had begun with the tank jobs, taking occasional dives for the fast long green. His father's friends would hand it over to Lenny, stuffed into white envelopes. Lenny the contender, a lightheavy with hands like lightning, sometimes getting two or three times more than his entire purse just to ensure that he didn't win. The first time he'd tanked, it had broken his heart. After a while though, it got easy, and it even became fun for him. There was one six-month period in his life where he'd made over eighty grand and didn't have to pay any taxes on it. He'd fight a couple of times a month, win five or six in a row, become a force in the division again, and get set up with a true contender. Then the men would come and see him.

He would gamble, too, Lenny had inherited that. He knew all about living high on the hog, then losing everything in the entire world that you owned as you sat at the gaming tables, with total strangers calling you "sir" and kissing your ass.

Age had a way of catching up to you, though, and after his legs went, his unbalanced record finally caught up with him, too. Who in his right mind would pay top dollar to sit ringside and watch as a perennial contender lost yet another fight?

He became just another tomato can, what was called in the game an "opponent." There were no more first-class airplane rides for Lenny, no more suites in fancy hotels, no more showgirls sent up by his friends. Just stifling hot Greyhound buses, and rented rooms in tank towns, where Lenny would train in somebody's garage or basement before fighting in VFW halls that didn't even have locker rooms, just bathrooms where all the fighters changed clothes at the same time.

Nobody came to him with envelopes stuffed with money anymore; nobody had to. Lenny had lost it, his purses were in the hundreds, and up-and-comers could take him out without half trying, no matter how hard he trained.

Lenny had never been ranked higher than fifth, and after the first few years of consensual losses, he never earned his way back into the top ten. Lenny never really minded the losses, though, or the self-respect he had lost along the way, either. Because his father had bet a fortune on Lenny's opponents, he would come into the dressing room after Lenny had dumped, and the old man would hug his son, tell him how good he'd done. It made Lenny feel good. That closeness, it was wonderful.

At thirty, when he retired, Lenny was broke and his father called him a loser, but some of his father's friends had remembered what Lenny had done to enrich them.

He got work breaking legs for a guy named Thomas Gerardi, back in the days before the guy had made it to the big-time by clinging to the coattails of the Eagle, the boss of all bosses, head of the second-biggest— but most violent—crew in Chicago. When that happened, Lenny's title was quickly changed; he became Mr. Gerardi's *chauffeur*. To Lenny that was good for a laugh.

It had been a good job, lasting seven years, until the Man had gotten tired of Lenny falling asleep at the wheel because he'd been out all night gambling the night before, losing the money that Gerardi had paid him at one of the gambling dens he owned.

He'd tossed around for a few years, dealing cards in a couple of joints, bouncing at some others, never marrying, hardly ever even getting laid. The cards and ponies were his lovers; seven face-up on a pair of dice his orgasm; small time street scams carrying him through when times were tough. Lenny had been pinched a lot, but he'd never done hard time; all in all, Lenny knew, he'd had a pretty lucky life.

But his luckiest break had come when he'd run into this guy, this wild motherfucker liked to call himself the *Collector*, the man an ex-middleweight he'd met when the guy was a kid and had been knocking around the South back when Lenny still had the punch, the instinct and the talent.

What the guy was doing now, Lenny was scared to think of it sometimes. Still, he stood up for the guy, and he ran his errands. He was paid well and he kept his mouth shut. And when Thomas Gerardi's boss had needed a favor last winter, Lenny had been glad to volunteer to do it; he thought it would get him his old job back, or at least score him a few extra grand.

The fact was that the favor he'd done hadn't gotten him shit except a nice payday from his partner, the Collector. Tonight Gerardi needed another favor, and the man who could deliver it wasn't anywhere to be found.

Lenny now stood in an old-fashioned phone booth in the back of a South Side bar, the door open so his cigar smoke didn't choke him. Lenny was no longer a light-heavy. His super-heavyweight belly leaned against the tiny wooden counter where you were supposed to lay out your change. He was listening to the ring of an unanswered phone on the other end of the line.

In the back room of this joint a high-stakes poker game was in progress, and Lenny had been doing good when the beep from Gerardi had come. He'd had to leave the game and go meet the guy, find out what the ungrateful fuck wanted of him this time. As soon as he had he would come back here, to a place where he knew that the line wasn't tapped, and he could get back to the poker game as soon as he passed on the word. But the guy wasn't cooperating, he wasn't answering his phone.

He was itching to get back into the game, too, his winnings burning a hole in the pocket of a pair of pants that were three sizes too tight, but he couldn't sit back down until he'd passed along the word, and this guy, he wasn't making Lenny's work any easier for him. Lenny didn't know what he was going to do.

Lenny didn't know where they guy lived, had never followed him trying to find out, either. This son of a bitch was a killer, the coldest man Lenny had ever known, even colder than his father, may the old man rest in peace. If the Collector lost out on tonight's action, he'd lose a major payday and have only himself to blame.

Thomas Gerardi, however, would not see things in that light. Gerardi, what he'd do was, he'd blame Lenny Roman.

Lenny had two phone numbers for the guy, had left messages at both of them, and although he had no idea where the man lived, he knew where he worked, had been there plenty of times. He wasn't at his place of business, either, though, and the more time that passed, the more Lenny worried. Gerardi didn't take kindly to failure. As far as Lenny knew, the man didn't even believe in the concept.

C H A P T E R
6

THE PAINTING WAS SMALL FOR ONE SO INCREDIBLY DETAILED, AND simple, after a fashion. It was a picture of a woman, seated at a tiny table, a glass of wine in front of her, looking off into the distance, perhaps at an approaching lover. At first glance you might believe that, until you looked at it for a while.

After prolonged study it was obvious that the woman was seeing God.

There was a detailed brooch pinned to the white lace at her throat, her cuffs were made of the same lacy material as the collar. Every hair was in place; under a magnifying glass, it appeared to be combed. Her face was lined with the commencement of early middle-age; this was a woman whose youth was about to pass her by, but she didn't seem to care. There was no bitterness about her. There were no rings on her fingers. Even her fingernails had been superbly recreated, down to the last detail. He'd seen the cuticles through his glass when he'd checked the painting before purchase.

There was a religious bent to the picture. At the very least this was a woman of spirituality, a three-hundred-year-old virgin captured forever in time by the artist, Vermeer.

How much effort had he put into his work? Three hundred and thirty-two years ago, a single man had sat by candlelight or perhaps in the mid-day sun, and had constructed this extraordinary recreation of a woman. Had he licked his brush to make it perfectly straight?

No. Vermeer would have worked with mineral spirits, as there hadn't been turpentine back then to cut the oil. How many painters had died over the decades, given up their lives, slowly poisoned by the lead they'd ingested while licking their brushes? Vermeer wouldn't have; he'd worked in oil.

But the Collector had no doubt that Vermeer would have died for his art. He would look him up tomorrow at the library, get deeper information on the man than the large amount he already had, the Collector now needing to find out even more, everything that he could. He knew from simply looking at this picture that the artist had had a total mastery of the color blue.

For now he would sit here, staring at the single tiny painting that somehow dominated the entire western wall of his cavernous apartment.

Looking at the picture made the Collector want to cry.

How few men knew what it was like to be a complete, dedicated artist, how few dared? He would wander, searching, into art gallery openings, and look with disdain upon what was passing for art today, being openly rude to anyone with the temerity to dare approach him. And approach him they did, for they knew who and what he was in his everyday life, knew how important he was, how a showing at his art gallery could make them stars. Women, mostly, approached. Men were often too intimidated.

There'd been a time, once, when he'd wanted to be a painter. Before he'd begun to collect. There was a correlation there, he thought, a bond between art and violence. Today, he had indeed become a great artist, but not in the way he'd imagined. He was a master at the art of violence. Vermeer would not have been familiar with violence. Vermeer would have known about love, about trust, and about what other men called hope.

One of the phone lines buzzed and he lifted his head and listened, knew what line was being called by the sound of the ring. He stood and walked to the bedroom that he'd converted into an office, scratched his cheek and strolled over to the phone, lifted it to his ear.

"Yes."

"Jesus Christ, thank God you picked up. Listen, I know it's late—"

"It's early. What can I do for you, Lenny?"

"I've been calling all night, leaving messages, calling the gallery, the other number you give me, shit—"

"Now you've got me, Lenny."

"Look, the guy, that party you did that thing for last December?" The Collector remembered, and he told Lenny so.

"He wants to reach you. Says it's real important."

"Did the—thing—not work out?"

"It ain't that, it's something else; someone else needs kind of the same favor from you."

"I'll speak to him."

"That ain't good enough. He needs to see you, *now*."

"You call him for me, Lenny, and tell him I'll be at his home in an hour."

"I don't know his home number, I didn't even know if this was *your* home number."

"I'll bet you that if you think about it, you'll know someone who can reach him. Call them, Lenny, and tell them what I said. No matter what happens tonight, you're down for a nice surprise."

"Thanks, I could use it."

The Collector cut off the connection without bothering to say good-bye.

C H A P T E R
7

T HE COLLECTOR WAS DISGUISED, ALTHOUGH NOT SO THAT A casual observer would notice. It was a subtle alteration of his features: his hair had been sprayed to a slightly lighter color, it was dishwater blond now, dye that was easily washed out, and he'd added clear-lens aviator glasses. Cheek padding made his face appear more full, and a heavily padded suit added twenty pounds. There were lifts in the heels of his Italian-made shoes, and he had put on a loud tie to distract attention from his face.

He'd also put on makeup, giving color to his usual chalky white complexion. Colored contact-lenses made his eyes light blue. On the rare occasions that he talked to such men as these he put a smoker's rasp into his voice, a gruffness that made them feel more comfortable with him. But he never said the word "ain't," and he refused to drop his "g's," or to curse the way they did. He could not bring himself to stoop altogether to their gutter level.

As long as he did the work they wanted, he had nothing to fear from them anyway. But still, it was good form to stay in character with them, none of them could be allowed to know him, to know who he truly was. *What* he was was all that they would ever have to know.

The Man in Winnetka had told him what he'd wanted, and now the Collector walked through the cool hospital corridor, searching for the proper room. An adhesive visitor's label was attached to the pocket of his suitcoat. He walked past the nurses' station without even a glance, his eyes on the room numbers. When he found the one he wanted, he stopped and looked in before knocking.

He saw the young woman on the bed, and he estimated how long she had left to live. There was no time to waste.

A heavyset older woman was sitting in a chair on one side of the bed, her hands folded as if in prayer. Her head was bowed. The mother. The man he'd come to see was sitting in a chair pulled close to hers, one arm on its back, as if trying to give her comfort without having to physically touch her.

The Collector tapped lightly on the door and entered, and the old woman jumped in surprise. The man, though, he didn't scare as easily, he just turned in his chair and looked at the door with cold, reptilian eyes.

"Doctor?" the woman said, and the Collector shook his head.

"No, ma'am, I'm sorry to have disturbed you." Then he said to the man, "Sir, could I have a moment of your time?" Slowly, with anger, the man rose out of his comfortable leather chair. The Collector watched him come toward him, admiring with detachment the physical presence he possessed.

It was as if death itself were walking toward the door.

There was no wasted motion, no swagger, none of the rolling hip and posturing shoulder movements seen in the typical gangster walk. This man moved with economy, as if floating, those hard cold eyes never leaving the Collector's face.

The Collector had to fight not to laugh; this man had no idea that the Collector's power was even greater than his own. Alleo was so used to giving orders and being obeyed that he never realized that he'd become a caricature of a real man. He was walking toward one now, though. From the way the man was acting the Collector thought that before this was over, he might have to be taught a lesson.

This man needed *him*, not the other way around. In a worst case scenario, the Collector could kill him without a second thought. A man this age, could he make the same claim? The Collector didn't think so; when Italian men got older, he knew, they worried too much about death and hell and eternal damnation and suffering. The house he'd just left in Winnetka had been filled with religious icons; they'd discussed cold-blooded murder in a room with a crucifix on the wall. No, this man's superstitions might be enough all alone to stop him from doing the Collector any physical harm.

As long as he knew that the Collector didn't fear him; he could not be shown that he was feared. Men like this took great advantage of such things. They were ignorant brutes, boors, and peasants, and they had to be kept off guard.

The old man came out of the room and closed the door behind himself, then waved for the Collector to follow him. He walked a few feet down the deserted hallway. He spun on the Collector, and when he spoke, his low, growling voice was menacing.

"You a reporter?" Alleo wanted to know. The Collector believed that if he were, he would probably be a dead man.

"I was sent by your friend in Winnetka."

"Oh." The man immediately relaxed. The Collector knew that this old man was an expert at what he did, but he was still not good enough to hide his relief, not good enough to keep the hope and desire off his face or out of the tone of his voice. The Collector adjusted his opinion of the man accordingly.

"What's your name?"

The Collector just looked at him. Alleo let it pass.

"Can you help her?" Said soft and low, but there was no hiding the begging. The Collector silently reveled in his power over this man, a man who'd ordered more men to their deaths than the Collector had had birthdays.

"I *will* help her."

The man seemed suddenly fifty pounds lighter. His shoulders slumped, and he leaned against the wall.

"How soon?"

"Tonight."

"How much?"

"It's been taken care of."

The reptile came back now, the deadeye stare of a lizard.

"By who."

"Come on, Mr. Alleo. You know by who. By your friend up in Winnetka; he said that you'd understand."

Was that defeat in the way the man sagged as he took in the words? The Collector knew little about the business of such men; he only knew that they were vicious in the way they conducted their trade, and that they paid on time. But he always doubted their strength, and certainly their intelligence. What kind of men depended on others to do their killing for them?

"So what do I do now?"

"You sit there, sir, and you wait. But first I need your daughter's charts, I need to know everything about her medical condition."

"I can have her doctor in the room in five minutes."

"We don't want him involved yet; he can't know about anything until later. Then he'll need to be a part of it. Bring me her chart, and I can go to work."

The Collector spoke in a flat, professional voice, showing no emotion to a man who would see it as a defect. He decided to show some humanity, though, as this man had shown his own. Later, after thinking things over, Mr. Alleo might decide that he'd given away too much. And then the Collector might have a problem. So for now he would operate on this killer's level.

"I usually know what to do far in advance; I pick the families I work for very carefully. I'll have to rush this one—" he saw the look on the man's face, and then hurriedly added, "—but that's not a problem. The problem is after the job is done. I can arrange for the donor to be brought to the emergency room of this hospital, but I can't do what I usually do in order to get you what you need; I don't have the time to set it up properly. I understand that you're on good terms with certain members of the city council."

"I own three alderman outright, and others owe me favors. I know the mayor, I know the police superintendent, hell, I know the *governor*. My daughter's on the top of the list for one of these transplants, has been for a month, but we can't find the right donor, nobody can match her blood type."

"Can you pull the strings you need to make sure that what I collect goes to your daughter?"

"You get the right party here, and watch me."

"I'll need a little time."

"I ain't got much time."

"It'll be tonight, Mr. Alleo. Don't worry. I understand."

"I don't think you do."

"Sir?"

"I know what you did for the Eagle, how you got him his heart. I got to figure he owns you." The Collector was glad for the makeup he'd applied. He felt the blood rushing into his cheeks at the mere suggestion of his being servile to anyone.

"Whatever they pay you, whatever they're giving you, I'll double it if my daughter lives, if you can save her life."

"That's not nec—"

"But if she dies, if you and the Eagle can't help her, you're both dead, you got me?" The old man paused, to give his next statment more weight. "You and everyone else in this entire world that you love. If Sophia dies, they die."

The Collector studied him, making no secret of what he thought. Here was a man who needed the services he could give, and he uttered *threats?* Was he that stupid?

One of the many defects he'd noticed in people was that they thought everyone else played by their rules; felt love and hate, anguish and desire; suffered the terrible trappings of an unchecked ego and the unquenchable thirst for revenge. The Collector knew that Alleo would think that even the worst of men had at one time or another experienced love.

The fool.

To Alleo, he said, "Your friend in Winnetka warned me that you'd threaten me."

"It ain't no threat, kid," Mr. Alleo told him.

The Collector smiled. He knew with a sudden clarity what he could do to hurt this man. Later, after things quieted down, after the daughter had been saved and his work had been forgotten, he would pay her a little visit, and undo the good he'd done. He'd teach this slithering snake of a man to make threats against strangers. He'd build up this gangster's hopes, let him see his daughter live, become happy and healthy again, and then he'd kill her in a way that would haunt the old man's dreams for the rest of his miserable life.

But for the moment he fought back his bitter words, and very softly said: "Mr. Alleo, believe me, I understand your pain." He lowered his eyes for a second.

"I lost my mother this way. I'll help you, and you don't have to threaten me, and I won't tell your friend in Winnetka what you just said to me. You doubt my work? I'll show you what I can do. You have a deal, Mr. Alleo; I accept."

Mr. Alleo nodded, foolishly gratified, not knowing what he was dealing with and secure in the knowledge that he still had what it took to instill terror in the heart of a hit man.

The Collector said, "Now, please, get me the chart, and I need a number with instant access to you, from now until the job is done."

The man looked at him, a short stout man having to crane his neck to do so, and he rocked on his toes as he made up his mind about how frightened the Collector was of him.

"Come on, but wait outside the door to the room. I don't need my wife any more upset than she is."

CHAPTER

8

THE YOUNG BOY'S NAME WAS RONALD; TULIO DOUBTED IF HE KNEW how to spell it. The twelve-year-old killer sitting across from him was slouched down in a high-backed chair, one hand idly rubbing his crotch while the other held a cigarette. In spite of the image he was trying to project, Tulio could tell that the kid was afraid. His knees swung quickly open and closed, open and closed, and his thumb was patting the cigarette filter in regular little taps. When he took drags off the cigarette, he sucked in hard, as if it might be the last drag he'd ever take on a cigarette in this life. The hair on his head had been cropped into what looked like a nappy box, with lines cut into it at regular intervals. His head smelled terribly, as if he'd used bacon grease to slick his hair back. Sweat poured off his face, down onto his undershirt, which was soaked. His over-sized baggy shorts were dirty, and he had them pulled down low on his hips, so that half of his underwear stuck out at the world. On his feet were a filthy pair of Nike Air Jordans. He wore an X hat, turned to the left.

His face showed outward calm, and the boy spoke as easily as he smiled. Tulio listened, trying not to appear as any sort of a threat to the kid. The lawyer would sense it and order him from the room, and Tulio wanted to hear this.

The juvie cop, Raleigh, who was sitting next to Ronald, looked as if he'd seen it all too many times to care. He sat back with his legs crossed, smoking in the tiny room with pink-painted walls, and the lawyer allowed it only because Ronald was smoking too. She couldn't tell one to put out his cigarette without making the other feel as if he were in command.

"I kilt her, so what?" Ronald said, half-smiling. "Bitch diss'd me. Don't *nobody* diss Taco."

Taco. His street name. Tulio faked a yawn to cover his growing anger. This punk was enjoying himself. The girl Ronald had sliced to death had been nineteen years old. The medical examiner would need some time to give them an honest count of the number of wounds, but it had taken some time and trouble to kill her; it hadn't been an act of impulse.

"Why did you paint your gang sign on her in her own blood?"

"That's how she *diss'd* me." Ronald shook his head and made a spitting sound, as if forced to deal with dolts. "I threw my hands down on her to see what set she played, and she laughed at me, told me I was too young to be a Maniac."

When she spoke, the lawyer's voice was soft, filled with a compassion that Tulio couldn't understand. When dealing with people like Ronald, he could only conjure up two basic emotions: terror and hatred, and whenever Tulio experienced terror, his survival instincts transferred it into a blind, unfocused rage. He looked at the lawyer, wondered how she could be so cool with a character like this.

"What else did she tell you, Ronald?" the lawyer asked, and the kid bolted up and leaned forward in his chair.

"You call me Taco!"

"Why's that?" Raleigh asked. "'Cause you look so much like a snatch?"

"Sit back," Tulio said, and everyone looked at him; they were the first words he had spoken since he'd entered the room, and even he was surprised at how softly they'd come out.

The lawyer said, "Taco, excuse me," and the kid smiled.

To Tulio, she was young; he'd never see his mid-thirties again. He admired her and respected her, and even though they were often on opposite sides of the fence, he was sometimes awed at the seemingly easy way she did her job; talking to and taking statements from preteenage psychopaths as easily—and with as much respect—as she did the highest ranking politician in the public defender's office. Her body was something to look at too—he noticed that Ronald agreed with him when it came to that. The kid was ogling her breasts.

She was wearing a summer dress that was loose and still professional; he'd seen her in a dozen interrogations and she'd never worn an outfit that could be described as seductive. But still, she made it seem so, in the way that she filled it out.

She sensed him looking at her, he could tell by the way she lightly but angrily tossed her head. Telling him to give it a rest; the kid would pick up on it and follow Tulio's lead. She had to have all the respect she could get when dealing with a mutant like Ronald. Tulio couldn't undermine her work; it was hard enough for her as it was. He made sure that his face showed nothing, and turned his eyes to Ronald.

"When I was cuttin' on her, she told me I was a no-good mu-fucker, *that* what else she say." Ronald smiled, the attention-seeking class clown scoring a point.

"Taco," the lawyer said, "you know you're in serious trouble this time."

"Sheet. I juvie, lady, you can't do *shit* to me."

"You can be put away until you're twenty-one years old." That hit home. It was too long a time for him to imagine.

"I want me a lawyer."

"You're not entitled to one, *Ronald*," Raleigh spoke up. "You're a *kid*, you said so yourself. Kids don't get no lawyers."

"I ain't go *no*wheres till I twenny-one, fuck that, lady."

The lawyer had had enough.

"Taco," she said, "I *am* your lawyer. This man's just busting your balls. I'm assigned for the moment, and I can help you if you want me to, but only if you'll stop acting as if this is a trip to Great America."

The lawyer looked at the kid with hard green eyes, her lips compressed into tight little red lines. She was about to drop the punch line and she wanted the kid to know it.

She said, "Taco, do you really want my help? Are you willing to try and work with some professionals? Will you help them to figure out not only what you did, but *why* you did it?"

"Tole you why I did it, lady. The bitch diss'd me."

"No, that wasn't it at all."

"Sheet."

"Look, kid," Raleigh said. "I can make you a deal right here, in front of witnesses." He smiled at Ronald, and Tulio stole a glance at the lawyer.

She was glaring at Raleigh, making no secret about how she felt toward his interruption, too much a professional to sabotage his authority in front of the boy. Appearances had to be kept up, and a kid like this would have learned how to manipulate before he'd gotten out of diapers. The three adults in the room had to show a united front. Ronald was looking at Raleigh, half-suspecting that the man was running a game.

But still, he was paying attention, and Raleigh continued.

"We know you didn't do this alone, no matter what you say. There were older boys involved, boys who can take the rap for you. Ronald, here's the deal. You give us the names of the kids that you were with, and we let you go, as simple as that."

Ronald smiled a smile of pure street ignorance.

"Okay. But then I be needin' a ride home."

"Stop!" The lawyer spoke the word loudly, and it rang off the walls like the report of a small pistol.

Raleigh jumped as if she'd slapped him. Tulio didn't move.

"Taco, he isn't telling you the truth. There's no way on earth he can let you walk away from this. No one's letting you go, no one's taking you home. If there's any deals made here tonight, only *I* am authorized to make them, in consultation with a lawyer who has been assigned to prosecute you."

"Hey, lady," Raleigh said, and the lawyer shut him up with a glare that seemed capable of melting stone.

"That's enough, Raleigh." Tulio could tell that she wanted to go on, but she stopped herself, and turned back to the kid.

"You killed a young girl, Taco, and you'll have to pay the price for that. But there's help for you if you want it; I know people who can work with you, and they *will* work with you. Together, along with a friend of mine whom you'll have to live with, in a controlled environment, they can find out what happened to you, what's wrong, and together you can work to fix it, but I can't do it for you, all I can do is help.

"Now, you want a deal? Here's a deal for you, Taco. You give these officers the names of the boys you were with, and I *can* promise you that the judge will sentence you to a restricted, maximum security juvenile detention center with an ongoing inpatient psychiatric facility."

"You call that a deal?" The boy was trying to sound cool and disaffected, but he was staring at the lawyer hungrily, seeing a way out. Tulio wondered if it was a manipulation, or if the boy actually wanted help, a way out of his life.

"That's the best deal you'll ever get. The detention center and help for your problem, and you better jump right on it, Taco. By the time the prosecutor gets here it might be too late."

"How you guarantee that? How you promise me that?"

"The judge is my father."

Ronald smiled, highly amused.

He said, "Your daddy the *judge?*" and threw his head back and laughed. "Ain't this a bitch? Your daddy a *judge.*" He shook his head as his laughter subsided, then reached across the table for his pack of Kools. The pack had been opened from the bottom, and Ronald tapped one out, stuck it in his mouth and lit it from the butt of the cigarette that was smoldering in his fingers.

"I go lady, to this joint you talkin' 'bout, you give me some *ong-ion?*"

"Some what?"

"Onion, lady," Raleigh said, then elaborated. "It means pussy." The lawyer at last seemed startled.

Tulio had seen and heard more than he could handle. He stood quickly, grabbed the kid by the front of his undershirt, and dragged him out of the chair, threw him hard up against the wall.

"That's it for you, Ronald. This is your last warning." The Kool was stuck in the corner of Ronald's mouth, and Tulio slapped it out from between his lips. It glanced off the wall, shooting ashes all over the room. Tulio held the kid against the wall with one hand, making sure his fingers never touched Ronald's face.

Tulio said, "One more remark, one more insult, and I'll book you as a John Doe and you'll spend the night in the County. I'll get in trouble, maybe even fired, but it'd be worth it, Ronald, to see what they'd do to you in there in just one night."

Tulio felt something plucking at his shirtsleeve, looked down and saw that it was a hand, clasped on his forearm. The lawyer had a grip on him, was trying hard to pull his arm free.

"Leave him al*one!*" He heard it from a distance. "Tulio!"

Tulio let go. Ronald wasn't acting so blasé now. His face showed shock, terror, and hatred at the same time.

Tulio watched, fascinated, as the kid's face communicated all the feelings that he was too inarticulate to express. Or it might be a lack of courage that kept him from speaking his mind; Ronald might be realizing that he had no knife in his hand; that this was no defenseless young woman standing in front of him.

Tulio said, "Stay in line, *Taco,* or you won't make it long enough to get into any clinic."

"Lieutenant, that's *enough.*"

Tulio looked at her, in contempt of her outrage, the woman taking sides against him with a vicious, heartless killer. Slowly, he sat back down in his chair. The lawyer firmly led Ronald back to his own seat, then sat down herself, composed and in control.

Raleigh said, "All right, kid, before your mind gets to racing, you should know there ain't no witnesses to that shit that just happened." The lawyer looked at Raleigh with contempt. "What happened was, you charged the Lieutenant here, and he pushed you against the wall."

"*She* my damn witness." Ronald jutted his chin toward the lawyer. "She seen it all." Raleigh snorted in disgust.

"And you're as stupid as you look, *Ronald*. You think any judge in this county's gonna believe your *lawyer's* word against two cops with forty-five years on the force between them?" Raleigh glared at the lawyer.

He said, "The deal's on the table, take it or leave it. It's the best you'll ever get in this lifetime, kid, believe me. Take it. You leave it, you go to the Audy home, and we all know what'll happen to you in there."

"No!" Ronald shouted, looking to the lawyer for help.

"Lady, all right, help me, get me out of here, will you? I don't want to go to no juvie joint, I ain't even in the set. I ain't no Maniac." His eyes were brimming with tears. Raleigh looked at him, bored, seeing him as a psychotic little killer who should be put away for the rest of his life. The lawyer looked at him, too, seeing a young tortured soul that needed nurturing and had never received it, but one who could survive if offered prompt and proper treatment.

Tulio also looked at the kid, and wasn't sure what he saw. He seemed pitiful. Or would, if Tulio hadn't seen what he'd done to a young girl in a hot, dark alley on the West Side of the city.

The lawyer said, "I'll help you, Taco, but only if you help these men clear up what happened tonight. You have to start making up for what you did by telling them who you were with."

"My homeboys, they kill me if they know I give them up." Ronald, defeated, was now bargaining for protection.

"I can't promise that they won't find out," the lawyer said.

"Where I go? To the Audy home with them?"

"No, they won't be near you. You'll be somewhere else."

"All right. I tell you, but I got a con-*dit*-ion."

"What's that, Taco?" There was exasperation in the lawyer's voice, that and curiosity. Tulio wondered how she did it. This kid should be told that he was in no position to make conditions or set terms. He'd just been handed the deal of a lifetime.

"*He* got to leave the room." Ronald pointed at Tulio. "He locked my brother, my boy's down for the rest of his life. He whomped me, busted my square. I don't say nothin' in front of him, uh-uh, or I wind up like Jamahl, I know how he do you."

"Lieutenant?" the lawyer said, and Tulio stood. He didn't mind leaving the room; the smoke was getting to him anyway.

CHAPTER 9

Jᴀᴋᴇ Pʜɪʟʟɪᴘs sᴀᴛ ɪɴ ᴛʜᴇ ᴄᴀʀ, ʙɪᴛɪɴɢ ʜɪs ᴛᴏɴɢᴜᴇ ᴛᴏ ᴋᴇᴇᴘ ʜɪs ᴍᴏᴜᴛʜ shut throughout Moore's entire tirade. He acted as if the words didn't hurt him, even though they did, even though he had to stop himself from punching Moore's fat face in. He didn't want to make any waves, had learned how the department worked at the knee of a man who'd been part of the problem for years, but shit if it wasn't tough this time, after this slob had given his pinch away just to get back at Jake for shaking Tulio's hand. Given it straight away to a couple of TAC slobs who'd been standing around, hiding out, using the murder as an excuse to get out of their car and off their asses. Now *they* had the pinch, and they owed Moore a favor, and what did Jake get out of the deal? Nothing, that's what.

They drove through the South Side, past burned-out buildings and storefront churches. There were groups of young black men standing on every street corner, and when they'd stop at a light these youths would stare at them in a way that frightened Phillips. They didn't seem to frighten Moore, though, he just ignored them, that or he glared right back. He acted as if his fat ass and badge somehow made him immune to gunfire.

As mad as he was, Moore would interrupt his harangue as he stared out at the alien, angry faces, speak to Jake as if they were pals, bound by the badge against the surrounding enemy. Telling Jake to look at 'em, bunch of ignorant welfare jigs. Telling Jake how he was going to get a T-shirt made up, one that said, WORK! then underneath: ɪᴛ's ᴀ ᴡʜɪᴛᴇ ᴛʜɪɴɢ,

YOU WOULDN'T UNDERSTAND. They'd pull away from the corner, and Moore, outside of the sight line of a race he feared, would turn his hatred on to Jake again.

Jake listened as Moore cursed him, berated him, asked him how the hell could he shake the man's hand after what he'd done to his partner.

At first he'd tried to explain things to Moore, but it was obvious that Moore wasn't listening, so Phillips sat back, his legs pushing him further into the car seat, looking out the window until this windbag ran out of steam.

Moore drove in silence for a while, fucking off more than anything else, taking them out on a wild goose chase, on their way to try and deliver a murder warrant to a man they both knew had given a phony address the last time he'd been arrested. He'd gotten the assignment after going back to headquarters and kvetching in the office with the captain for a while. Probably ratting out Tulio, the son of a bitch. He liked Moore silent. It was better than the shit he'd been talking earlier, about Tulio's girlfriend, the lawyer he'd met back at headquarters. Suddenly Moore broke the silence, his voice now seeming more hurt than angry.

"You shouldn't'a done that, Philly. I know you're new, I know you lack experience, but you always got to back your partner up, you shouldn't'a shook his hand."

Was he expecting an apology? Jake couldn't tell. If he was, he shouldn't wait for one with his hand on his ass; it would grow there before Jake would apologize for what he'd done. He wanted to tell him that he agreed with Tulio, that he thought that Moore was an asshole, but he didn't. He was new, this was his first day in Homicide, he didn't want to make any waves, did not want to rock the boat. Because he knew that if he did, and if he caused the boat to turn over, *he* would be the one to drown, because Moore had been swimming in shit for so long that he could win a gold medal for it if it were an Olympic event.

"I'm doing you a favor, you know," Moore went on. "I ain't trained nobody in ten years I been working the death squad. The captain asked me specifically if I'd let you ride along, and I told him okay, 'cause now you both owe me."

This was not a belief that Phillips felt he could afford to let the man harbor. He said, "*He* owes you, Moore, if anyone does. The *captain* owes you, not me."

"What? What did you say?"

Moore took his eyes off the road and gave Jake an intimidating stare. Jake shook his head, breathed deep.

"If you did the captain a favor taking me on, fine, he owed you one. I don't owe you shit until you do something for me."

"So, you think so, huh?"

There was no coexisting with some people. With guys like Moore, everything had to be spelled out; subtlety would never be understood.

Phillips said, "I think you haven't done anything for me, yeah, I think that's the case. I ask you questions, you either ignore them or find some way to insult me when you answer them. That's not doing me much of a favor, Jerry. You call me by a name that's not mine, you disrespect me like I'm some street punk suspected of something instead of your partner."

For a second Jake thought that Moore was going to pull the car to the curb and punch him. He raced the engine a little and half-pulled over, then slammed on the brakes as cars swerved around them. The sound of bleating horns and harsh black voices cursing came to him above the rush from the air conditioner, right through the closed window of the sedan.

Then Moore got control of himself and pulled back onto Drexel. When he spoke his voice was wheedling, thinking he knew the score.

"You got friends somewhere, don't you, Phillips? Guys looking out for you?" He paused, deep in thought. Moore proving to Phillips exactly the type of man he was: one who thought that no one would ever speak up to him without having a powerful friend in the department. "You some-body's son, Phillips?"

"We're all somebody's son, Jerry," Phillips said, and relaxed in his seat. Rock the boat or not, he'd ask for a new training officer the second they got back to headquarters.

He sat in a room by himself, Lieutenant Anthony Tulio all alone, with no one around for him to dazzle with his alacrity, wit and knowledge of the erratic criminal mind.

Around crowds of his fellow officers he'd keep his face impassive, but he was always warmed inside by the knowledge that he impressed the shit out of them, that they knew that he, Tony Tulio, was the best Homi-cide detective there was in the entire Chicago Police Department. Even a slob like Moore would have to be impressed by Tulio's quick solution to the murder on the near South Side.

Jake Phillips, for one, had been awed by Tulio's solution, but that awe would be tempered soon by the habitual criminal's propensity to speak nothing but lies, and Jake would learn the hard realities involved in fighting crime. They'd find the murder weapon, Tulio would bet on that, and the killer would be faced with the fact that he was caught, but he'd come up with a story that no lawyer—even the hellcat in the interrogation room with Ronald—could break; it was the way it was these days, in the victim-saturated city he lived in.

The killer would say that the man in the car had waved something at him that looked like a pistol, and he'd fired in response to what he'd thought to be an attempt at a drive-by homicide. The victim was a white man in a black man's neighborhood, and he'd been driving a shiny new Cadillac. The killer would cry on the witness stand, and if the jury didn't let him go then they of course would find him guilty, but not of murder, Tulio knew, and not of murder-burglary. The killer might even cop to manslaughter before a trial, and do three years, and the victim would be forgotten before the killer hit the yard.

Jake's awe would be forgotten, too, as his desire to see justice would be greatly tempered by a judge or a jury or a plea bargain from a lawyer in the State's Attorney's office.

The disposition of a case rarely mattered to Tony Tulio, though; solving the crime was what he was really all about.

That was where he did his job better than anyone else could do it. No one on the force even came close. It made Tulio believe, just for a little while, that what he did was important, and therefore that he was, too. He was still the best, in the eyes of the rest of the force. But now he was alone, and being the best at what he did didn't seem to count for much.

No one was really predictable, that was the entire secret. People might be expected to act in a predictable way if treated in a certain manner; that conformed to human nature. But every person—cop or crook—was unique, driven by things that they truly believed no one else could understand.

Cops could sometimes be lazy; they looked for the easy way out. And—thank God—most crooks were incredibly stupid human beings. He'd had too many experiences with them to ever believe otherwise.

When he'd been working Homicide, before the inception of Special Victims, he'd solved a murder quickly, had the name of a suspect, but the suspect had taken what on the street was called an Outie 5000: had split after the crime, and Tulio couldn't find him. The papers had run the suspect's picture, and had quoted Tulio extensively. Tulio had gone on and on about the homosexual aspects of the homicide, how the killer had obviously been striking out as a way to prove his manhood and to hide his effeminate qualities.

Gay activists had gone berserk, but the killer had read the article— or had someone read it to him—and he'd called, as outraged as the activists seemed to be, and as he'd cursed at Tulio and told him that *he* was the faggot, that his *momma* was the faggot, as he'd bragged about how he would never be caught, Tulio had calmly traced the call and the killer had been captured while still on a pay phone, in the lobby of a fleabag hotel, three blocks from police headquarters. He had gotten the job done, and he'd lost no sleep over his tarnished image in the gay or any other community.

That crook, like most of them, had been pretty damned stupid.

But narrow frames of reference cut both ways, and what the public rejected from one group, they would easily accept from another. Especially if they could be convinced that they were getting insider information. Just throw a little psychobabble in and watch the sheep line up for your shears.

Tell them that as a working cop you knew a way to tell if a suspect was guilty. Tell them that the guilty ones, they always go to sleep in their cells after they've been processed. See the big eyes and the look of enlightenment come over their faces as they digest what you have told them, and hope that none of them have the sense to think the matter through. It looks good on paper, but Tulio hoped that such enlightened viewpoints would never be taken as evidence in a court of law.

He'd been there, a long time ago. When becoming a cop was the furthest thing from his young and immature mind. Tulio knew what it was like, because, unfortunately, he'd had to live through it.

You get arrested and you're scared to death, there are people with power and authority over you who are pointing guns at your head. For the minimum of an hour—sometimes much longer—you live in a state of pure, raging terror. Depending on your background, you are called an asshole, a shithead, a shine, a spic or a guinea, over and over again by people who make it clear to you that they want you off the street for the rest of your natural life, even if they have to kill you to meet that agenda. If you've never done any serious time before, they will try and terrify you with stories of what the niggers will do to your asshole once you hit the county lockup. If they think they can get information from you, they will tyrannize you with stories about the penitentiary, trying to get you to squeal. Your entire existence is compressed into seconds; there is no past, no future. There is just now, and the feeling of steel handcuff ratchets biting into the skin on your wrists. Just these people who can show you kindness if you give them what they want, or who can cause you untold grief and pain if you dare to take an attitude.

They throw you in front of a camera and snap pictures, they roll ink onto a blotter and shove your fingers into it. Then they lock you up in detention, usually in a tiny cell with cheaply painted brick walls and thin disposable mattresses atop old and squeaky springs, with plastic blankets to cover you and a toilet that has no lid. The door slams shut and the adrenalin stops flowing, and, if you're lucky, you find that you are alone.

You lie down on your "bed" and cover your eyes with your arm and you try and block out the panic.

Within minutes you are asleep.

Then a cop looks in on you, sees the state you're in, and can proclaim you guilty as hell because as soon as they locked you up, *bam*, man, you fell right to sleep.

For him it was just another night on the job, you were just another failed player that he'd put away for a little while.

To you, however, things looked a little different.

Perspective was the answer.

These days the stakes were higher than ever before, and the killings more coldblooded, and not as easily figured out. The further away he got from what he'd been, the harder it was to remember what it had been like.

Unlike most cops, Tulio never looked for the easy way out unless it was completely obvious to him that there could be no other solution. It had brought him a measure of unwanted fame, but more importantly, it brought him autonomy.

He was the actual head of the Special Victims squad, even though he had three men of rank to whom he answered. Even though he had more enemies than friends within the department. Even though the press believed that he was a homophobic, racist, fascist pig. That was all right; he used them more than they used him.

He was the boss, the man the men believed in, and after twenty-one years of standing alone he now had a squad who counted on him. The problem was, he wasn't really sure if he wanted it anymore.

Ronald was sitting in the next room over, giving his statement to a kiddie cop and a lawyer who wanted to help him, who was only there at Tulio's invitation, extended because Tulio wanted to get the Homicide cops' goat for calling him out on a simple killing that they could have handled without his help.

The bulls on that one hadn't even bothered to hang around.

Ronald would be in there embellishing things, playing down his own personal role in the brutal, ugly crime. The lawyer would be nodding her head, at least pretending to believe him. Ronald would be staring at the ceiling, making it up as he went along, rolling his eyes and smoking. The lawyer would be taking it all down, looking to help the monster, encouraging Ronald to give her more and thinking of a creative way to get her boss to stand up to the deal she had cut for the kid.

Everyone in the room had been seeing Ronald as something different. All of them would to some extent be right, yet all of them would be wrong.

Ronald was, to Tulio, the face of things to come.

How long could you be expected to look at mutilated corpses and teenaged killers? There was a growing number of stone cold killers who were only upset by the fact that they had somehow screwed up and been caught. Tell them that the life they took was as valuable as their own, and they would look at you and sneer, they could never grasp that concept.

Was it lack of imagination that made things the way they were today? Or laziness? Or maybe just a casual attitude toward violence, the dehumanization of every other person in the world except themselves.

Few people suspected this about Tulio, and even less would believe it if you told them, but sensitivity had been the thing that had really made him successful, and when he was confronted with the total lack of it, he became, inside, enraged.

It was what made him a good cop, and what made him a candidate for an early retirement. If a heart attack didn't get him first. Or a bullet from a pistol aimed by a son of a bitch like Ronald. Score him a cop, that would get him into the set.

He'd thrown himself into his work immediately after the accident that had changed his life, had worked long, fierce hours, and sometimes that would work.

It seemed to be working less and less though, these days. The challenge didn't seem to matter to him as much as it had before the accident.

But that challenge, being smarter than they were, had at one time been of the utmost importance. Beating them at their own game and seeing the looks on their faces when he came calling at their door, with his badge swinging loosely from a chain around his neck. Proving the crime was the prosecutor's job, solving it was his. And he had loved to solve crimes, there was no doubt about that.

Since Martie and Jess's deaths it had become a lot less important.

The door opened and he started, did a quick reality check, made sure that his face was blank, that the thought of Jess and Martie hadn't caused his eyes to water. He looked up, coldly, to see Raleigh standing in the doorway.

"Hey man," Raleigh said, his voice cold and angry. "What the fuck's your problem, bringing that bitch into the interview? She wasn't the defender on call tonight—you know how her fucking heart bleeds."

Coolly, Tulio said, "I didn't bring her, I only asked her to sit in. Blame Homicide. If they'd have handled it themselves instead of calling me out, you could have told that sorry-ass kid all the lies you wanted to and gotten away with it, Raleigh. As usual. *And* you could have called the Assistant State's Attorney in, the way you're supposed to, to counteract what she was doing."

"Yeah, I'd'a done that, and *two* lawyers would'a seen you assault the kid. You'd'a been in jail by now, and Taco'd be roamin' the 'hood."

"I did that for your benefit. I know it's SOP in juvie."

"Man, *fuck* you." Raleigh slammed the door shut and Tulio felt himself loosen up, but then the door reopened almost immediately, and he made his face blank, expecting Raleigh again, and so he was surprised to see, instead, the lawyer.

C H A P T E R

10

Tulio nodded to her, one foot resting on a chair, knee up, his forearms across the knee. He lifted his hand in greeting. She walked over to him, pulled the chair away from under his foot, and sat down on it, shaking her head at him sadly.

"Why did you do it?"

"Do *what?*" he said, though he knew what she meant.

"Why call me in? You know what will happen tomorrow? The hell we'll both catch? I'm a public defender, for God's sake. This is bad, Tony."

He used his favorite excuse, one he spoke aloud plenty of times, whenever he was asked to justify his behavior. "Sometimes you have to do bad things in order to get a good thing done."

She shook her head in exasperation; it wasn't the first time she'd heard him use the phrase.

"You'll never learn, will you Tulio?"

"Learn what?" Tulio was all innocence now, raising his eyebrows quizzically.

"Raleigh's really pissed."

"At you, counselor, not me."

"He knew what I'd say, how I'd play it, the second he saw me walk into the room. It's not as if we'd never seen each other before. He took a shot at lying to the kid, hoping I'd give him one, that I'd keep my mouth shut, but he knew, which was why he didn't complain when I brought him down. But *you're* the one who called me in, and he's mad at you, Lieutenant."

"He'll get over it," Tulio said. He leaned forward in the chair, reached out and touched her face. "You're so damn beautiful."

She pulled away, quickly.

"Tony, stop it."

He leaned into her, tried to kiss her, sensed her reticence and reluctantly pulled back.

"Come on, Marian, don't you think everyone knows by now?"

"I think some of them might. Do you know who I just saw in the hall? That fat, miserable, piece of garbage excuse for a man, Moore. He introduced me to his new partner, staring at my breasts the whole time, leering at me. Tells that kid, Jake something or other, he tells him I'm your old lady."

"That fuck. What did you say?"

"I told him that I wasn't anyone's old lady, and I walked away. What was I supposed to do, scream for you and let you beat him up? Twice in one night? I'm still a professional, and so are you. So don't treat me like a squeeze, all right? I'm not gonna be ripping off quickies in interrogation rooms."

"What? What the hell did you say?"

"You heard me, Tony."

"I heard you, but I don't believe you. When'd I ever act like that? It was just a happy birthday kiss."

"And you called me in on this case to spend time with me on my birthday."

"I called you because that kid's barely out of diapers, and he's a cold-blooded, heartless killer. He needs someone like you."

"Is that it? Wow, have *you* changed! Imagine that, Tony Tulio, all of a sudden caring about the disadvantaged youth of our city. I know better, Tony. The only question is, did you do it just to piss off Raleigh, or to get back at Homicide for calling you out tonight? Either way, I'd like you to know I don't appreciate being used."

"I've *never* used you."

"Well, I think you have. And I resent it."

"Is this what's called getting in touch with our feelings? *Sharing* with each other?" Tulio regretted the words the second they were out of his mouth.

"Don't you dare analyze me. You resent me when I do it to you, and you're less qualified to do it than I am, pal."

Tulio let the insult to his education pass, just looked at her quizzically, said, "Then what the hell is it? What's been wrong with you lately?"

He watched her, suspecting certain things, but not accusing her of them, wanting to hear them from her. If she confirmed his suspicions then the two of them would be through, he'd walk, though it would hurt worse than anything had hurt since the accident two years ago.

He'd ask, and if he thought that she might be lying to him, he'd check out his suspicions, see if they were true. He didn't know how he felt about that. He was afraid of what he might find, and even more frightened of what he might do if he found the wrong thing.

If he couldn't trust her, what good would it do for them to stay together? But it was too much for him to think about, he had to concentrate on what was going on right here, right now, this minute.

Marian said, "Nothing," and sighed, and Tulio was careful to keep his face blank. She was lying to him, and he knew it. Something was wrong, and he thought he knew what it was.

He had to be careful here, he didn't want to blow what he had with this woman. Or, rather, what he used to have, before she'd begun to change.

Still, he had to know. Keeping his voice level, showing her none of the panic he was feeling, Tulio asked the question that he wasn't sure he wanted an answer to.

"Is there someone else, is that it, Marian?"

All she could do was look at him.

"Will you at least *talk* to me about it?"

He was begging now, he could hear it in his voice, but he didn't care, he loved her. He sat in the chair, didn't want to make any move that she might perceive as threatening.

"Will you come and get a cup of coffee with me?"

He felt his face twisting, fought to control himself. He did not want her to stay with him out of some sense of pity. And she might, she had that much compassion in her. He watched her, saw her fighting, struggling with something inside.

Softly, in a low tone, she said, "Tony, let's just call it a day. It didn't work. We tried, but it didn't work."

When he didn't answer, when he just stared at her, Marian continued. "You're too—in*tense*—too focused on your work."

Tulio took a deep breath. "I've never pushed you, Marian, in the year we've been seeing each other, I've never been like that with you." He tried to make himself stop, he sounded like an imploring fool. And she was staring at him as if she saw him that way, too. Look at her. She could act as sensitive and caring as she wanted, but it was clear from her expression that on some level, she was enjoying this.

"I'm sorry, Tony, I don't want to hurt you. But it's over. It has been for months."

"Months? You owe me the truth, Marian, I got that much coming to me!" He was shouting now, and she looked at him, hard.

"Don't you dare yell at me! And I don't owe you anything!" She paused, as if worried as to how far she should go. "You're right, okay? There is someone else." She watched him, waiting to see how he'd react. He felt himself slump, as the truth hit home. "There has been for a while. I just didn't know how to break it to you."

Tulio was disgusted. "Then go to him," he said.

Marian lifted a hand, tentatively reached out, as if to touch him, then pulled it back when she saw his eyes.

"You heard me," Tulio shouted. "Get out of here. Go to the mother-fucker!"

Without another word, Marian left the room.

C H A P T E R

11

THE COLLECTOR SAT AT HIS DESK, FLIPPING THROUGH FILES THAT had been transferred onto computer memory. He wasn't flying through them, but still, he was in a hurry. This Alleo was not a man who would take kindly to the Collector should he fail to perform the task he'd been paid to do.

Nor, for that matter, was the Eagle. He had paid in cash, money that was now hidden away in the Collector's office safe, to be invested tomorrow, a little at a time so as not to draw attention from the IRS. He smiled as he figured out that it would take him over three weeks to invest it all at $9,900 at a time. But he would have trouble investing it, or anything else, ever again, if he didn't save Sophia Alleo.

Which might not be as easy as he'd thought it would.

Her blood type was rare. He had been searching through his files for an hour and had not come up with a match.

On the computer screen was a picture of a pretty woman in her mid-twenties. Next to the picture was a partial history: height, weight, hair color, eye color, age, date of birth, social security number, marital status and address. Her blood type was on the bottom right hand side: A Positive. This one would be allowed to live another night.

Rapidly, the Collector scrolled. Down a page, looking quickly at the blood type, then he'd hit the button to erase the picture and bring up another page. He had several thousand files in the machine, which were added to constantly, with files dropped from time to time. He carefully watched the Chicago papers, and he had hired a clipping service that sent him the obituary pages from newspapers statewide so he could delete certain files when the situation called for it. Everyone in the computer was currently alive and living in the state of Illinois. Every time a driver's license was granted to an organ donor, he got a copy and it cost him fifty cents. The process was expensive, but worth every penny.

How many had he looked through already, a thousand, two thousand? What if he couldn't find a woman with Sophia's blood type? Or what if he found her, and she lived downstate, a six-hour trip one way if he were to drive? It might be too late to call a pilot. He forced his mind off that problem; if he needed one, he'd find one, there were plenty of people willing to do anything for anyone, as long as the price was right. He'd cross that bridge when he came to it; for now, he just had to keep going, had to find a suitable match.

For the best possible result, he would like to have someone as near in all physical aspects to Sophia as he could find, but so far the best match he'd been able to come up with was an Italian male who lived in Southern Illinois. Sophia might have to settle for that, but the optimum result would not come from an organ whose donor was much older than herself. Still, ape livers had recently been successfully transplanted into humans; if push came to shove, she would have to settle for the male.

The Collector didn't panic; it wasn't in his emotional makeup to do so. He'd find a donor or he wouldn't, and if he couldn't, he'd return the money. Maybe he'd even have to take back the heart that he'd given the Eagle last winter, using his own brand of surgery; he could do that if they pushed it.

The Eagle, this Alleo, he hated working for such men. For mobsters who thought that they could intimidate everyone. They couldn't intimidate him, he didn't think it was humanly possible.

Still, he didn't want to fail. Nor did he wish to kill the Eagle, Alleo, and everyone who knew of him and what he'd done for the Eagle. All those killings would be risky, and worse, they'd be done for free, and he didn't like to work for free, although he would if he had to. He was a professional, an artist. There was no emotional involvement on his part. For him, it would always be a matter of artistic perfection.

Fifteen pages later, the Collector found his match.

Thank God that the woman lived near enough so that he could drive over to acquire her. In his career he'd sometimes had to rent planes, the pilots being the type who were used to strange requests. They asked no questions and saw nothing, took their money and forgot all about the strange, tall, slender man who carried sacks of things back from various parts of the state.

He had a couple such pilots whom he knew he could count on, but tonight he wouldn't be needing them. The woman was close, in the northern suburbs, in a village called Lake Forest. He was vaguely familiar with the area, had attended parties there back when he was still trying to fit in.

The Collector was driving a stolen plumber's van with plates that weren't originals. He drove the posted speed limits, and, even this late at night, people flashed their bright lights at him from behind and were ignored. As were the honking horns and the raised middle fingers as the cars flashed passed him. He had no time for egos, so he wasted no effort on response.

Things were far different up here than they were in Chicago.

There was no noise to speak of. These were people who would sue each other over loud lawnmowers or mufflers. The only buses that passed this way stayed to the main streets, dropping off and collecting the minorities who worked as domestsic servants. Their major noise problem would be the acorns rolling across their slated roofs each fall. Maybe a dog barking, if left out unattended at night. He would have to be careful to adjust to that; he could draw attention in this area.

He hated this, doing rush jobs, without time to prepare and draft plans. Usually he had the neighborhood down in his mind, a map right there in his head, escape plans drawn up, extra getaway cars on side streets, in case of emergencies or an unexpected change of plan. He would know everything about the intended victim: if they had kids, how many; what the spouse's name was. Where the parents lived. What security they had. He'd know these and thousands of other details before he'd go out to make his acquisition.

Tonight, he had nothing. Only a name—Carole Conners—and an address. And a blood type. In a way, though, it made the acquisition more of a challenge to him. Could the local Lake Forest police stop him? Could they even stand a chance? If they came near him he would kill them, and *still* take this Conners woman home with him in a bag.

He forced himself not to think about it, he had a job to do, and he hadn't picked the circumstances. He would be paid double his usual fee because of the extra risks involved, and now he had to live up to them, had to take them as they came.

The Conners residence was a wooded estate in an area filled with houses that could quite properly be referred to as mansions. Not that anyone in this area would ever refer to them as such. He pictured them as the types who would tell their colleagues that they had "a place" in Lake Forest. Say it like that to show that they themselves were old wealth. New Japanese cars lined the curbs, with a few Cadillacs and Lincolns thrown in here and there for variety. There were many trees on the Conners' property, and a long curving driveway that led up to the mansion itself. The Collector cut his lights and drove slowly up the driveway. When he was halfway up the drive, he parked the van and hurried silently into the woods.

A convertible Pontiac Sunbird was parked in the driveway. That would be her car. The one she'd driven home from college just a few short weeks before. A light was on above a side door; he could see it burning brightly through the gaps in an old iron fence. Was the side screen door open? He stood there, hidden by trees, until his eyes became acclimated to the darkness. Yes, the door was open. He could see a woman's silhouette in the doorway.

It was her. He stood looking at her, at the woman who, in just a few minutes, would become his latest acquisition.

What did she do in the summer, his Carole? Did she hold down a job, was she learning the value of money? Or did her parents allow her the luxury of simply doing nothing? He hoped that the latter was the case. Hoped she'd been enjoying her first summer break away from college.

She was nineteen years old, with blond hair and rich green eyes. A stunning combination. He'd once had a woman who'd looked almost exactly like her. Hanging, framed, on his living room wall. Just the sight of Ms. Conners on the computer screen had stunned him for a second, and when he'd finally looked down and had seen her blood type, he'd known that it was destiny.

He was excited, in the darkness, smelling freshly mown grass and the mixed scent of a variety of flowers. This was his most wonderful moment, the artist about to create. He heard the sound of a small dog barking and he circled the mansion, went around back, then walked boldly through the gate that led to the pool and toward the house.

• • •

Carole Conners harshly whispered Muffin's name, angry at the little dog, this poodle that her mother loved so dearly. Why didn't Mom let the dog out herself? One of these days Carole would ask that question; she wasn't about to spend her summer taking care of her mother's dog. She stopped thinking that way, cursing herself; her mother was good to her. What was wrong with her expecting Carole to let the dog out before she went to bed during the summer? Carole stayed up much later than her parents. Besides, Muffin wasn't so bad, she was actually pretty cute. She'd sure been excited enough to see Carole when she'd walked through the door in June, hailing the hero college freshman returning for the summer.

Carole heard Muffin barking, fitfully, and in spite of her annoyance, she smiled. Little Muffin, little nervous, rat-looking Muffin, was barking madly at something out there on the property, as if she were capable of scaring some neighborhood cat away.

"Muffin! Come on, come *here!*"

For as long as anyone could remember, Carole had been thoughtful, appreciative of any kindness shown her, large or small. Even the snooty neighbors in this exclusive area had always doted on her, on Marge and Ben's little girl. Marge and Ben's only child. It could be a drag at times, living up to her parents' expectations, but it was fun, too, seeing the pride on their faces whenever she surpassed their already high hopes.

There was always something in it for her, but that wasn't why she'd accomplished what she had. The Sunbird had been promised to her five years ago, on the day that she'd graduated grade school. Four years of High Honor Roll, Carole, her father had told her back then, 4.0 grade point average, and any car you want is yours. Within reason, of course.

She'd gotten those straight A's, and had been a social whiz to boot, had grown into a woman during her high school years, and her father had presented her with the car on graduation day.

Was something out there? Carole felt a soft stirring of fear. She shook her head and made a face at her foolishness. Where did she think she was? This wasn't the campus, where you had to be careful all the time. This was Lake Forest, for heaven's sake. There wasn't any crime in Lake Forest.

Carole turned her head to the side, stood silently listening.

What had happened to the dog?

"Muffin?"

Carole walked toward the side of the house, whispering the dog's name.

The low-wattage light bulb from above the side door didn't shine out this far. Back here, the night was black. Carole Cummings shivered, in spite of the horrible heat. She hugged herself, and chided herself for being afraid of the dark. What could happen here? What on earth could possibly happen?

Suddenly Carole couldn't breathe.

Someone had her by the throat, was choking her with a powerful hand, and in her panic she saw that it was a man, a man who seemed entertained by her flailing, by her desperate attempts to push him away.

What turned her fear to terror was the way that he was smiling, looking at her in reflective contemplation.

Oxygen deprived and rapidly losing strength, Carole began in her mind to pray.

The last thought she had as blackness swarmed over her was concern for her mother's dog; she hoped he hadn't hurt Muffin.

C H A P T E R 12

He HADN'T ACTUALLY HURT THE DOG; HE'D KILLED IT BEFORE IT even knew that it was in danger. The Collector had it in the back of the van now, lying in a loose-limbed bundle beside the bound-and-gagged form of what was still a living and breathing Carole Conners.

He'd carried her to the van and had put her in the back, then returned to the open side door, had gone stealthily into her house to find and search through her purse. Her wallet was now stuffed into the back pocket of her jeans. It would not seem out of place to the hospital attendants, nor to the police. They'd know that she'd been murdered, but they'd never suspect why.

Behind him, Carole Conners was breathing raggedly, banging around among the pipes and the various plumber's tools. She'd panic when she awakened, but she wouldn't be able to do much to relieve that panic, nor would she be able to scream. All she'd be able to do would be to make nasal sounds of fear, sounds which wouldn't be heard above the noise of the van's stereo. She'd spot the dog beside her in the light from a passing car's headlights, and she'd become aware of the fact that she wasn't going to be just another victim of random crime. A statistic, sure, but this certainly wasn't random.

What would she think? he wondered. Would she think that he was kidnapping her for ransom? He'd let her believe that for as long as he could. He didn't want her knowing the truth. Not out of pity, but rather because someone who thought they were about to die could sometimes gain the strength of five men. If she thought that he was just holding her for ransom, she'd try and reason with him, try to make him see her logic. If he wasn't under such a tight time schedule, he might take her somewhere and let her try and talk him out of it. He'd done it before, when time permitted. Once he'd even let an acquisition go free.

The Collector pulled off Lake Shore Drive, and drove carefully until he was only a block away from the filthy, rat-infested building that housed his secret office. He would do the job there. This was the sort of neighborhood where his work would go unnoticed.

He pulled into the alley on 13th Street, drove halfway down and into the customer parking lot of a black hairdresser's studio. On the back of the building was a billboard with a beautiful black woman, ten times lifesized, smiling down with perfect teeth upon the lot, one eye half-winking. Her hair had been straightened, and she was sharing the secret with the patrons. The Collector rolled the windows up and shut off the ignition. He turned in the seat and looked carefully through the small, square back windows of the van, made sure that he would be able to see car headlights coming from either direction.

The heat was suddenly cloying. The Collector began to sweat. He could smell her, and she was foul. It would, he knew, get worse.

He had to be careful. He had to do his work here, where there would be no interruptions, then deposit the acquisition almost three miles north, in an alley close to the hospital. It would ensure that the acquisition would be taken to the proper Emergency Room.

Sometime during the drive Carole Conners had become an impersonal thing to the Collector, no longer a human, just slightly more valuable to him than the small, dead poodle. She wouldn't even have that much status if someone had been willing to pay him to kill the poodle instead of her. Art was art, and its value wasn't ascertained by anything as simple as humanity.

He stepped through into the back of the van, got down on his knees, taking the disposable plastic gloves out of a pocket in the jumpsuit, pulling them back on over his hands, slowly, snapping them at the wrists the way a doctor does before surgery. Sweat was now rolling down from under his arms; the creases of his groin felt soaked. With the windows closed, it had become claustrophobically hot inside the van.

He smiled when he saw that his acquisition was awake and staring up at him.

"Hello," he said, softly, almost seductively. "Are you all right?" He marveled at the sound of his own voice; at the way he could emulate emotion at such a time.

He watched as it nodded its head vigorously, tears flowing down its cheeks. He reached over and rubbed at the tears, held the wet fingers before his face and squinted at the fluid. He rubbed his fingers together, thinking, wondering which of the very many ways at his disposal he should use to gather in the acquisition.

In an emergency such as this, it was best if a heart was needed. He could gutshoot almost carelessly, and keep the acquisition alive for hours at a time. But he couldn't shoot at the belly this time, not when a liver was needed. Bullets could do untold damage, they often bounced around inside the body, destroying tissue. He could risk no insult to the acquisition's lower body organs.

The acquisition was making sounds at him now, straining at bonds that would have held men ten times as strong as the acquisition itself. The acquisition's terror floated out to him in waves, he could feel it assaulting his skin as strongly as he felt the heat. The fear had less meaning to him than the heat. It has as much effect on him as rain does upon a sidewalk. Its begging eyes pleaded with him, and he smiled down at it, gently.

He would not sexually assault the thing that had once been a woman named Carole. He did not enjoy visiting unnecessary pain upon his work.

"I'll be asking for a half-million, do your parents have that on hand?" He watched as hope filled the large green eyes, as it nodded its head with vigor.

"I'm sorry about your dog, Carole, but I didn't have much choice."

It shook its head, trying to show him that it didn't care about the dog. It thought it had connected with him, was waiting for him to remove the tape that covered its mouth. He'd be doing that soon enough, but by that time the vocal cords would be of little use to it.

He looked at it, almost longingly. He would soon make it achieve perfection.

The Collector shut his eyes and shook his head, grabbed his temples and squeezed them tightly as he whined in agony. There was something tearing at his chest, an inner pain that was foreign and strange. What was wrong with him? The Collector felt terror. He took several deep breaths as the pain in his head and his chest subsided.

This had never happened before. Was it physical? What could it be?

He heard the thing that had once been Carole Conners making nasal sounds beneath him; whining, squealing noises that made him feel a sense of compassion at its ignorance because it would never know what it was about to become, and wouldn't appreciate it, even if it did. He looked down upon it. He cautioned himself to be exceptionally careful; he could not allow what was happening inside him destroy what he'd come to collect.

He had to show it a merciful passing. It was part of what made his work beautiful.

He touched its throat, gently, caressed it with strong fingers. Felt around in the back, until he had a grip on the bones he needed.

Then he squeezed once, with all his might, and felt the thing beneath him go limp in his hands, and he knew that it would take at least half an hour for it to die.

He pulled the van behind the Maternity Ward building, parked in the delivery zone and put on the van's flashers. He pushed open the back door and looked out, both ways, back and forth, saw no one.

He removed the tape from her mouth, arms and legs, and kicked her out into the alley, and was back in the driver's seat with the van in gear before her body rolled to a stop. He pulled away from the scene with haste, turned out into the street and smiled.

The Collector reached into the top pocket of the jumpsuit and removed a cellular flip phone, popped it open and dialed a number. He heard Alleo answer, let him say hello three times.

"What you've been waiting for is in the alley behind the Maternity Building, that's Prentice Hall. I'll call you tomorrow to set up a time to collect what you owe me." He broke the connection before Alleo could respond in any manner.

Less than an hour later he was showered, relaxed and content, sipping a glass of wine and gazing at his newest painting with as close an approximation of love as he would ever be able to summon.

CHAPTER 13

MARIAN THOUGHT ABOUT TONY, SAD AND A LITTLE HURT OVER what had happened, as she stepped out of the shower in her North Side apartment. She shouldn't be thinking about him, she didn't *want* to think about him. She wanted to think about Paul, about how happy he'd sounded when she'd returned his call a few minutes ago.

He had almost choked up, he was so happy to hear from her. She'd asked him, a little coyly, if it was too late to see him, and he'd told her to hop in her car and come on over, they'd worry about time when they were old. It had been so sweet of him to call because he was worried. Tony would have called just to find out where she'd been.

It was only one of the many differences between the two men.

Tony was exciting, in his own way, but he was focused on only his job, had no cultural awareness, didn't care about anything but hunting down and arresting killers. He often dressed more like a street bum than a police lieutenant, didn't shave for days on end; he slept little and ate terribly.

Paul, on the other hand, was just this side short of being a health fanatic. Always impeccably dressed, with manners befitting royalty. He always seemed to know the right thing to say, was the least self-absorbed man she'd ever been involved with, yet the one with the most actual reasons to be egotistical if he so chose.

He had the class, the wit, the intelligence and the style. The money he made wasn't important to her; she made a good living herself. And if she wanted to make more she could go into private practice; she could defend the criminals, the same way she did now, only as a private attorney she could make a hell of a lot more money.

But that wasn't her style. She was doing well enough.

Doing even better now that she was sure that she loved Paul Harris. It was the single most important reason that she'd cut Tulio out of her life.

He was so different from Tony, so much more *alive!*

She'd already lain out the clothes, the casual pants and blouse she would wear when she went out on this night that she turned thirty-five. Thirty-five had always seemed so old to her, and now that she was there, she understood it wasn't really that old at all. She smiled. Middle-aged, her father had often said, is always fifteen years older than you actually are.

She toweled herself dry and quickly began dressing, not liking the look that she saw on her face when she caught sight of herself in the mirror.

It had never before been this difficult for her, breaking up with a guy. She could usually walk away without a problem, but with Tony it had been different. Because he wasn't like most of them, he wasn't some ladder-climber, some yuppie only looking for a good time from her. He was deep, he was smart as a whip, and he'd been through so much, had suffered such a terrible loss.

Yet tonight, she'd had no choice. She'd finally summoned the nerve she'd needed to tell Tony Tulio goodbye. Because he was right, there *was* someone else. Someone she'd been seeing for a time, someone she thought might at last be the real thing.

Marian combed out her hair, a little put off at the late hour. She should get undressed and fall right into bed, but how often did you turn thirty-five? And besides, after a night like tonight, she needed someone to talk to. Someone who would understand. Someone who would commiserate.

Paul never judged her and they never argued. She'd never seen him angry, he was always reasonable and *calm!* He was a refreshing change from the passionate Tony Tulio.

Paul had understood for some time now that there would be no sex until the situation with Tony was resolved once and for all. He'd been patient, had told her he wanted her company for a lot more reasons than just physical intimacy. Well, she'd show him some physical intimacy tonight. She'd tear his ass up, is what she would do. Marian smiled. She felt like celebrating now that Tony was finally out of her life. Tonight, all bets were off.

She thought of Paul, of that body, those *muscles*. He was an incredibly well-built man who wasn't some half-assed jock. Mature enough to know who he was, needing to prove himself to no one. He'd pull away from a gentle kiss and look at her with a special sadness, as if wanting more and knowing she'd give in if he pushed it, but too gallant to go against what she had stated to be her wishes. She'd done a lot in her life, made some bad mistakes, but in this day and age it was suicidal to sleep around. And even though she'd been a little wild as a teenager, she had never slept with two men at the same time. Had never led one on, either. She had stopped sleeping with Tony Tulio a couple of months ago. She felt that she had to break it off clean with him first, before she started an affair with Paul.

He wouldn't have to wait much longer.

Marian grabbed her purse and made sure that the apartment was double-locked behind her. There'd been a series of break-ins recently in the neighborhood, and a monster that the cops were calling the Locksmith Rapist was prowling the area. He'd committed six rapes in the last month in her neighborhood, always managing to get into apartments and houses that had been securely locked.

Marian walked three flights down the stairs rather than waiting for the slow, rickety elevator. She got into her car, made the turn onto Cornelia, drove to Southport and headed south.

She hadn't heard from her father today, nor had she expected to. He wasn't much for remembering birthdays; she was lucky if he sent her a Christmas card.

She'd only been three years old when her mother had died, and she didn't remember her, had no warm memories of the woman, nothing for her to hang onto. Only what her father had told her, and he had not been kind. Her mother had been content to sit home, to take care of the house, and later, of Marian. It was what her father had expected of his only daughter, too, Dad wanting Marian to finish college more to impress a man than for an education. As for a career in law, that was out of the question to him. He'd been so dead set against it that she'd had to work like a dog in order to pay her own way through law school. He hadn't helped one bit, and she hadn't asked him for a cent, not once.

Was he afraid of the competition? Was he insecure about that? A man like her father could be that weak, she knew. Women seemed to intimidate him; she knew that he far preferred the company of other men. He still didn't seem to know how to respond when she put her arms around him and kissed his cheek as she entered his house. She suspected that he would have been a far happier man if his wife had given him a son.

And now she practiced law before him, and Christ, did he enjoy busting her ovaries on the rare occasion that he caught her in error.

She made the turn onto Division, and automatically touched the electronic door-lock button. She drove for a while and then there they were: the Cabrini-Green high-rises. The most poverty-stricken high-crime project in the city, and Jim Harbaugh could throw a football from the roof of her boyfriend's apartment building and break one of these windows. So much wealth mere blocks away from so much devastation. No wonder her case load was full. She looked straight ahead, and was relieved when the light turned green and she finally turned east.

Marion forced thoughts of her father and everything else out of her mind, as she pulled into the recessed circular driveway of Paul Harris's building. She got out of the car and gave the parking valet Paul's name; each penthouse came with two spaces for the owner and a free space for the owner's visitors. She gave the valet two dollars and accepted her yellow stub, nodded to the doorman as he held the glass door open for her, then walked through the lobby, feeling a little ashamed at the snobbish thrill she felt going past the regular elevators to the one that serviced only the top floor. She had to wait for the doorman to hit a special button that would open the penthouse elevator's door.

The elevator was incredibly fast, and it swayed just a bit as it rose. It was a silent ride too, with none of that stupid Muzak. She could do without the small couch in the rear, that was a bit pretentious, but she was grateful for the mirror, it gave her a chance to check her appearance.

She looked confident. Strong. Capable and competent. The type of woman who belonged in such a building's penthouse. But it was not at all the way that she was feeling inside. It was just like being in the courthouse; facade was everything.

The doors whooshed open and she stepped out onto deep pile carpet, turned right toward the first of the two penthouse suites. She touched the lit doorbell button, heard nothing from within. But in a matter of seconds the peephole went dark, and she heard the sound of locks being turned.

The door opened, and a smiling Paul took her into his arms, pecked her lips and quickly squeezed her hello, then escorted her inside.

He didn't even seem to want to relock the double oak doors, did so hurriedly and then rushed her over to the far wall. Marian was out of her element, had never seen him so animated, so excited. He gently propelled her forward, her eyes going, as always, to the breathtaking view of the city, to the vast blackness that was Lake Michigan at night, then she heard his proud voice, asking: "Happy birthday. What do you think?"

Marian looked at him, gave him a skeptical smile. She turned toward what he wanted to show off, the small painting on the wall, with the tiny brass light shining down on the canvas. She looked at it, at the painting of a woman sitting in what seemed to be a blue room, looking patiently off into space.

"Vermeer," Paul Harris said to her.

Marian looked at him in astonishment, feeling disoriented and frightened. She had to look at it again, squinting, then she shivered. She leaned against him, her knees weak.

"Three hundred some odd years old," Paul said, his words coming to her as if through a long tunnel. Marian nodded her head slowly, staring at the painting.

It was such an exact replication of her face that she might well have posed for the artist.

"It's you . . ." Paul said, and she could only nod in agreement.

CHAPTER
14

Marian sat on the leather sofa, recovered now from her shock, but still astounded at the likeness of herself hanging on the wall. She could see it from here, the little brass-covered light shining down, radiating upon it. Paul brought her a glass of wine, and she sipped it, then placed the glass on the end table and shook her head as if to clear it.

"I was raised Catholic," she said.

"Hannerty."

"Yes."

"So it doesn't fit your concept of a hereafter?"

"I haven't been inside a Catholic church since the day I graduated high school, except for weddings, funerals, and christenings. But from the time I was five years old I was told that you died and went either to heaven or hell, depending on your behavior."

"And you rejected that."

"I never spoke up about it—it's not a topic of debate with the nuns— but I couldn't see my erotic fantasies about David Cassidy causing me to be cast into the same hell with Hitler, it just didn't make sense."

"Religion is superstition, weak people need to it to stop them from eating their young."

"*That's* a pleasant way to put it," Marian said. "I haven't given it a thought in years, but the indoctrination, the concept, it's there, ingrained in my head. I never even seriously considered reincarnation before just now."

"But you agree it's you."

"My God, it's as if he painted it from a snapshot."

"No cameras back then." Paul smiled at her, so she'd know that he was joking. "I believe you sat for him."

"For Vermeer. Me."

"Yes, you. And you came back again and again, across three centuries, until we found each other."

Marian sipped her wine; a deep sip this time. She gave a melancholy laugh.

"Thirty-five doesn't seem so old anymore."

"The painting's roughly ten times that age, Marian." Paul got out of his chair and came over to her, took the glass out of her hand, and put it back on the end table. He sat down beside her, and put an arm around her shoulders.

"Do you think that maybe back then, *I* was Vermeer?"

"To be honest with you, it's not something I *want* to think about right now."

"Does it scare you, the thought of having lived before?"

"No, but dying does scare me, and tonight I feel old."

"Thirty-five? Come on."

"It's not just that. I told Tony goodbye tonight."

"You did?!" He smiled broadly, and Marian felt proud. This rich, successful art dealer was happy that she'd dumped her boyfriend and was in his apartment, telling him about it.

"How did he take it?"

"Not very well."

Paul snorted. "It doesn't matter, as long as you're happy."

"He knows about us. Not your name, but he knows there's someone else."

"Did you tell him?"

"I didn't have to."

"He'll get over you."

"There's no telling what he'll do."

"I'm not afraid of him. And he's not your problem. Nor is he mine. If he comes here, Marian, I'll deal with him."

"The thought of him hurting you . . ."

"He won't hurt me. He *can't* hurt me." Paul nestled his head on her shoulder, kissed it. Marian felt herself begin to tingle.

"The only thing that might hurt me," Paul said, "is if you left me. That might hurt me." He brushed his lips against her neck again. "That might even kill me."

"That won't happen," Marian said. She was weak, excited, a little overwhelmed. She thought of Tony and felt a pain in her chest, felt tears well up, and she wiped at them quickly. Paul sat up and looked at her, concerned.

"He's not worth tears."

"He's so old-fashioned, so chivalrous. In his head he's in the fifties."

"He wanted to control you, to own you."

"And you don't."

He looked at her as if she'd slapped him, his eyes showing his pain.

Paul said, "Never," softly. "I love you, Marian. All right? For who you are. Not for what I can mold you into. He wanted a little cop's wife he could control, so he could think himself more of a man. Mr. Macho. As for me, I learned a long time ago, you never really own the world's most beautiful artwork. You just, if you get really lucky, only savor it for a time."

Marian let her look apologize for her. She reached up and touched his cheek, let her hand linger. He turned his head and kissed her palm. He'd told her he loved her. She'd heard him.

Across the room was a painting that he must have paid a fortune for, one he'd sought out and bought for her, to show her how much he cared. He'd been behind her all the way, since the first time she'd told him of her doubts about Tony, had never judged her in any manner, had been willing to wait until she was ready before he pushed her into a commitment. She had evidence of how he felt; he wasn't just speaking words.

How many questions had he asked her? It had to be hundreds. Cogent, intelligent questions, about Tony, how he was. What he might be working on that was causing him all the stress. How his mind worked, what he was really like when the TV cameras were not glaring in front of him.

And he'd never criticized their relationship, either, the way that some men would. Some men, hell. The way *most* men would. Paul had never tried to undermine what she and Tony had, he'd always made it clear that he was there to support her, standing in the wings. He allowed her to make her own decisions, without letting his personal judgments and feelings cloud up hers.

Marian said, "I love you," very gently, then leaned into him, kissed him on the lips. He kept it gentle, didn't push.

He broke away from her and wiped away what was left of her tears. He said, "Stay here tonight."

"You bet your ass I'm staying here tonight."

Paul smiled, then laughed out loud.

He leaned into her again, and this time his kiss was more urgent. Marian pressed into him, kissing this man who wanted nothing from her but the opportunity to be with her, the pleasure of her company. She knew that if she pushed him away now, he'd apologize, move back to the chair, and easily change the subject. Tony would pout and be silent, thinking that it had to be something he'd done. Paul was far more secure than Tony, knew who and what he was. There wasn't any doubt in his mind about his manhood. Paul had nothing to prove.

Marian let her hand drop to his and lifted it, placed his fingers on her breast and felt him stroke it, softly. She placed her hand on his crotch, gave him a little squeeze. She felt him break the kiss off, felt herself being lifted into the air, and she opened her eyes and saw that he was carrying her as easily as he would a pillow, in no hurry, toward the bedroom. She wondered if he'd kick the door open, and stifled a laugh at the image.

He didn't. He pushed it open with his back and kicked it shut behind them, flicked on a light with the back of his arm, and carried her over to the bed and gently placed her down upon it. She began to unbutton her blouse, and he touched her hands.

"Let me."

He unbuttoned the top button slowly, licked at the skin behind the blouse. He looked at her.

"Let me do it all, Marian. You just lie back and let me."

He had throughout his life been a highly sexed man, but Harris's strongest sexual urges always came upon him immediately following an acquisition. He'd played it cool, as if it didn't matter to him, but Marian would never know how much he'd wanted to grab her the second she'd come through the door.

Now he licked her breasts, his finger busily working lower down, Harris planning on making his way down there with his mouth. He loved her. *He loved her!* He wanted to give her a night that she would remember for the rest of her life.

He was even overwhelmingly glad that she'd finally dropped Tulio. He had initially sought her out solely because of her relationship to the man, but it had become far, far more than that. In spite of himself, it had become a lot more. He never thought it would happen, but Paul Harris was in love.

Joyfully, he licked his way down her body, wondering about that. There were new feelings, emotions, attaching themselves to him the way pilot fish attach to a whale, alien and completely new sensations that he had to think about rationally, had to try and figure out.

He felt strong protective urges toward her, to be gentle with her, and kind. He would look into her eyes and *feel*—exactly what, he did not know, but something would tug at him, pull deep within his chest.

At first, last fall, back when he'd cultivated her, he'd seen her as dumb, as a stupid, weak, silly little woman who could give him all the information he would need on a man Harris suspected was working hard, trying to arrest him for murder. Back then he'd had specific questions that needed to be answered. Tulio had been the investigator on one of Harris's acquisitions, a case that Harris had thought to be long closed. Tulio had suddenly reopened it and he'd mumbled some psychobabble on television about Harris's relationship to the victim. Had he known that it wasn't isolated? Was he aware that there were other acquisitions, that they were all connected to him?

Harris had to know, and Marion had been his pipeline into the mind of the investigator; it hadn't taken Harris long to decide that he had nothing to worry about. Tony Tulio was a self-absorbed, ego-driven publicity whore, trapped in self-pity over the memory of his dead family. He had important enemies within the department, and when he was away from the job, all he seemed to want to do was try to get a commitment out of Marian.

Now Tulio was gone, no longer a part of her life. And Harris would quit, the Conners girl would be his last official acquisition. That part of his life was over. He knew that *now*, now that the most important artwork he'd ever see was squirming under his tongue.

Harris took his mouth away, and softly said to Marian, "I love you." He felt her hands dig into his neck. He didn't think that he'd ever spoken words that were more sincere and honest.

He did love her. My God, he did. What sort of woman was it who could turn him around like this? Harris smiled as he licked her, feeling a sense of contentedness, a sense of true devotion. He was doing something he had never done before: bringing pleasure to someone he loved.

He worked his tongue into and all around her, half-listening to her guttural moans of pleasure, wondering if Marian was even aware that she was making them. He was delighting her, and that made him happy.

Strange, strange things were happening. He'd think about them later.

C H A P T E R 15

TULIO'S HOUSE WAS ON A QUIET SIDE STREET, JUST A STONE'S THROW away from Comiskey Park. When night games were played the neighborhood suddenly wasn't so quiet; after the game, well-tended lawns and gardens were watered with piss from the suburbanites who parked in the driveways then saw the homes as their own personal urinals. If you were lucky, as Tulio was, your backyard was fenced. The stink took forever to wear off when these people pissed on your central air-conditioning unit. Tow trucks worked the street nonstop during those night games, costing sixty-five dollars out of pocket for some goof who'd been trying to avoid a five-dollar parking lot fee. In the summertime, it seemed as if there would never be peace in the neighborhood again; in the wintertime it seemed desolate. At least to Tony Tulio. At least these past two winters.

He silently entered his house through the garage, as if there still might be someone inside in danger of being awakened. The attached garage had been built in the spring, just before the accident, Tulio not wanting his family to have to walk from the backyard garage, through the yard, then on into the house. It took his wife forever to transfer groceries that way. A lavish expenditure for a man of his means, but one he'd felt, at that point in time, that he owed to the woman he loved. There wasn't much doubt in his mind back then that he hadn't given her much of anything else in their years of marriage. That was when he'd first been trying to sober up and change his life, when thinking about her, giving her things, had been of the utmost importance.

What had he given her? There were so many things . . .

Headaches, yeah, he'd given her plenty of those. Heartaches, too, truth be told, when he'd been out all night drinking, leaving her home alone with the indisputable and undenied knowledge that he was out cabareting with some other woman.

It took him too long to mature, to see what he had at home as more important than anything that the street had to offer, but she'd never complained, never once called him on it, and by the time he understood what he truly had, it was too late . . .

Tulio stepped into the house, reached out blindly and flipped the air-conditioning on, stood there in the dark and looked around, trying to sense their presence, that of his wife and daughter. He walked into his bedroom without turning on a light.

In the dark Tulio noticed the flashing light of the telephone answering machine, blinking once, and he wondered if it was Marian who had left the single message. He walked over to it, hit the Play button, and turned his head away in disgust when he heard a man's voice coming over the speaker.

It was Hal, the man who used to be his sponsor in Alcoholics Anonymous. Sanctimonious prick. "Just checking in," Hal said, as he said every time he called. Hadn't seen Tulio around, wondered if he went to meetings anymore. Couldn't those people take a hint? What did he have to do, *shoot* one of them before they understood that two years of their deal was enough? He rewound the tape, shaking his head. He wouldn't return the call.

He walked into the living room, at last turned on a light, and stopped in front of a family picture that had been taken during a heat wave a few summers back, snapped by a neighbor as the family had returned from a Saturday afternoon at old Comiskey Park. Back when they were putting the finishing touches on the new stadium, and the old one stood almost in its shadow, an anachronism, a dinosaur facing extinction. It had saddened Tulio to see the new place built, had hurt him to see the old one torn down, to drive past it every day as the wrecking ball destroyed it, the place where, as a kid, he'd seen Nellie Fox and Louis Apparicio play, and so many others, a lot of them gone now, as dead as his wife and daughter . . .

In the picture, the three of them appeared forever happy, Tony and his wife and daughter smiling at the camera. Tulio grinning half-drunkenly, macho, his chest stuck out, one arm around each of his girls, telling all the world that these were *his* women, and that if you messed with either of them, you'd have to deal with *him*. It was one of the last times he'd gotten drunk, right at the end of it, when he'd started to wise up.

In the harsh sunlight in which the picture had been taken, he could see that Martie's light brown hair had been turning lighter in shade, with many strands of white-gray in there, gray that he had caused her. But she held her tall, thin body with dignity, with a grace that couldn't be faked, and she was smiling broadly, she had had fun that day. She'd had two or three beers right along with her husband. He looked at the picture longingly, at all that he had left of the only woman that he'd ever really and truly loved.

Martie had been thirty-three at the time that the picture was taken. Her breasts had been beginning to sag, and there was a softness to her belly that she'd worked hard to overcome. The gym equipment was still in the basement, home for spiders now, barbells and an exercycle, a rowing machine covered with silken webs. What a beauty his Martie had been, and how proud he'd been to have won her.

It was only later, after their deaths, that he'd learned that she'd never been a prize that he'd truly ever captured.

Jess, too, he stared sadly at her now. How much he'd loved that child! Tall and thin, like her mother, wearing a purple halter-top in the photograph, captured forever young behind glass that each Saturday morning was wiped clean of the week's accumulation of dust. When she'd been a toddler she had been without shame, would climb up into his lap for a hug and kiss whenever she'd felt the urge, and back then she'd felt it often.

Later, she'd learned not to come too close when there were too many empty beer cans lying crushed in the kitchen garbage can. By that time, the smell of his breath had become offensive to her.

But in the picture there was no sign that she was the teenage daughter of a falling-down drunk. In the picture, his little Jessica was alive and smiling, budding breasts pushing out of the tight halter top that her mother had insisted it was all right for her to wear. He remembered the bright red anger that had filled him when he'd seen men look at his daughter with glances of carnal appraisal.

Tulio reached out a hand and lightly touched the picture, saw his reflection in the glass, the look of ugly, pained sadness, so different from his appearance in the photo. The card from their funeral was beginning to curl now, yellowing with age. He would leave it in the frame until it collapsed into ashes.

He should have given her more of himself, should have been a better man. It wouldn't even have been that hard a thing for him to do. He'd always taken her so much for granted! A mistake, he knew now, something he understood, now that he was well into the middle of his life and was truly all alone. The pain of that loss was something he appreciated daily, more and more as he grew older. How rare was the sort of total, forgiving love that Martie had once given him? And how long, he wondered daily, had it taken for that love to be wrenched from her heart?

He made his way to his bedroom, the one he'd once shared with Martie. There were times—more and more frequent times, of late—when, depressed, he would go into his daughter's room, sit on her bed, and just stare at the posters she had hung up on the wall. George Michael posters; some other old ones showing a bunch of young, posturing studs who had back then called themselves the New Kids on the Block. Contemporary Elvis's, programmed to stimulate hormones.

Tonight, he wouldn't dare wander into that room. Tonight, Tulio wanted to remember his wife. And, too, he wanted to torture himself. As if losing Marian forced him to do additional penance—by remembering the way his wife and child had died.

He sat over on her side of the bed, where Martie had once held his naked body to her own, picked up the pillow which he had rarely touched since her passing. He had never changed or washed her pillowcase, believing he could smell her perfume and hair spray upon it, captured for all eternity in the soft, thin fabric. He put the pillow to his nose now, took in a deep breath.

"Martie . . ." Said on the exhale, Tulio breathing in again and again, remembering her. Remembering what he'd learned after her death. What he could never discuss with anyone. Not even with Marian. Marian, whom he'd thought he'd loved.

How could he have believed that? Believed himself to be in love with a selfish, self-absorbed yuppie female lawyer? *That* was a cause of shame. She'd used him, toyed with him, all the while searching for another man, the right one for her. Discovering that was more than he could bear.

Because it wasn't the first time he'd been treated in such a manner.

Tulio rose from the bed and walked over to a small table set next to the closet, between the corner and the dresser that still held all of Martie's underclothes. He unlocked the small drawer, and removed a letter that had been rubber-stamped by somebody in the post office. It depicted a hand with a finger pointing in bold red ink at the return address. Under the finger it was marked RETURN TO SENDER, INSUFFICIENT POSTAGE. The fact was, in her haste and confusion, Martie had forgotten to put any kind of postage on the letter. It had come back to the house on the day of the double funeral, Tulio finding it lying on the floor as he'd returned from the post-funeral luncheon, where friends he hadn't known he had and family members he hardly knew had acted as if they'd really cared about his tragic loss. He'd read the letter at least a hundred times that first day, trying to figure it out. Sometime that night, at last, he was finally able to halfway understand what his wife had been trying to say.

Tulio looked at the name and address on the envelope, the letter having been sent to a man he had never met, and never intended to meet. He hadn't shown up at the funeral, and he had never tried to call. Which was a very good thing. If he had done either, Tulio might have been compelled into pulling his gun and killing him.

He walked heavily back to the bed and sat down, opened the envelope, took out the letter, and for the thousandth time in just over two years, he read his wife's last thoughts.

> Dear Scott:
> I cannot believe that you lied to me, that all we ever had was a sham. I loved you—I still do! And Jess loves you more than she loves her own father. Our plans, our dreams, they were shattered last night. How could you let me go, how could you say that you never really loved me? I was willing to sacrifice everything for you, to start over again, my daughter and I, and now you tell me that I was nothing more than sex, a trinket that you played with.
> I have never felt this humiliated.
> The child within me will never know its father. You've broken my heart, you've devastated my daughter, but you won't ever get the chance to hurt this infant, not in this life!

The letter was signed, simply: Martie.

Tulio slowly blew out his breath, folded the letter and put it away.

He'd been working on a stakeout the day his wife and daughter had died, had been gone from the house for the better part of three days, trying to set a trap for a man who'd killed a young girl by the name of LaFeit. He'd gone to the press, told lie after lie, carefully laying the bait in the trap, bait that was never taken. As hard as he tried to remember, he could recall no bitterness in those three days, no moodiness on Martie's part, no unhappiness on Jess's.

They'd both betrayed him, stabbed him in his heart, his wife with her blatant cheating and his daughter with her accepting, conspiratorial silence. Martie had found a lover, and Jess had grown to love him. More than she had loved her father. It would not, could not have been some casual affair. That, Tulio had convinced himself, he would have been able to forgive. But this, her planning on leaving him, her wish to begin anew, as man and wife with someone else . . .

How could Jess have done it, why hadn't she come to him? Had he been that terrible a father? He knew he'd failed as a husband.

And Martie had been pregnant when their car had hit the concrete underpass, carrying the fetus of a man she thought she'd loved.

Tulio had considered killing the man, immediately following the accident. Killing him and then turning his pistol on himself. He'd lain in bed and fantasized over it, about the death of a stranger named Scott. But he hadn't acted on the impulse, not even after he'd truly figured out the letter's brutal, hidden truth:

Their deaths had been no accident; Martie had killed them both.

Had she shut her eyes and pressed her foot to the floor? Screamed as the car raced over the shoulder, in the nanosecond before the vehicle had impacted with the underpass? What had Jess done? She surely couldn't have been a part of it.

For a time, he'd hated Martie, wished her in hell for the terrible thing she'd done. And then he'd hated this bastard Scott, the man who'd boldly lied to Martie, had impregnated her, then abandoned her.

But finally, after months had passed, he put the blame where it truly belonged. On his own shoulders, on the shoulders of the man who had driven Martie over the edge, into a suicidal lunacy.

She'd tried, so many times, to be the perfect wife for him. And the more she gave the more he took, even more so after he'd cut way back on his drinking. He'd seen that as some accomplishment that needed to be rewarded, as if Martie owed him heavily for his putting down the bottle. He was staying home more often, and he wasn't cheating on her. Didn't that deserve some extra credit, didn't she owe him for that?

Tulio's beeper went off, and he jumped. He turned the device off, checked the number, then replaced the beeper on his belt. Gratefully, he reached over to the nightstand and grabbed the telephone.

CHAPTER 16

MARIAN WAS LOOKING UP AT THE CEILING, LISTENING TO PAUL'S soft snores as he lay on his back beside her. She smiled. He was so shy, in his own way, so eager to make her happy. She was thirty-five tonight, and for the first time all day, she realized that she was blessed. She had a good job, a good life, and now, it appeared, she had found a good man.

That last part she'd always wondered about, hadn't been sure it would ever happen. She seemed to mainly attract men like Tony Tulio, men with flaws that made her want to heal them at first, flaws that later proved fatal, were poison to a relationship.

But Paul seemed so different. He didn't seem to need her. Paul seemed, instead, to want her.

What a refreshing change *that* was.

She sat up in the bed, unable to sleep in such strange surroundings. Paul's bedroom was larger than her entire apartment. It was like trying to sleep in the Grand Canyon.

Funny, she had never spent the night at Tony's house, had rarely even been inside the place. They'd only had sex at her apartment, and he only occasionally spent the night. It was as if his bed had been forever reserved to the memory of a woman who was a year dead before she and Tony had even met.

Marian shook her head to clear it of thoughts of Tony Tulio. She knew that if she let herself, she would start feeling sorry for the man. He was wild and manic, not yet healed enough from his loss to be able to have a healthy relationship. She would have walked away from him months ago, if Paul had pushed the issue. But now she was glad he had not. It had been *her* decision to cut Tony loose, and she knew it had been the right one. She would not think of him again tonight.

Tonight, she would think of Paul. Paul, who was so different from Tony, with his high-class job and all his money, with his apartment in the sky. No bus, car, taxi or other street sounds made it up this high. It was as if they were in a cocoon, quiet, safe and warm. Up here, Marian knew, she would never be able to hear anyone scream.

Not exactly the type of environment that Marian was used to at night.

Nor was she used to the darkness. When Paul had turned off the small night-table light after making love to her, it was as if, all of a sudden, she had gone blind. The room was in instant, total darkness, without even the red digital flashing of an alarm clock to give her some bearings. If he hadn't been beside her, she would have panicked.

She eased her way out of the bed now, groped around in the intense darkness, found the door where she'd sensed it would be. Thank God. Paul's white ankle-length terrycloth robe was hanging from a hook on the back of the door. She put it on, smelling the rich scent of some expensive soap in the cloth. She opened the door just wide enough to slip through, closed it softly behind her, careful not to let it click; she didn't want Paul disturbed.

Marian stood in front of the large glass wall of the living room, staring out at the blackness where she knew there was a lake. She couldn't see it now, there were no streetlights out there on the water, nothing but blackness.

She should head back to her apartment, get some sleep. But her clothes were in Paul's bedroom, and she couldn't dress in the dark, probably couldn't even find her clothes.

She turned from the window, avoiding the painting. She couldn't look at it anymore, too afraid of what the ancient art implied. She walked the length of the apartment, to a large oak door, turned the knob and felt inside until she found a light switch. She flipped it on and discovered that Paul had a personal, well-equipped gym.

She turned the light off and closed the door behind her, vaguely troubled. It was the first gym of its kind she had ever seen that did not have a single mirror in the room.

There was one other door, plus the one that led to the bedroom where Paul slept. Out of boredom more than anything else, she wandered over and entered the room. She flipped on the light, saw a computer on a desk in the corner. It was a strange room, and she looked around it, puzzled. There were four different phones on a low table opposite the one the computer was on, each phone hooked up to a separate answering machine. Was he doing some sort of art telemarketing from here? Two of the machines had message lights blinking. She wouldn't listen to the messages; they were Paul's personal business.

Marian went over to the computer, noticed that it was quietly humming. It was on. She sat down and turned on the monitor. It immediately snapped to life.

There, before her, was a full-color, somehow familiar photograph of a beautiful, smiling young woman. The picture was a full-face shot, the smile showing her promise, the mark she intended to leave on the world. Was this someone Paul knew? Next to the picture were several lines of information: name, address, date of birth, hair and eye color. The woman's eyes were green, the same as Marian's own. Down at the bottom, in different-sized type, as if added later, an afterthought, typed in using a different font: her blood type. Strange. So many things tonight seemed odd.

Marian felt, for the first time since leaving Tony, afraid. Of what? she wondered. What did she have to fear? She felt a quick shiver and suppressed it, fought the fear and told herself that it was foolish. But she couldn't shake it.

A hand fell on her shoulder and she jumped, grabbed at her throat.

"Looking for something?" Paul asked her, and she had to take several deep breaths before she could find the strength to answer him.

"My God, you scared me."

"I'm sorry, Marian." His voice was low and calm, relaxed, the words spoken in a tone she'd never heard from him before. She decided that she was being silly; the man had just wakened, and she'd never spoken to him at that time of day, that's all. The hand on her neck moved over slightly and began to massage her shoulder; she closed her eyes and leaned into it, trying to let go of the irrational sense of dread.

"Mmmm," Marian said. "That feels good."

"What were you looking for, Marian?" Said evenly, slowly, with just the slightest rise in intonation when he spoke her name. He sounded like an angry parent who was trying to restrain his annoyance.

"What?"

"I asked you, what were you looking for?"

"Nothing especially, I just couldn't sleep, and I wandered in here, that's all." She heard the resentment in her voice, tried to fight it off. "The computer was turned on. I wasn't prying." He didn't answer her, and she decided to take the offensive.

"What is this, anyway?"

"Just an experiment some starving artist wanted me to look at."

"About the belittling of women," Marian said. "How they're treated as objects in today's society."

"Something like that."

Paul's finger came into her vision, and he stabbed off the monitor button.

"Hey, I was looking at that."

"I'm sorry. I hate to bring work home. If you want, I'll turn it back on, you can watch it while I try to go back to sleep."

Slightly mollified, Marian said, "That's all right, I've seen enough."

Did his hand squeeze harder when she spoke? It seemed as if it had, just barely, almost imperceptibly. What was wrong with him?

"Come on," Paul said, "let's go back to bed, Marian."

She got up, thinking that he thought her a snoop, feeling slightly ashamed of herself, an intruder now more than an invited guest. And feeling that way made her angry.

Marian said, "I can't sleep here, Paul. It's too big, too quiet, too dark." She faked a shiver. "Too cold."

"You should stay, Marian. Sooner or later you'll have to get used to it."

Was that a marriage proposal? Or was he asking her to move in? She felt a little better now.

But not so much better that she didn't notice that as they left the room, Paul locked the door behind them.

CHAPTER
17

TULIO RACED THE CAR BACK DOWNTOWN, GOT ON THE RYAN AND at this time of night he, along with maybe a half a dozen other vehicles, had the whole thing pretty much to himself.

Ahead of him, the Sears Tower beckoned, watching over the city, or maybe preying on it, Tulio couldn't tell. The lights of the world's tallest building were the best advertisement the city could ever have; for some reason, looking at them, Tulio always felt safe.

He drove up to the alley behind Prentice Hall, got out and for the third time that night walked under yellow crime-scene tape. It had been left up here, but it was guarding nothing. The alley was empty; it was the cleanest alley Tulio had ever seen. Except for the bloodstains. He locked the car and walked the two blocks to the Emergency Room entrance.

The doctors had been interviewed by the responding detectives, as had the patrolmen who'd found the young woman's body, and they'd decided, in their wisdom, that this was a Special Victims case. For the first time this evening, they had been right.

She'd been dead for less than an hour, her organs given for transplants, taken from her body after the surgeons were sure that they'd lost her. What was left of Carole Conners that was functional had gone to help somebody else. What remained would be autopsied, to find the cause of death.

It was something he was getting used to, now that such organ donations were common. But he'd be looking for a lot more here tonight, he knew. Locked in his desk were five files where the victims had been donors. He hoped that it was not what he'd been suspecting for the past two years. Hoped that it was just coincidence, the fact that the victim was a donor. As cynical as he'd become in his life, he was still aware of the fact that, even in their darkest hours, human beings could come through, wanting to help somebody else. It helped them to overcome their grief. He hoped that Carole Conners's death was just an ugly, normal killing.

But she was only nineteen, Tulio thought. He'd been an Army veteran for three years on the day that she'd been born, had already been on the force for two years. There were scars on his body that were decades older than she was.

He hoped that his suspicions were wrong, that there would be an easy solution to this one, even though it would probably not prove itself to be a slam dunk. This time, he suspected, there would be no license plate number conveniently punched onto the keypad of a cellular telephone.

On first sight it appeared to be an accident, a lover's quarrel, perhaps. Carole Conners strangled in the heat of an argument, and then the killer had panicked, raced her to the hospital and dropped her off in the alley. He couldn't have taken her inside himself, he would have had to explain how it had happened. As if the police couldn't find out on their own.

Her boyfriend would be the most obvious killer. If she even had a boyfriend. At the moment, they weren't really sure. There was someone she'd been seeing from school, but in the reports, the parents were vague. Nor could the theory be discounted, due to the area in which she'd been found, that it was some kind of drug killing. Rich kids from the northern suburbs, fancying themselves to be street smart, had a habit of underestimating big-city desperados.

No matter who had killed her, it was a Special Victim's case. She'd been found in the city of Chicago, and her father was a man of power and position in a town where who you knew was almost as important as what you had or how much you made.

Tulio looked in his notebook, made a few notations to pass along to whomever he would be assigning the footwork later, after he was done here at the scene. He would leave a note, and all the reports. He himself would not work this case; it was late, and he was tired. He believed that there'd be no solution tonight, as there'd been in the two earlier cases. The boyfriend—if there was one—would be the first suspect spoken to, and he would have to be found, brought in, and it would take hours of interrogation before he was either charged or cleared. Tulio wasn't up for that, he'd collapse from exhaustion during the initial phase of questioning.

He would speak to the parents tonight, though, then make a decision, maybe even call in two of his squad later on and give them what he had. By the time he wrapped things up here, it would be close to dawn. He wouldn't be robbing his detectives of too much sleep. He liked to do the initial work himself whenever he could. Get a grasp on things, see how they felt, then pass his impressions on to his subordinates. He would do that with this one. Then he would go home, take a shower, and go to bed. He hoped he'd be able to sleep.

The parents were sitting off in a corner by themselves, seated in molded plastic chairs that they hadn't pulled close together. He looked at his notes: Benjamin and Marjorie Conners. Older people to have a daughter so young. They had waited until they were sure they could give her the best before they'd decided to have her. And now their daughter was dead. As dead as his own daughter was.

Benjamin Conners was very short. A hotshot professor at the University, though, head of some department or other; a word that Tulio had never seen before. He was some sort of 'ologist. The man was soft, but not fat. An elitist, North Shore snob, to the manner born. A man who used his brain rather than his body to get things done. If he needed physical labor, he'd hire it. He had wisps of still-black hair combed across a mostly bald head.

He wore heavy, thick-lensed glasses that gave his eyes the illusion of wisdom. He had a heavy, graying, walrus mustache that curved up at the ends. Tulio would not have liked the man if their meeting had been social. He was the type who hid in an ivory tower and passed judgment on the lower classes who didn't have his education and money. And those who had his education would of course not have his intelligence.

The woman, Mrs. Conners, was the sort who married such a man. Tall, classy and elegant heading into her golden years, Mrs. Conners had graying hair that had been carefully finger-curled. Her face was far more lined than her husband's. She'd be long-suffering and strong, would have made a number of compromises to maintain her life's station. Tulio could see her hosting a faculty wives' tea, speaking at libraries about the importance of great books, encouraging the reading of Plato to minorities, and hating every minute of it, wishing she were somewhere—maybe even somebody—else. Such as a member of the faculty, rather than a member's wife. She would have worked hard in the early years, so that he wouldn't have to, while he was doing post-graduate work, back in a time when she wasn't supposed to do such studying herself.

She seemed to be bearing up a lot better than her husband. Their daughter's death would be, to her, a tragedy. To Professor Conners it would be not only tragic, but also an embarrassment.

Tulio walked over to them with his head bowed respectfully, introduced himself, and immediately knew which parent he would deal with. The mother looked at him with a depth of sorrow in her eyes that he could relate to, but her eyes were dry. The father was shaking; his hand trembled as they shook hands briefly. His eyes were red and his cheeks were streaked with tears. His voice broke as he said hello. Even in his moment of greatest loss, the man was condescending, saying the word "lieutenant" in a way that told Tulio what his status truly was in the man's wide, wise eyes.

"Mrs. Conners," Tulio began, and saw the quick resentment pass across Professor Conners's face. He didn't have time to worry about the man's feelings, would have to speak to the parent who obviously had it most together. "I'm sorry to intrude on your grief, but I have to speak to you."

"We understand." She patted her husband's hand. Tulio wondered if the man would ever forgive her for that gesture.

"I've read the initial reports, but they don't mention a boyfriend, just someone she might have been seeing during the semester . . . ?" He saw a quick, furtive look pass between them, and knew that the next words the woman spoke would be a lie.

"She wasn't seeing anybody right now." Tulio let it pass; he was used to people lying to him. His people would canvass their neighborhood, they'd find out who it was the young girl had been seeing. Neighbors of homicide victims and suspects loved to talk to detectives and the press. It made them important for a day, gave them a chance to share their insights into the character of the people next door. They were almost always wrong, but they did know facts, which was what the detectives needed, while the amateur psychological reports would be eaten up by the reporters.

For the moment he hunched down so that he was below Mrs. Conners's eye level; he did not want to seem intimidating when he asked the next question.

"You told the detective that you said good night to Carole after the 'Tonight Show' came on. That's eleven-thirty. The call came in to nine-one-one at a little after two. Do you have any idea where she might have gone, who she might have been with?"

"She didn't go *any*where."

"Ma'am, she was found almost twenty miles from home."

"She was reading a book when I said goodnight, she wasn't going out tonight, she would have told me if she were."

Right. Tulio had heard variations of these words more times than he could count. He had stood in front of the parents of kids who'd died of drug overdoses, and even with the needle still stuck in their arms, the parents had denied that their kids had ever used drugs. Demanded that the case be classified as a murder. Someone had *done* this to their baby. No parent wanted to think the worst of their child, and Tulio understood that.

No husband wanted to think the worst of his wife, either.

He wouldn't be getting much from these two, and prayed that Carole had had a boyfriend these people were trying to protect. If there was no bodyfriend, the trail could grow glacial by the time his detectives reported in in the morning. He wouldn't be calling anyone in tonight. The Conners, through their behavior, had made that decision for him.

"I'm sorry about your loss," Tulio said, and handed Mrs. Conners a card. "Somebody from my department will be contacting you early tomorrow morning." Tulio nodded at them, and stood.

"Wait!" Professor Conners said, and Tulio looked at him, hopefully. The man was having a hard time articulating his thoughts, that much was obvious, his lips moving soundlessly, forming words he couldn't yet bring himself to speak. He was probably trying to figure out a way to express himself in a way which an illiterate copper like Tulio could somehow understand. Tulio looked at him, wondering when compassion had been surgically removed from his heart.

Around them, all was chaos. He could hear screams from the Emergency Room; cold, loud voices of the hospital personnel, calling the suffering by their first names. Personalizing them, showing them that they were friends.

At last the professor spoke.

"Will you get him, will you get the man who killed my daughter?" The man was begging, maybe for the first time in his life. He wanted assurances after offering only evasions. Tulio looked at Conners, at a loss for words himself.

"*Please?*" Conners said. "Don't let her be a statistic."

"I'll get him," Tulio said, in a tone of voice that he hoped would convey his contempt for men like Conners. He looked at Mrs. Conners, felt a twinge of sympathy. Carole had been *her* daughter, too, but the man had said, "My daughter."

"I'll get him," Tulio told her, with feeling this time. "We'll be around to talk to you tomorrow, ma'am," he said, and turned to leave.

"Wait!" This time it was the woman's voice that stopped him. He turned to her, looked down, saw her rise quickly without checking with her husband. Conners watched his wife's back as the woman approached Tulio, then buried his head in his hands. Tulio saw his shoulders shake, and looked away. Mrs. Conners took Tulio's forearm and walked him several steps down the corridor. He could feel her fingers trembling on his bicep.

"Lieutenant."

"Ma'am?"

"I know what you're thinking. That this was some drug deal, or that Carole had a crazy boyfriend. You're thinking that she didn't tell us about the bad things in her life, but you're wrong." Tulio was moved by the strength in her voice.

"She told me *everything*." Mrs. Conners whispered the last word. When she spoke again her voice was low, so her husband couldn't possibly hear what she was saying to the police.

"I knew when she had her first love affair, knew about it when she smoked marijuana her junior year in high school. I was her best friend from the day she was born until the day she was killed." Mrs. Conners paused, unused to speaking of her daughter and death in the same sentence. She pulled herself together. Tulio admired her fortitude as he envied her her courage.

"My husband's afraid that you're going to sweep this case under a rug, that you'll see it as some yuppie murder and pretend it didn't happen. I know he offended you when he said what he did about statistics, I could see it in your face." She paused, uncertain as to how she should continue. When she spoke now it was hesitantly, with a slight touch of chastisement in her voice.

"I can see what you think about people like us, Lieutenant."

"My opinion's rising with every word you speak."

"He's afraid that your—distaste of us would stop you from finding the—Carole's killer."

"It won't."

She stared into his eyes hard, the power of her glare touching him. Her husband might, over the years, have broken her heart, but he'd never gotten to her spirit. Tulio suddenly wished he had met her when she was thirty years old.

"*My* daughter was a good girl, Lieutenant, always thinking of others, since the time she was little. And she had the opportunity to do so. Carole had a rare blood type, you see, and ever since she was twelve years old she would donate it to help others." The woman paused, instinctively reached out and touched Tulio's forearm. "Are you all right, Lieutenant?"

"Fine." Tulio said, his mind racing. Not another one, he thought. God, no, not again.

"She loved to do that, Lieutenant. She still has the letters that the Red Cross would send her, thanking her, telling her how special she was. She didn't do drugs, Lieutenant. My Carole was taken from our home, against her will, and murdered."

"Ma'am . . ."

"Please don't 'Ma'am' me, Lieutenant. Our dog's missing, too, it's in the report. Do you think *he's* a junkie, run off to buy drugs? My daughter was taken, and the more time you waste pretending that anything else is the case is time that her killer will have to get away." Mrs. Conners paused as if to see if she had offended Tulio. He just stood there, looking down at her.

"Will you help us, Lieutenant? My daughter was no junkie, and she wasn't seeing any crazy man. She was killed by a stranger. Will you find that man?"

"Yes."

The woman signed in relief, at last believing him. "Thank God. My husband's a powerful man, Lieutenant, in his field, but he's not strong. By tomorrow he'll be on the phone, talking to the mayor, to your boss, demanding action that will only cause you resentment. It will be his way of dealing with what happened, trying to control something. Do you understand?"

"Yes."

Mrs. Conners took his hand and squeezed it hard, sealing their pact. Her husband would raise hell as soon as he stopped crying, but Tulio couldn't hold the professor's actions against his wife. They had a bond between them. He'd given her his word.

"Thank you, Lieutenant." Mrs. Conners said. "Thank you so very much."

C H A P T E R

18

PHILLIPS SAT IN THE WATCH COMMANDER'S OFFICE, UNCOMFORTABLE, unsure of himself now, too, knowing that he was pushing his luck by coming in to complain. The captain sat behind his desk, nearly smirking at Phillips. Phillips had the urge to just get up and leave, right now. Not say anything that would alienate the man.

"So, Phillips, we got trouble already, or what?"

The guy was solid, built like a linebacker, with a full head of graying black hair that was cut very short. His weapon was carried on the left, inside his pants, with the clip over his belt. As if he needed it anymore. Jake felt small in his presence, like a kid sent to the principal. His bachelor's degree wouldn't carry much weight with an old-timer like the captain. The captain would respect a high-school dropout with good instincts more than he would a cop who had a doctorate in police sciences.

Phillips said, "Captain," and nearly lost his nerve.

"You ought to know, right up front, Phillips," the captain said. "The guy, he's doing me a favor."

"There're other detectives who could train me."

The captain didn't respond. He tapped a nonfiltered cigarette out of the pack on the desk, lit up, and blew the smoke away from Jake. The white walls of the small room were discolored from the captain's habit. There were small brown spots of congealed nicotine on the filthy yellow window directly behind the captain's head. Phillips concentrated on the spots, on the captain's weakness. Jake could smell the stale tobacco from the butts that overflowed a large, round, brown glass ashtray on the desk, right behind the cursive lettered sign with his name on it, *Captain*

Merlin Royal. He didn't want to look at the man, didn't want to see the way that the captain might be looking at him.

"I want to work with Tulio." There, it was out. But the captain wasn't happy.

"You pick and choose your own assignments around here, do you, Phillips?"

"Sir, it's not that—"

"Then what is it?"

There was no hint in the captain's voice to tell Phillips how he felt. The guy spoke in a flat monotone, without inflection, in the tough ghetto cadence of a black man who'd been raised on the West Side. Every word he spoke, however, carried with it an implied warning. Phillips was scared, but had come too far to back out now. If he did, he'd look like a coward. And the one thing you could never live down in a department that prided itself on machismo was cowardice.

Phillips went for what he thought would be the captain's soft spot. He said, "Captain, the guy's a bigot, he's a lump. Every word out of his mouth is nigger this, baboon that. First homicide we pull up on, he tells me what happened, tells the whole *world* what happened, while he's cursing at the neighbors who're standing around watching. Tulio comes, five minutes later, the thing's solved, and Moore was completely wrong."

The captain ignored what he'd just been told, didn't even make mention of Moore's bigotry. Maybe it was such a well-known fact that the captain didn't even give it serious thought anymore.

"That five minutes count the time Tulio spent attacking your training officer?" Royal said.

Phillips was stunned. Word traveled fast, and the captain had to have snitches. Or maybe that's what Moore had been doing in here earlier, snitching on Tulio after the man had solved their case. That fat piece of shit. Phillips didn't answer, just spread his hands, showing his impotence, then quickly changed the subject.

"Captain, he was so pissed off at Tulio that he didn't even let me have my pinch. He sent two plainclothes TAC guys who were just standing by watching all the action, and *they* got *my* pinch."

"Now we're getting to the bottom of it, aren't we?" the captain said. "Penny-ante, petty-ass, hurt-feeling bullshit. I don't care *whose* kid you are, Phillips, I ain't got time for this."

"Captain, it's not like that," Phillips said, disappointed in the watch commander, running out of words. All he could think of to say was the truth. "The guy, Captain, he scares me."

"So who do you want me to hook you up with? And forget about Tulio, he don't work with nobody. Not even his own crew. They take orders from him, they don't work with him." The captain was enjoying himself now; there seemed to even be a hint of cruelty in his voice.

"Who you want to work with? Someone who owes your father? Someone who respected the old man so much he wouldn't watch his own ass out there, on account of he'd be covering yours?"

"Sir—"

The captain slapped one hand down hard on the top of his desk.

"Sir my ass. Who do you think you *are*? Moore's testing you, seeing what you're made of, and what do you do, right off the bat? Come running in here to bitch to me, crying 'cause your Field Training Officer gave your pinch away to somebody else. After Tulio gave it to you in the first place. This is the way to act, Phillips, first day on the squad. It'll endear you to the rest of the guys, this sort of behavior."

"I don't need any of them to be—"

"The hell you don't. Get it through your head, everything you say or do, how far you go here, Phillips, depends on your relationships." The captain paused, waiting, and when Phillips didn't respond, tried again.

"Look, Phillips, let me tell you how it is. You don't get along around here and your life, it starts to get miserable. Your life gets miserable, you don't focus on your work. You don't focus on your work, you don't solve homicides, and if you don't solve homicides, you don't stay on the squad. Moore's locked in with everybody in this department worth being tight with. I've known him almost twenty years myself. He knows the superintendent, he knows the fucking *mayor*. You want to piss him off? For what, to work with Tulio? Get this, Phillips: Tulio's days are numbered. He's been stomping on his dick so long it's a shock it ain't fell off. The guy's a dinosaur. You're with a thoroughbred. Bigot or not, I don't got time to worry about accusations. The man, he performs. Now listen carefully, son: There ain't no problem, Phillips, you hear what I'm saying? 'Cause if there is, it's *your* problem, not Moore's."

"Sir?" Phillips said, and the captain held his hand up.

"Wait, Phillips, wait just one minute. Before you say another word, let me tell you something. You mention Moore's name again to me, you're off the squad, tonight. You can go and get some sleep, report back to TAC tomorrow." The captain lowered his hand, crushed his cigarette out in the ashtray without looking down at it, keeping his eyes on Phillips the whole time. His eyes were cold and unforgiving; brown, wide, the whites streaked with red lines.

"Now, you wanted to say something?"

Phillips said, "No, sir."

"Good. Then get the hell out of my office, I got other things to do besides babysit your ass."

Phillips walked into the dayroom and interrupted Moore in the middle of a sentence. Moore looked at him from the table, sitting so he could see whoever came through the door, and shut his mouth. Phillips got the feeling that Moore and the other two bulls in the room had been talking about him.

Moore said, "You done with the captain, Philly?"

"No problem, Moory," Phillips said, and one of the other bulls laughed. Moore didn't crack a smile.

"Didn't I tell you? This one needs work. Come on, Philly, we got a call. Nigger stood in front of the trigger down on Twenty-third and Michigan." Moore looked at the black detective leaning against the coffee counter. He said, "No offense, Rosy."

The black bull said, "Why I be offended these young niggers want to kill each other?"

Moore told Phillips, as they drove down Michigan Avenue, to look on the bright side, they could be working a West Side district. If they were, Moore assured him, they'd be elbow deep in the shit.

"Every one of them got a pistol, got to have them a 'nine, though Uzis are just now starting to come in as a close second. Motherfuckers can't read their driver's licenses or spell their names, but they can turn a weapon full automatic in five minutes, blindfolded." His tone of voice was friendly; Moore complacent, sure of himself. He waited a minute, making sure that Phillips knew that he was about to impart another dollop of wisdom.

"Your new best friend," he said, "is about to lose his ass."

"Who's that?"

"Tulio." Moore gave Phillips a look and smiled. "One of the rookie uniform guys filed a report on him attacking me. Office of Professional Standards wants to talk to him tomorrow, Internal Affairs too. They'll be wanting to talk to you, too." Moore chuckled. "You'll have to tell them the truth and rat out your hero. Ain't life a bitch?"

"You sure you didn't turn him in?"

"Me?" Moore said it with studied exaggeration, telling Phillips that he'd certainly been the dealer of the cards. "Naw, Philly, I couldn't do that, not after your buddy solved the shooting for us. See, it's the way it works, you do me a favor, I got to do you one in return. Naw, some young stud complained." Moore shot him a sly look. "They do that sometimes, young guys. Bitch, I mean."

Phillips let it go. "So he solves our homicide, and then we try and get him fired."

"Hey, all I'm gonna do is tell the truth. And you better, too, Philly. Tell the truth. This time. Instead of the fuckin' bullshit you was spreadin' around the captain's office."

Phillips looked at the street sign as they passed. Twenty-first Street. Only a little way to go. He could see a crowd gathered up ahead, a block up and across the street, civilians drawn like moths to the blue-and-red flash of the responding squad cars. Phillips didn't know if he could keep his mouth shut for the rest of the ride. In an unmarked squad with a bigot, having been chewed out by a black man who was more politician than cop, who was himself afraid of the bigot. While the only good homicide cop he'd seen in action all night was in the middle of being set up by the bigot and his flunkies.

Phillips took a deep breath, silently hoped that his father, wherever he was, would forgive him. The old man was probably laughing his head off; he'd told Jake to stay in patrol. He blew his breath out slowly, his cheeks puffing out, then spoke.

"Hey, Jerry?"

"What's that, Philly." Smug bastard. Phillips waited a second, making sure that he could control his anger, before he continued.

"Pull the car over, would you please, Jerry?"

"Now why would I do that, Philly?"

"Cause I'm walking back to Eleventh. I've had it, I'm through with this bullshit."

"You're gonna walk?" Moore was having fun now, playing with the new guy. "Don't you know it's downright *danger*ous out there on those mean streets in the middle of the night, Jakey?" He dragged Phillips's first name out, *Jay-key*. "Young, good-lookin' guy like you could get himself hurt in this neighborhood. Shit, you might even wind up bein' sex-u-ally assa*ul*ted."

"Moore, I'm not telling you again, pull the car over, *now.*"

Moore pulled to the curb, in front of a broken parking meter on a deserted South Side street. Phillips could see, on the opposite corner, the old Lexington Hotel, where Capone had once held court. He took inventory of his decision, felt right about what he was doing. He opened the car door and looked out, down at the gutter littered with trash. A wino slept in the doorway of an abandoned building across from him. The wide sidewalk was heavily cracked. A shopping cart lay on its side a few feet from the wino. Jake put one foot out on the street, then turned halfway back toward Moore.

"I'm going back to TAC where what you do matters and you don't have to work with assholes."

Moore didn't seem at all offended, in fact, he acted as if Phillips couldn't possibly have been talking about him. He said, "Bad career move, kid. But probably good for you. You ain't cut out for the death squad, I don't think."

"But I'll talk to the Internal Affairs guys, Jerry. I'll tell them the truth, how you almost pulled down on Tulio. Tell them what you said about Baboon Island, and the T-shirt you want to have made up, too. The papers, they love to hear about shit like that, even if your captain doesn't care. Reporters, liberal as they are, they eat that stuff up. See you on the front pages."

He was disappointed by Moore's reaction. Instead of getting mad, the guy was just smiling at him.

"Tell 'em anything you want, kid, who you think they're gonna believe? A guy with ten in on Homicide and his *black* shift commander, or some wet-behind-the-ears punk who couldn't cut the mustard on the squad for even one day."

Phillips closed the door on the rest of it, heard Moore race away from the curb and felt gutter dirt tear at his trousers legs. Some of it went far enough to spray the guy in the doorway, who sat up, quickly, thinking himself under attack. The man threw both hands up in front of his face in a protective gesture, looking up at Phillips, seeing him in the glare of the streetlight, probably only able to see a tall, threatening shadow.

"Don't hurt me, please don't hurt me," the man cried, and Phillips stood there and stared at him for a second, then turned, shoved his hands in his pockets, and, with his head down, started walking back toward Police Headquarters.

CHAPTER
19

THIS WAS NUMBER SIX, TULIO KNEW IT IN HIS HEART. HE HAD THE files, the information, the experience and expertise to have no doubt that the killings were being performed by only one man, some maniac out there for hire, killing to get organs and money. Destroying two families every time out.

The only thing Tulio didn't have before tonight was a suspect and hard evidence. So far, he still didn't have a suspect. But he finally had some evidence. There were voices on tape, calls to police emergency.

Death due to generosity. What kind of an animal did it take to commit such an act? Not a serial killer. Rather a hit man, glorified perhaps, but no more than that. One who liked visiting cruelty upon other human beings. A man who would see them as a means to an end, and the end for this killer, Tulio knew, was money.

The question that disturbed him most was: Was it a national network for hire? He had facts only about a few of the murders that had been committed in Chicago. He could put a call in to the feds, to VICAP, the FBI's Violent Criminal Apprehension Program, and find out if they had other cases like this anywhere else in the country. For all he knew, the feds were already in place, working around the clock trying to hunt down this killer. They might see him differently than Tulio, might even be referring to him among themselves as an organized serial killer. It was the sort of exotic game the government liked to play in order to make themselves seem romantic and fascinating, and invincible to the public. They might already have a profile made up, and they would come damn close, too—the profile being based on his crimes—to the way he looked and acted, what he did for a living, how he'd been raised, even (as they'd done more than once before) the type of clothing he wore. The fact that he hadn't called them in bothered Tulio, but if he did that he'd have to ask his superiors for authority, and he didn't want to go that far, not based on what he had.

The suspicion had begun with a young woman named Latetia LaFeit, found just over two years ago, dying on a cracked sidewalk on the far Southeast Side. Latetia had been carefully shot once in the neck, nicked just a little bit, but enough to cause her to bleed to death, which she did while she was being transferred to South Chicago Community Hospital, which was less than a block from the spot where the teenager had been found. A panicked male voice had made a call to 911, and the responding officers had found a living, breathing Latetia, although the girl had been unconscious.

Latetia's father was a retired police officer, and it was he who had planted the seed of suspicion in then Homicide Sergeant Tony Tulio's mind, had asked him if he saw the coincidences there, the girl dying, shot down at seventeen, a young woman with a future, with no gang affiliations, her car missing, no marks on her body and no sign of a struggle, found slowly dying so close to the hospital where the wealthy, elderly woman who was on top of the list for a kidney-heart transplant lay terrified and in waiting.

More than a coincidence, Tulio had decided.

He had planted one of his specialized stories with the reporters, had gone on about the psychic state of whoever had shot the kid, in a way that would not panic the city, but still, he'd gotten his point across. He'd used himself as bait in a game in which there were no second chances to win. But nothing had come of it, not that time. The bait had not been nibbled.

Which had disappointed him. Had he been so far off the beam in his investigation? The least that he'd expected would have been one phone call, and Tulio had been ready for that, with a trap of his own. Criminals being basically stupid believed what they saw in the movies and on TV, thought that it took three minutes to run down the phone they were calling from.

Wrong.

In his office, Tulio had a computer monitor that was hooked into the 911 system. He could have the phone number and address of any phone caller who dialed his special emergency number from outside of police headquarters, the information coming up right there in front of him as soon as the call was taken, blinking on the computer screen.

He hadn't told anyone of his suspicions, not even Martie. He had, however, tried to talk to the husband of the organ recipient, a wealthy construction contractor who had gone dead cold on him. When Tulio had gotten hard, the contractor had told Tulio to speak to his lawyer, who'd threatened to take it to the papers and TV.

That same afternoon, he'd gotten heat from the bosses: Who the hell did he think he was, what the hell did he think he was doing, harassing a man like that? Didn't Tulio know how many hundreds of thousands of dollars that man had donated to the last mayoral campaign? He'd been ordered off it, told to leave the family alone, but even then he had not told his superiors of his suspicions. He'd kept them to himself, would have strong and solid evidence before he came forward.

It was the way Tulio operated, always played his cards right up tight, next to his chest.

Three days into the investigation, Martie and Jess had died.

It had taken him some time before he'd even thought of Latetia again, although her father had come to the Tulio funeral, had stood at one end of the room and had looked at Tulio through hooded eyes with a sad expression that told Tulio that in the man's heart, he knew the investigation into his daughter's death was, for all effects, now over.

Later, on his own time, Tulio had begun to do some checking into what was really not much more than a hunch. It became in effect a hobby, something to help him keep his mind off the booze. Off Martie and Jess, off what had happened. And off thinking about the wasteland that his life had become.

It was a big order, too, this grand new hobby of Tulio's; there were, on average, two and a half murders committed every day in the city.

Tulio went over every homicide that had occurred in the city of Chicago in the past five years.

He excluded vehicular homicides and homicides where the killers had been caught or where the killer had paid scant regard to the damage that was done to the victim. His killer, if there was one, would be a perfectionist. He would not kill in a way that would damage useful organs. Tulio began an investigation of the dozens of victims that were left, found out how many of them had been organ donors.

Eleven.

Of those eleven, only three (along with Latetia) had died under circumstances that still remained suspicious, in almost the same way: their bodies found close to a hospital, their organs donated to help somebody else. The other eight had been unsolved homicides that remained officially open. A little further checking revealed that in each of those cases, there were strong suspects. But not enough evidence to bring the suspected killers to trial.

Despite the year he devoted to the project, he could find no real link between the dead and any single individual. And how he'd looked, the hours he'd put in! Particularly before he'd met Marian Hannerty.

The project became his obsession, especially on the nights that Marian couldn't see him, or when he had strong urges to drink. It was like a game to him, a puzzle, one to which he wasn't sure he knew the rules or had all of the pieces; for all he knew he might really only have a head filled with paranoid suspicions. That certainly would have been what anyone else would have thought, if he had taken what little he had to his bosses. They thought he was crazy enough without his going to them and proving them right.

He'd gone a long way toward proving them right, later, when he'd reopened the LaFeit case, had taken it right to the press without even bothering to check with his bosses. When had he done that, a year ago? Right about the time he'd been made Chief of Special Victims, a year after the accident, about the time he'd started seeing Marian.

He'd told them he had new evidence in the LaFeit slaying, that he was expecting an arrest at any moment. Told them that the killer had made a fatal mistake, had left behind identifying evidence that had been misunderstood until now. He'd done everything but say they had the suspect's name, Tulio trying to spook the killer, wanting him to make a move. He felt sure that someone the killer knew would call the special number he'd given out to the press, someone who might have been involved in the case, but who until now hadn't come forward. Someone who was willing to come forward now, though, and get that all-important immunity from prosecution in order to give up the shooter.

The number had gotten plenty of calls, and every single one of them had been run into the ground by the new, elite Special Victims Squad. None of them had panned out. They were no closer two years after Latetia's death than they'd been on the day her body had been found. The only thing going public had done was cause him more grief with the ass-covering brass.

Tulio now came to a long hospital corridor with a finger-sign pointing him in the proper direction: SURGERY. He walked slowly toward the waiting room, savoring the encounter he would be having in the next few minutes. As he walked he remembered the one special death that had occurred that had convinced him beyond any doubt that he had indeed been on the right track, right from the very beginning.

The Eagle—Carmine Venicie—had been dying of heart disease.

Chicago's second most powerful, but without doubt most notorious and vicious gangster, the brutal, venerated patriarch of the outfit who'd been suspected of committing thirty-four mob hits himself, had, at fifty-six, been about to meet his maker. In the law enforcement community, it had been cause for celebration, but the brass had gotten worried, because rumors had begun to circulate.

The word was that some of his friends were about to find the Eagle a heart.

The thought was ludicrous, would have even been funny if the outfit didn't have a reputation for being efficiently, pragmatically brutal in achieving their desires. It wasn't above them, any copper knew, to kill a total stranger in order to get their boss whatever he might need in order to prolong his miserable life. The fact was, it might have even become a contest, with every mob punk in the city bringing in three hearts, hoping that one of them would be compatible.

The rumors came in from reliable street sources, and the U.S. attorney himself was looking into a way to stop the murder before it happened when the problem was taken out of their hands: a donor had been found, far outside of the city.

Nobody was fooled. No one thought it was an accident. Not the feds, not the cops, not even the Eagle pretended otherwise. But nothing could be proved, no evidence was at hand. The worried doctors, to stave off their fears, had put the Eagle on the top of the donor list, and a suitable, twenty-one-year-old donor had been found in a downstate farm town emergency room, dying of a mysterious gunshot wound to the head that had caused massive, fatal trauma.

There was an investigation, of course, but it was at a local level. As it was far outside of the city, Tulio had some trouble learning the details, but he'd gotten them nevertheless.

The donor had been a gun nut, a farmer's son who'd been hunting and target shooting since the time that he'd been old enough to walk. Not the type to have an accident cleaning a .22 handgun, but that's what the investigation had concluded, and nobody wanted to argue.

Except Tony Tulio. He believed he'd found number five.

But he kept his mouth shut, he had less than no evidence. The farmer and his wife had been in an upstairs bedroom sleeping when the gunshot had awakened them. They'd seen or heard nothing out of the ordinary either before or after the shooting. There had been no sign of forced entry into the house, and there were no tire tracks outside that did not conform to vehicles owned by the occupants of the farmhouse. The case was closed, but the suspicions lingered.

Over how the heart had been rushed to the Eagle, by special helicopter, the boy's heart on ice.

How it had been a perfect match, how his body hadn't rejected it.

And now the Eagle was as dangerous as ever, running his criminal empire from a mansion in Winnetka, the man taking to wearing black silk pajamas around the clock.

Rumors naturally flew, but none of them reached the citizenry, and few had reached any members of the popular press.

But the Eagle knew, and the cops suspected, and they all knew he'd gotten away with it. Tulio still wasn't completely convinced on that last point. It was something he was looking into.

Tulio had the tape at home, a copy of the 911 call that had come in after Latetia's murder. He'd check it after he confronted Alleo, against the call about the victim that had come in tonight. He would have to wait until tomorrow, but he'd bet he could get a voiceprint match. If he did, he'd have his evidence, he could begin to formulate a plan of attack. Even the cynical, nonimaginative people he worked for would have to cut him loose full-time to hunt down a man who could murder with such cold calculation. He'd bet that he could even talk them into letting some of his team work with him exclusively, on a task force of his own. The bosses would not want the feds sniffing around any more than Tulio did. The bosses of both agencies could tell all the lies they wanted about interagency cooperation, but that was bullshit, and every working copper knew it was. If you could keep the feds out, you did. They were good for crunching numbers and for following paper trails, but when it came to investigating murders, there wasn't one of them who could hold a candle to what Tulio was capable of.

And if the brass didn't go for it, he would go to the newspapers and to television, terrify the city with the story he could tell.

Tulio didn't know it, as he walked down the final corridor to the surgical waiting room, but his lips were twisted into an anticipatory snarl as he prepared himself for combat.

C H A P T E R
20

Tulio saw the old woman look up, and for just an instant he had the urge to back out of the room. She was old and in tears. The hope on her face when she first saw him was painful for him to observe. He then saw Alleo glaring at him, and decided to stay in the room.

"What do you want, Officer." Alleo didn't take a wild guess. The badge was still hanging around Tulio's neck on a chain.

"Your ass, Alleo, in Stateville for thirty years."

Alleo slowly stood as the woman reached out a cautionary hand that was gently pushed away.

"You didn't have that badge around your neck, I'd have thought you to be a stewbum. Look at you. I can smell you over here. What are you, some burnout undercover? Do you know what you're doing? Get out of this room, you don't know what you're getting into."

"Put me out."

"You think I can't do it? You think I don't have it in me?"

"Arturo . . ." the woman said feebly, and Tulio and Alleo both ignored her. Tulio didn't worry about what she might hear or see. She'd made her bed when she'd married the man, she had to know what he was.

Tulio said, "Where'd you get the liver, Alleo?"

That stopped the man for a second. As good as he was, he wasn't good enough to keep the suspicion and fear from crossing his face.

"How should I know where the liver came from? Some donor, I don't know."

"The doctors didn't tell you what happened?"

He stared at Tulio, wondering how to play it. At last, he said, "As a matter of fact, they did."

"Then why did you say you didn't know?"

It was too late, he'd had the guy for a second, but now Alleo had it back: his arrogance, that particular superior audacity that made simple and stupid men like him believe themselves to be smarter than the law.

Alleo said, "I don't have to tell you anything. Go on, get out of here, you forget about me and I'll forget about you." He walked away from Tulio, went over and sat back down in his chair. His wife was looking at him, greatly relieved. Tulio took his last shot.

"Come on, Alleo, we're gonna take a ride." Alleo simply smiled.

"Not tonight, I don't think. Not ever, as a matter of fact." The old man's voice hardened, and he sat up straighter in his chair.

"You have nothing, you have never had anything, and let me tell you something, son, you are never *gonna* have anything." He turned his head away from his wife and dry-spat toward the floor between his feet. "You'll never get me to go anywhere with you. Not now, not ever. Understand that."

Tulio stared at him, the old man not giving an inch. He could see how Alleo had gotten where he had.

"Please, Officer, our daughter's in surgery!" The woman again. Tulio kept staring at Alleo, did not even bother to look over at her.

He knew there was nothing he could do, that Alleo was right. He'd told the man to come take a ride to try and spook him, try to goad him into physical attack. It hadn't worked.

"I'm going to find out where that liver came from, Alleo."

"You go ahead and do that, you be my guest."

"Did you order the girl killed?"

"You gonna question me, Officer, take me in and read me my rights. I'm not saying another word to you until you do. In about fifteen minutes after that, you'll be out of a job, and a lawsuit will be in the works, against you and your entire department. Now for the last time I'm telling you, get your ass the hell out of this room. All you're doing is upsetting a couple of senior citizens who are waiting to hear how their daughter's doing in surgery. You have no right to harass us."

Alleo was letting him know how it would play on the four o'clock news, and in the morning papers, too. Alleo would have his lawyer go to them if he felt that he had to. As much as he hated publicity, he would do it to get Tulio out of the room and away from his wife.

Tulio knew that he must have a very good reason to make such a threat. He felt a shiver of glee, but kept his face impassive. He was on to it, finally. *He was on to it.* He could not allow himself to do anything that would put the outcome in jeopardy.

Tulio smiled at Alleo and said, "I'll be seeing you again, soon."

"No, you won't," Alleo said, then immediately asked, "What's your name again?"

"Tulio, my name is Lieutenant Anthony Tulio. Why, you going to file a complaint? Would you like my badge number?" Alleo was looking at him cautiously now, ignoring the sarcasm, maybe remembering things he'd heard.

"I know who you are, Lieutenant. You're the one shoots all the *tuit-soons*. Why are you bothering me?" He made the universal Italian gesture for confusion with his hands and shoulders. "You, you're Italian; me, *I'm* Italian. Lieutenant, we're almost *paisan*."

"I'm no *paisan* to you."

"Lieutenant, come on, blood's thicker than water."

Tulio saw red dots in front of his eyes; it was an expression his own father used to use after a beating, when he'd calmed down and become panic-stricken at the sight of what he'd done, trying to convince young Tony that he had to keep his mouth shut and not tell anyone what had happened to him, how he'd gotten the bruises. So he kept his mouth shut, now, just looked at Alleo, then backed out of the room with the two of them locked in a stare that didn't break until the door closed behind him.

Tulio let out a slow, long breath, standing with his back to the door, his eyes tightly shut. He was the closest he'd ever come to cracking this case, and he knew it. Knew he had the lead he'd been seeking for two years. All he had to do was think this through, and he would have it all together in a way that he hadn't for two years. Tulio pushed away from the door and walked away from the room. All he had to do now was not blow it, not lose his temper, to remain in control, and he'd have him.

"There is a man who is out of control," Mr. Alleo said into the pay phone on the wall across the room, after checking to make sure the cop was gone. "And I need him—spoken to."

Mr. Alleo was whispering so his wife would not hear. He had never discussed business in front of her, and he wasn't about to start.

"This is important, do you understand? Get down here right now, tonight." He listened for a moment as the man on the other end argued with him. What was this, idiot night? Had the man forgotten where the bulk of his earnings came from? Mr. Alleo *owned* this man.

"Get down here, now," Mr. Alleo said, then hung up.

Mr. Alleo went into the bathroom, thankful that tonight he and his wife were the only people in the surgery waiting room. He locked the door, went over and sat down on a toilet seat, thinking about his options.

Should he call someone of importance in the department, report the impertinence of this Lieutenant Anthony Tulio? No, that might be a mistake; he should just have him killed. It had been so long since he had given an order to murder, and here he was tonight, giving two such orders in a matter of hours. Neither of which was business, nor brought the family any money. The irony of it all almost made Mr. Alleo smile.

Mr. Alleo couldn't have this lieutenant killed, at least not yet. He may have reported where he was going, what he was doing, who he was seeing. He had to think this through as he would have done when he was a younger man. He could not use the passing of time as an excuse to act impetuously.

Of course, back then, no policeman in the city of Chicago would have dared try to question him without ten members of the FBI right behind him for backup. He had owned too many of them; that or he had owned the bosses of the ones he couldn't buy.

But that was all a long time ago. Today he was respectable and the law and lawmen had changed; he could not act like he used to. And his problems were here with him tonight, twenty years after such a time had passed. He had to think this through, make sure that he hadn't acted in haste, because he could never, ever allow this Tulio to know how he'd gotten the liver. His daughter, his wife, they could never be touched by the reality of what he was. He owed them that, and he was, above all, a man who looked out for his family.

So, what should he do? His options were very limited. Then he sat up and smiled; the solution to his problem was so simple, had been right in front of him all along.

He would call every bigshot he knew in the department, from the superintendent to the captains in the individual area precincts, shout his outrage at how, in his time of greatest suffering, some lowly *lieutenant* had intruded upon his grief, insulting not only him but his distraught wife, as well. He would call his lawyers and have them tell it to the reporters they held in their pockets like the small change that they were, willing to sell their very souls to get an exclusive story about a man such as himself. He would raise all sorts of hell, a tremendous, powerful stink— but he would wait until after he saw the man he had called on the phone.

Because all this complaining wouldn't do him any good if this Lieutenant Anthony Tulio were around to tell his side.

First, Mr. Alleo would have to have him killed.

The finger of the investigation would never point toward him, because if it did, he'd have the perfect alibi, and everyone would know it: If he were going to have a man murdered, why would he have been so incredibly stupid as to call the man's superiors and complain about his actions?

He would begin the calls, wake people up, as soon as he gave the killing order.

CHAPTER
21

Jᴀᴋᴇ's ɴɪɢʜᴛ ᴡᴀs ɢᴇᴛᴛɪɴɢ ᴡᴏʀsᴇ, ᴡʜᴀᴛ ᴡɪᴛʜ ᴛʜᴇ ᴄᴀᴘᴛᴀɪɴ ɴᴏᴡ pissed off at him and not caring if Jake knew it. He stood in front of the man's desk, the captain having given up all pretense of friendship, Jake listening to it, having to take it. He had not been asked to sit down this time. He wanted out of Homicide, but he had no desire to be thrown out of the department, so he had no choice but to wait the man out.

"You want *out* of *Homicide*? You want to leave *my* command? What're you, *stupid*?" The captain seemed in awe of Jake's request. Still, Jake didn't open his mouth, although he wanted to point out that an hour ago, this guy had used sending him back to TAC as some sort of terrible punishment that Jake might have to bear. Now that Jake was volunteering, the man seemed to see him as some sort of irreplacable asset to the Homicide unit.

Smoke filled the captain's office. The ashtray had been dumped into a round metal can beside the captain's desk, but it hadn't been wiped or washed; black ash spots filled the bottom of the glass.

"Phillips, how long you been on this department?"

"Four years," Jake said, then quickly added, "Sir."

"Four years. *Four fucking years!*" The captain finally made it, he was shouting now, managing to be in Jake's face even from across the desk. "There're people been waiting four*teen* years, twenty-*four* years, to get on Homicide. You ignorant son of a bitch!"

Jake didn't get a chance to defend himself.

"You know how many *minorities* get promoted into this division every year, Phillips? Too few, and every time I get a chance to try and sneak someone in, to replace the Moores in this goddamn division, I get told to hold off, to wait a while, somebody's *kid* gets the first shot, some hot-shit punk with four years on the job somehow *earned* his opportunity at the Homicide division. Well, I had to take you, and I'll be a son of a bitch if I'm gonna let you walk the hell away from *my* command after less than one full shift on the squad."

"Captain, *why?*" Jake had to speak up. "Look, just let me out of here, transfer me, get me away from this guy and bring in one of your minorities who deserves it more than me. What do you want to do, punish me?"

"I wanted to punish you, I'd walk around this desk and slap the shit out of you, Phillips. And who the hell are you to come in here and question my decisions?"

"Sir—"

"Sir, shit! You want to know why I won't let you go? I'll tell you why, Phillips. 'Cause there's too many goddamn pigs like Moore waiting to get into this squad, too." The captain nodded his head, the cat out of the bag.

"Like Moore, but thirty years younger, with his attitude and beliefs. Guys who wouldn't have a lick of trouble relating to that bastard."

"You can't keep me here if I want to leave, sir."

"No, but I can make your life in TAC miserable, Phillips, I can make every second of it so goddamn painful that you'll quit and go be a school-teacher somewhere. In the suburbs, where you belong, shit, with your sensi*tiv*ities. Get it through your head, Phillips; this is a tough unit, but it's the best. I worked my ass off for seven years to make this group what it is today. I won't let you or anybody else fuck it up."

"Then why do you—"

"I'm through answering your damn questions. You want to ask questions, get a job as a census taker." The captain sat forward in his chair, stabbed his cigarette out hard, left it smoldering in the ashtray, then leaned back and looked at Jake cynically, nodding his head, as if coming to some inner agreement with an earlier assessment. When he spoke this time the anger was out of his voice, the captain speaking softly, with just a hint of disgust in his tone.

"I knew your daddy. Stayed away from his type, but I knew him, who and what he was. I was handed you, and you better believe I looked into you, Phillips. You ain't like him. I even thought that, eventually, you might be an asset." He paused for effect, then said, "I was wrong." He pointed his chin toward the door as he reached for another cigarette.

"Go ahead," the captain told Jake, "get on out of here. Get some sleep and report to TAC in the morning or whenever the hell time your old squad is working. I'll make a call before I go home, let them know what's going on. You won't have any trouble, either." The captain grunted. "God knows who's looking out for you, might want my ass hanged if I beef you."

Phillips looked at the captain, stunned. What was it the man was saying? He was throwing out so many confusing signals. Had he misjudged the captain, was he more than just a politician putting in his time? He didn't want any junior Moores under his command, he had told Phillips that. So why hadn't he explained things to him earlier, when they'd first discussed Moore?

Then again, who was Jake to question a captain? He thought about how it must look to the man, how his coming into the squad must have seemed. A young guy, educated, but with only four years on the job. Pushed into Homicide, against the captain's wishes. The captain knew of his father, the type of cop his dad had been. He didn't hold that against Jake, had gone to the trouble to learn that Jake was honest. What the hell was he doing? Jake felt he'd made a big mistake by being so impetuous.

Jake felt ashamed, belittled. The captain had at first thought him to be a crook, like his father. Well, he found out that he was wrong. And he had said, straight out, that he thought Jake might be an asset. He'd been waiting, willing to sit back and watch, not giving Phillips anything until he had proved himself and what it was that he could do.

Jake had proven himself, all right. He'd sure shown the man what he was made of, running out at the first sign of trouble.

The captain finished lighting another cigarette and grunted.

"You still here?"

"Uh—Captain?"

"What now?"

"What, uh, what would you like me to do until my training officer gets back from the field?"

The captain looked at Jake for just a second, then swiveled around in his chair, stared at the filthy window for a minute. Phillips could see the top of his head shaking up and down, as if he were dancing to some inner music. Or he might be pulsing with anger and didn't trust himself to look at Jake until he calmed himself down. At last the captain swiveled back to face him, flicking ashes in the general direction of the glass ashtray.

"You walked away from your partner," the captain said. "Left him out there to dry, all by himself."

"There were plenty of uniformed officers on the scene, squad cars, paramedics, it wasn't like he was out there all alone, or in any danger."

"That's how you see it. Ask Moore how feels about it when I tell him you're still on the squad."

"Captain—"

"Shut up. Go up two floors and wait. Special Victims office is on the right. I'll beep Tulio. If he's still out on the street, I'll tell him you're waiting for him. If he ain't, you go on home and come back tomorrow, early afternoon. You don't want to drag him in here to interview you if I pull him out of the sack." The captain caught Jake's expression, and the man grunted, half-smiling. "His department gets its share of pressure too, you know."

"Captain—thank you."

"Talk to Tulio, he might not want you. Even if he does, don't thank me 'till you been there a while." The phone on the desk rang, and the captain reached for it, still talking to Jake.

"Man hangs onto his job long enough, he'll have you thinking I'm the best boss you ever had in your life." The captain barked a "Yeah," into the phone, and Jake turned to leave, had taken a couple of steps when he heard the captain's voice change its tone in a hurry.

"Yes sir, this is Captain Royal."

As he walked out the door Jake looked back shortly, noticed that the captain was now sitting up straight, looking completely revolted. He heard the man say, "Sir, I don't have the authority to suspend—" then, a second later, "Yes, yes sir, that's true, but only nominally, he heads his own—" Jake closed the door just in time, but before he did he heard the captain softly say, once again, "Yes sir."

Jack was walking down the hallway, toward the stairs, when he heard the loudly screamed, vicious curse that must have shaken some of the dirt off the captain's dirty window.

CHAPTER 22

Mr. Alleo stood in a dark, empty room in a deserted corridor of the hospital, one that was under construction. The strain of the night—of the past months—was beginning to get to him. His daughter might well be dying, his wife was having her doubts, and he owed allegiance to that maniac, the Eagle, for saving Sophia's life.

And now, here this bastard was, acting as if he were doing Mr. Alleo a favor by showing up to see what he wanted. Not only that, but throwing his weight around, wanting to know *why* Mr. Alleo needed this cop, Tulio, killed.

How dare he question an order? Had he so soon forgotten how he'd gotten the huge suburban house in which he and his wife lived? Forgotten who had shown him how to earn sums so vast that he had to be taught how to hide it all from the Internal Revenue Service? If it hadn't been for himself, this slob before him would be making forty-five thousand a year, barely eking out an existence, instead of living like a king in a house with an in-ground swimming pool.

"We don't have to kill the guy, Mr. A," this dog of a man now said to him. "He's gone, anyhow, I guarantee it. Between you and me, what we did, he's out of a job. By morning, he'll be through."

Mr. Alleo did not allow his anger to show on his face nor in his voice. When he spoke it was very softly. He forced himself to smile a little, to show the man what he thought of his argument, the degree of seriousness with which it was taken. Did this peon expect to be told Mr. Alleo's personal strategy? Perhaps it was time to consider having this idiot killed and replaced.

He said, "Don't argue with me. I want him dead, tonight. I want whatever files he might have destroyed, all of them, whatever's in his office or in his home. You get into both places somehow, how you do it is your own business." Mr. Alleo had to crane his neck to look way up to stare into the man's eyes. The man lowered his own. Submissively. Good. He wasn't going to take things any farther.

Still, even looking down, the dog had to argue. He said, "Mr. Alleo, excuse me, please, I know I'm speaking out of turn, but I gotta tell you, it's a mistake. The guy's a cop; we can't kill a *cop*." He raised his eyes and stared into Mr. Alleo's own, trying to project his sincerity and to take the sting out of the words he was about to speak.

"Sir, again, excuse me, but Mr. A, you've been under a lot of pressure. This thing with your daughter, it'd make anyone think funny."

Mr. Alleo nodded, as if thinking over the man's words. He half-turned, stroking his chin, then turned back quickly, the back of his hand cracking against the man's left cheekbone. The man stepped back, in shock at what Mr. Alleo had done. Mr. Alleo lifted his hand again, as if about to slap the other side of his face, and the man, dog that he was, cowered away, half a whimper escaping from his lips.

Mr. Alleo lowered his hand and turned the full strength of his personality on his subordinate. He glared at him from under half-lowered lids, aware that his lips were snarling, showing bared yellow teeth. He was grateful that he no longer carried a weapon. If he did, this man might die right here, tonight. Mr. Alleo controlled himself. Again, he made sure that his voice was calm and low. But it carried his intentions well; the mutt would not misunderstand him.

"You small-time, low-life, *disgracia!* Who are you? Who *are* you! Are you somebody now, are you a power, my *partner?* You're my fucking lapdog, you hear me? That's what you are, that's *all* you are! If I want to hear anything out of you, I'll give the command for you to speak!"

The man stepped back against the wall and tried to hide within it. Terror filled his eyes.

"I gave you an order, and you're gonna do what you're told. Now. Tonight. As soon as you leave this hospital!"

"Please, Mr. Alleo, I had no right, forgive me—I'm sorry, I'm sorry, sir, for*give* me."

"Go ahead. Get out of here. Do what I told you. Tonight. Now leave me, get out of my sight."

Without another word, the dog ran out of the room. Mr. Alleo heard his footsteps racing down the hospital corridor.

If he had been any less repentant, Mr. Alleo would have made him bark, would have made him crawl on his knees and bay at the moon. The sight of such unmanly cowering disgusted him. This dog of a man had been so afraid, he would have taken Mr. Alleo's sexual member into his mouth, had Mr. Alleo told him to do so. The type of person it was good to have working for you, but never one that you could trust. In fact, you killed them when they discovered things you didn't want them to know.

He forced himself calm, left the room and turned and walked down the empty corridor, back to the surgical waiting room, where his wife would still be fingering her rosary, saying her prayers for Sophia. He would tell her nothing of what had happened, nor would she dare to ask him. She knew better, knew how far she could go, and stayed well behind the line. Not like the arrogant dog, who, in order to live with what he was, had to pretend in his mind that he was an equal, instead of the servant, the lackey that he truly was.

Then again, Mr. Alleo thought, cops could sometimes be like that. They got to thinking that because the civilian population was terrified of them, everyone else was, too. Especially when they took your money, they thought it gave them some power over you instead of the reverse being true. Sometimes, these cops, they had to be taught harsh lessons. The way this one had just been taught, and he'd learned. This fat Jerry Moore, this cop who was more of a dog than he was a man.

Mr. Alleo stepped back into the waiting room, and felt a huge shiver of fear race down his spine when he saw the two doctors in the white coats, their backs to him, leaning down, talking to his wife.

CHAPTER
23

LENNY ROMAN HAD WAYS OF PROTECTING HIMSELF THESE DAYS THAT went far beyond the prowess he'd once had with his fists in the ring. He'd learned, he believed, to use his head every bit as well as he'd once used his fists.

The City Council of Chicago, in its wisdom, thought they had found a way to enrich the city coffers and fight street crime both at the same time; they decided to take away your car for whatever shit they caught you doing.

Lenny thought it was cute, especially the way that the press had taken to it. If you got caught driving around while carrying a gun in your ride, *ba-bing*, they took your car away from you, made you pay through the nose to get it back. It cost you six hundred dollars flat just to get the heap out of the city's hands, plus you were responsible for the towing and storage fees. You were looking at a total of a grand out of your pocket because you were carrying a gun around in your Chevy. Or, rather, because you got *caught* carrying a gun as you tooled around town. The fact was, Lenny didn't know a lot of guys who didn't regularly pack.

It was the same with running with the hookers, you couldn't let one into your car. The morality police would take your car away from you and it would be the same deal as when they caught you carrying a piece. They'd take the car, and it would cost you. Roughly a thousand dollars per blowjob. At that price you were better off staying home and begging.

They already had a deal if you were caught carrying dope, only then they didn't hold your vehicle as a hostage. If they caught you with dope, they kept the car, unless it was rented or leased. Lenny had spent considerable time trying to figure that deal out: if some punk was driving Daddy's car in from the suburbs to try to score some pussy, the car got taken and held for ransom. But if some killer from the Murderous Monster Cannibals streetgang had an Avis rental Lincoln filled to the roof with stolen Uzis and crack cocaine, the player got the car back as soon as he made his bond. To Lenny's way of thinking, that didn't make a lot of sense.

What *did* make sense to Lenny was the fact that if he had himself a car, sooner or later some cop from the city would set him up just to take it away from him. So to protect himself—and to save a lot of money, considering gas, parking fees, insurance, and the price of a sticker— Lenny didn't drive. He hardly ever carried a piece and stayed away from dope as if it were a proven carrier of AIDS.

Cops loved to hassle Lenny, they were always busting his balls about something, and if they pinched him tonight they'd hit the jackpot; he was masquerading as one of them. He had the badge and fake ID in his pocket to prove it. Hanging from his belt, on the left side, was a useless two-way radio that had been stolen from a construction sight. The batteries had long ago worn out, and Lenny had never replaced them. On the other side was his beeper. Also hanging from his belt, in back, was a pair of silver handcuffs for which he'd lost the key. With the exception of a gun, he was decked out pretty much like a bull. At least enough like one so that someone who was afraid of the law wouldn't be able to tell that Lenny wasn't a cop.

He had made a lot of enemies within the Chicago Police Department. Usually it started out as D&D and quickly escalated from there, a squad dispatched to some fancy lounge to deal with the disorderly drunk who'd punched out a bouncer or two, and the next thing you knew, Lenny had popped one of them, and then there were battalions of cops called in to try and bust his head, with nightsticks getting broken over a skull that was harder than their round pressed wood. More than one cop had told him, after Lenny had walked on an I-Bond, not to ever let him catch Lenny alone on the street without any witnesses. Lenny's response at such times was always: Why, you want to suck my dick without losing your tough-guy image?

For these reasons, Lenny rarely got behind the wheel of a car. He generally took cabs, wherever he went, no matter how far, unless he could talk some hero-worshipping geek into giving him a ride for free. There were plenty of those around, guys who got some kind of cheap thrill by basking in the reflected glory of Lenny's illustrious past. Who'd want to know what it was like to get beat by such great lightheavies as Foster and Victor Galindez. Lenny as a rule tried to stay away from such people, because he was often tempted to show them just exactly how it felt, and he had enough trouble in his life without beating up groupies who asked him stupid questions. But sometimes he was in a hurry, or maybe he felt like talking of the past, and he'd let them zip him around the city, Lenny pretending that he was Thomas Gerardi and this *schlub* behind the wheel was his personal driver/bodyguard.

But not tonight. Lenny wasn't in the mood, and besides, there was no one around to give him a lift down to Halsted. After meeting with Gerardi and finally getting hold of the Collector, he had gone back to the game and quickly found out that the luck he'd been having earlier that night had gone south on him. Lenny had lost his ass. And now he had to hustle up some money, and fast, too.

He would have to lay low if he were going to get through it this time. Gerardi might understand that he was a standup guy, and he hadn't pushed Lenny too hard for answers because Lenny had once worked for him and the man knew Lenny's ways. But that Alleo, he was a tough one, Lenny knew. Someone who had to know everything about everyone who ever did a job for him. The stories about him were legend; the guy could go from being a gentleman to you one second to your killer in the next without even blinking his eye.

Back in late September, when Lenny had first approached Gerardi about getting the Eagle a compatible heart, he'd lain it all out for him, what the guy he worked for could do. Gerardi had been interested, intrigued, and wanted to know more about the man, but Lenny wasn't giving it up; he had his loyalties, too. And somewhere in the back of his mind was another reason to keep his mouth shut, even after Gerardi started making threats: If he told Thomas the guy's real name, what was to stop him from approaching the Collector all by himself, and cutting Lenny out altogether? The Collector, Paul Harris, was as steady as a man like him could ever get. If Lenny put him together with Gerardi, Harris would come through for him, give him a piece of the pie. But he was also a businessman, and as coldblooded as any snake. Lenny never got a piece of anything that he wasn't involved in right from the beginning.

He'd been able to hold Gerardi off from hurting him last fall, and maybe Thomas hadn't had him hit simply for old-time's sake. But he had no old-times to fall back on with Alleo, there was no shared history to keep Alleo from having him tortured to find out the Collector's true identity.

Which meant that Lenny needed money in case he had to lie low, and he'd get some tomorrow, from Harris. It could be any amount, though. Lenny wasn't even sure what Mr. Alleo wanted. Nobody ever told him anything; he was a go-between and nothing more. For all he knew, Gerardi wanted to kill Harris, and had used Lenny to help him do it. Which scared him. If Harris died, there'd be nothing in it for Lenny. Except maybe a hit order on his head, and a million guys willing to take it for nothing, to do Alleo or the Eagle or Thomas Gerardi a favor.

Lenny had thought at first that he'd be on easy street, that there'd be something nice in it for him from Harris in the morning, but the more he thought about it, the more afraid he'd gotten. What if Gerardi had only mentioned Alleo's name as a dodge? What if the Eagle's new heart was giving out, and he wanted his last act to be that of killing Paul Harris with his own two hands?

There were too many what-ifs in this entire deal for Lenny. He didn't like playing in this league, knew that he was good at running errands and small-time cons, but this was too much; guys like Alleo had always scared the shit out of him. Nor did he like the way his mind raced when he tried to out-think guys who came out of the womb with more smarts than Lenny would ever have. They were too good, knew too many angles for a guy like Lenny to ever be able to beat them. So what he'd have to do was get some dough together, lay low and wait until he heard something from Harris.

But he'd lost his ass in the card game tonight, and he knew only one other way to make a good score fast without having to take a couple of days to plan it all out in advance.

And so it was that at 4:35 A.M. on Monday morning, with his life savings of two ten-dollar bills still left in his pants pocket, Lenny sat in the back of a shit-beaten cab, on his way to find the whore who could help him out of his trouble.

CHAPTER

24

JAKE TOOK THE STAIRS UP TWO FLIGHTS, CONTROLLING HIS NER-vousness, telling himself that everything was going to be all right. What had Tulio said to him, over at the South Side murder scene? "You ever need anything, look me up." Well, Phillips needed something now. He needed an assignment to Special Victims.

He expected the bureau to be empty at this hour. Tulio had to be in bed. The door to Special Victims was made of light wood, installed when the new addition to the building had been built. This door was unlike the heavy wooden door to the captain's office, or the thick steel firedoors that they had in the stairways, all of which had been hung when the building had first been built. Jake pushed it way too hard, and it flew wide, slammed against the wall. He was glad that no one else was around to witness his first clumsy entry to what he'd hoped would be his new assignment.

He shook his head at his own stupidity, turned to close the door, and when he turned back he jumped, startled, because Lieutenant Tony Tulio was standing in the doorway of the bathroom at the far end of the room, pointing a 9-mm Browning at Phillips, and even from this distance Jake could see that the hammer was pulled back and Tulio's finger was on the trigger.

Tulio immediately jerked the weapon into the air, holding it with both hands, relief and anger in his expression. He lowered the hammer, put the safety back on, shoved the pistol back into its holster.

"Sorry," Tulio said.

"Who'd you expect to be coming in here, for Christ's sake?" Jake said the words before he could stop himself. Tulio had scared him; he was angry. "This is a police station, Lieutenant."

Tulio didn't get mad or even respond in any way. He simply stood there looking at him. Phillips watched as Tulio shook his head just a little, then walked over to a desk in the center of the room, the only one in the place that didn't have another desk pushed up next to it, front to front. Judging by the arrangement, Phillips guessed that with the exception of the boss, Special Victims worked in teams.

Tulio sat down in a high-backed leather swivel chair, turned on the gooseneck green-shaded banker's lamp on his desk, and quickly closed the covers on a half-dozen yellow files that had lain open on his desk. He stacked the files, then looked up at Phillips, quizzically.

"What can I do for you, Jake?"

It threw Phillips off balance for a minute. Captain Royal was supposed to have told Tulio what it was that Jake wanted. He said, "Did Captain Royal beep you?" and watched as Tulio shrugged.

"Maybe." That was it, no explanation. Was his beeper turned off? Was the battery dead? Or had Royal called and spoken to Tulio, but the lieutenant wanted to hear what Jake had to say from his own mouth? There was no way to tell from the expression on Tulio's face. It was blank, except for the eyes. The eyes were alive, boring into him with intensity.

"Sir?" Jake said, trying again and fighting the impulse to forget the entire thing and just apologize and leave the office; his being a member of Homicide didn't seem to be written in the stars. "I blew off Moore. I did what you said, requested a new FTO, but Royal wouldn't let me go, said I had to stay with Moore."

Tulio watched him, as if he didn't care one way or another about what Phillips might be saying. Yet he didn't tell him to get lost, didn't even seem impatient. The man just sat there, impassively, watching and listening.

Phillips swallowed, growing increasingly more uncomfortable. "He got mouthy again with me, in the car, on the way to a murder scene? I made him pull the car over and I got out and walked back here."

"Jake?"

"Yes, sir?"

"Why are we talking?"

Jake suddenly felt incredibly nervous, felt his palms sweating and rubbed them down the sides of his pants. He opened his mouth to speak, decided to think over his answer a bit more carefully, and closed it, swallowing hard. He managed to shake his head in misunderstanding.

Tulio said, "It's late and I'm tired, Jake." Spoke the words and then let them hang there in the air between them, thickening the atmosphere. He'd let Phillips know that he was wasting the great man's time. Well, fuck him, Jake thought. Who the hell did he think he was?

Jake said, "Look, Lieutenant, I dumped my training officer, the way you told me to. Now I can't stay in the squad, and I want to be in yours."

"We're all full up," Tulio said.

Phillips watched Tulio's lips twitch, then relax. Was the bastard fighting not to laugh at him? It looked that way to Phillips. This was getting worse and worse with every second that passed. Maybe he'd be a lot better off just forgetting about Special Victims altogether and just going meekly back to TAC. But Homicide! It was the cream of the crop of the entire department, and Special Victims was the most elite squad within an already elite unit. Phillips decided to give it one more shot.

"Lieutenant, I can be an asset to your squad. I'm loyal and I'm honest, and I work like a dog, and I want to work with the best. With you, Lieutenant. My old man always told me that you were the best he'd ever seen, and you proved it tonight, out there in front of God and everybody when that art guy got shotgunned."

Tulio looked at him, as if once again sizing him up, and Phillips stood tall, staring back at him.

Tulio said, "Jake, I owe your father. And I don't want to hurt your feelings. But I'm up against something here, something and somebody so big, that if I play my cards the wrong way he could ruin my career. It's a chance I'm willing to take, but I won't put you in that position. I've got my twenty in, I can go to Stateville tomorrow and they'd have to send my pension checks to the commissary. You don't have those guarantees." Tulio nodded once, and when he spoke again, his voice was ice.

"The biggest favor I can do your dad is to get you as far away from me as possible. You don't want to be around me. You can't handle what might come down. If Royal doesn't want you, then pull some of your father's strings, do anything, but for now, Special Victims, Jake, it's not where you want to be."

Tulio's phone rang. He glanced at it as if it were an intruder, then shrugged and picked up the receiver.

"Tulio." Tulio's impassive face gave away nothing. Jake couldn't hear the sound of the voice coming out of the receiver, had no idea if it was Captain Royal on the other end, lobbying on Jake's behalf. Tulio listened, and the impassive look on his face was replaced by a melancholy, knowing smile.

Tulio said, softly, "Merlin, did you send this kid up to see me?" He paused, then, "Do me a favor, will you? Take him back, put him with Renelli. Tell Renny I said to help him out, would you do that?" Tulio winked and nodded at Jake; Royal had obviously okayed it.

But from the look on Tulio's face, the captain was now telling him things that he didn't want to hear.

Jake watched Tulio listen for a while. Tulio looked like an old man gradually accepting the fact that he had a terminal disease, his stubbled face stamped with that sad, weary smile. It reminded Jake of fighters he'd seen, sitting on the stool after having gone the distance. He'd fought the good fight, and now it was over, the decision was in and about to be announced, and he knew that it wouldn't be going in his favor even though he'd fought his heart out.

"You can't do that," he heard Tulio say. "You know better than that, Merlin." He listened for a minute, then said, "Bullshit, you *can't* relieve me of my duties. You don't have the authority. Listen, you want me out of here? Here's what *I* want. I want a hearing, I want representation, I want to face my accusers. I want to tell them to their faces, in front of the whole world, that they're lying, thieving, dirty, crooked, corrupt pieces of shit. And I want something else, Merlin. I want to know if you're with them."

Phillips watched as Tulio took the phone away from his ear, replaced it while Captain Royal's voice was still yelling something at him. Tulio kept his hand on the phone for several seconds, as if drawing some sort of warmth from its plastic. He looked up at Jake, seeming surprised that he was still there.

"Look, Jake," Tulio said, then seemed to discover that his voice was cracking. He stopped and cleared his throat. "All hell's about to break loose up here. I'm catching it in the neck. They'll be coming up here pretty soon, and you don't want to be around when it happens; they'll remember you if you are, and believe me, they'll hold it against you. Come in tomorrow afternoon, talk to Vince Renelli. He'll look out for you better than a hundred Moores."

"I'm staying." Jake spoke without thinking. What the hell had he said? He wasn't a member of the damned squad, didn't owe this man anything. Why was he willing to throw away his career for Lieutenant Tulio? He wasn't sure, but he felt good with his decision.

"You're going," Tulio said to him. His tone of voice made it clear that he didn't doubt his words for a second.

"Lieutenant, let me tell you something," Jake said, feeling more relaxed than he had since he'd stepped into this building to begin his first shift in Homicide. "All night long, I've had people breaking my balls, calling me names, insulting me and treating me like a goddamned half-retarded stepchild. All hell's gonna break loose? Fine with me. I like it when it's warm."

"Too bad." Tulio nodded his head in approval. "Too bad I didn't find you a couple weeks ago, even a couple of days ago." He pushed away from his desk, got up out of his chair, stretching muscular arms, his shirt riding up out of his pants, showing well-defined stomach muscles that Phillips was surprised to see. The guy, he had to be at least forty-five years old. Tulio shrugged the tension out of his shoulders, then shoved his hands deep into his pockets.

"I have eighteen people working for me, and tomorrow there won't be three of them who're upset that I got canned. You know what they'll be upset about? They'll be upset that their jobs might be in jeopardy, that they might get tainted with the same brush that painted me, that they'll lose their spot in the unit. Next week, next month, hell, the day after tomorrow, it'll be as if I was never even here."

He walked over to the door, put one hand on the knob, squeezed it tightly. Phillips could see the whiteness of Tulio's knuckles. He appeared to be fighting for control of his emotions.

"When I started this squad, you know what I was looking for? A dozen guys like you, Jake. Loyal and smart, knew what they wanted. Knew how the game was played, too. Cops who wanted more out of the job than a pension at twenty and all that they could steal in between. Too bad we didn't hook up sooner." Tulio nodded his head toward the doorway.

"But we didn't, and now its over. So you get the hell out of here, before I throw you out."

"Lieutenant—"

"Shut up." Tulio's voice was low and cold, he wasn't going to argue. "I haven't had a hearing yet. For the moment, I'm still a lieutenant, and you're a junior officer. You get the hell out of here, right now, Phillips. I mean it."

"All right, Lieutenant, I'm going. But you should know, Moore's setting you up. One of the uniforms at the scene already beefed you to IAD and to OPS. That might be what the captain's pissed off about."

"Fuck the captain," Tulio said. "And fuck Internal Affairs and the OPS vampires right along with him. They're the least of my worries. Your loyalty's appreciated, but you go on now, Jake. Go on. Get the hell out of here."

Jake Phillips nodded and kept his face straight, walked quickly past Tulio without looking back. He'd go home to his wife, give the kid his 5:00 A.M. bottle, give Marsha a break. When she got up he'd put on the coffee, and they'd sit down at the kitchen table and he would run all this by her, and together they'd come up with a game plan, figure out what he should do next.

CHAPTER 25

THE HOOKER'S REAL NAME WAS LaMAR DeWITT, BUT HE LIKED TO be called Diana, because he thought that, when made up, he looked like Diana Ross. LaMar wore the same kind of slick straight wig that the singer used to wear back in the 1960s, and he was thin enough to pass; he had the thick pouty lips, the high forehead, and he wore the right kind of makeup, artfully applied. To Lenny, however, LaMar did not look much like Diana Ross. He had to admit, though, that in the right light, with enough drinks in him, he might confuse LaMar with Gladys Knight.

But he'd never want to get it on with LaMar when he was dressed up. Lenny never got that drunk. To Lenny, LaMar was a transvestite whore, nothing more, and nothing less. There was no attraction there for him, although LaMar liked to act as if the two of them were destined to be together someday, pretend it would have happened already if Lenny had ever acknowledged his true sexual identity.

LaMar would talk like that and it would be all that Lenny could do not to whack him one, a single hard shot to the sculpted chin, just to straighten the faggot out. But he never did, because there weren't a lot of whores around who were willing to take the kinds of risks that LaMar thought nothing of. Most whores were stupid and lazy. LaMar, though, he was a real good worker.

If you put a gun against his head and told him to tell the truth or die, Lenny would have to admit that if he ever had to do any serious time, he'd want LaMar for a cellmate. But outside of the joint, forget about it. Lenny wasn't interested, and sooner or later LaMar would just have to get that through his head.

But he hadn't yet, Lenny guessed, judging by the way he greeted Lenny when he spotted him. LaMar broke away from the rest of the girls he was speaking with, strutted toward Lenny quickly, high heels click-click-clicking on the broken cement under his feet.

"Hi, baby!" LaMar was happy to see him, but smart enough not to say his name in front of the others.

A steady stream of cars cruised the area, late workers or early risers, looking for exotic action and willing to pay the price. If they got caught by the law, they'd try to talk their way out of losing their cars, tell the cops that they were writers, out here soaking up some street reality, doing research for their next novel. They wouldn't know, as Lenny and LaMar did, that they all had the same story, and the cops didn't believe any of them for a second. *Whoosh*, there goes the car. A thousand-dollar business expense that wasn't even tax-deductible.

"Hey," Lenny said. He caught the look LaMar gave him, and quickly added, "Diana," and watched as LaMar smiled.

Was he something, or what? He was dressed totally in black, from wig to shoes, the dress a heavy sequined thing that glittered in the headlights of the cars that were cruising the street. LaMar's black hose had a run down the side of the left leg. An occupational hazard. The exposed skin was smooth and hairless.

"We working tonight, honey? Tell me we working tonight. This corner all used up for me now, anyway, it all blowjobbed out. Now all we got is these burnt-out crack bitches strollin' the avenue. Look at them, don't even look up when a man look like a cop come walkin' up to one of they own."

Lenny said, "I'm up for it," and smiled as LaMar laughed. It was a good laugh, feminine yet hearty, and it made Lenny feel good to have made LaMar laugh. Why, he did not know. He didn't even want to think about it.

"How they hanging?" he said now, and the smile dropped off LaMar's face.

"You gone' too far wit' it, now, you know that shit true, Lenny." Lenny knew that LaMar had spoken his name as a warning: Mess with me, and I'll hand it right back. The balls on this guy. LaMar nodded, then said, "We gonna work together anymore, though, honey, we got to re-ne-*go*-tiate, get the percentages right, you understand."

"Come on . . ."

"*You* come on, motherfucker, what I look like, a door prize to you? Want me to work for a quarter? I'll be damned if that's so anymore. I need more than a fourth, I can make more money than that any night out here on my own, and don't got to hide for the rest of the night in case the John gets wise and come around back, lookin' for my ass, while you in some bar, drinking up my hard-earned money."

"Yeah, but this is for one John only, Diana, you make your cake and retire for the night, don't got to get all the sticky stuff in your mouth."

"Don't I wish I could still catch a taste now and again." LaMar made a face that told Lenny how wrong he was. "Shit goin' 'round today, a girl in this business'd be *crazy* to not use a rubber."

Lenny looked at the skin-tight dress. LaMar was not carrying a purse. "Where the hell you carry them?" And where did he keep his money?

"You let me worry about that. We got other business to discuss. Baby, I gots to get half."

"Half? Diana, you're nuts."

"It's half or it ain't nothin', honey. I won't be mistreated or underpaid."

"Jesus, you want me to pay for the operation for you, all out of my own pocket."

"Ain't no use arguin', honey. Half, or get your white ass on away from around here, let me get back to work. Time stand still for no girl, and I gots me a livin' to make. I got an operation comin' up."

"LaMar, what's wrong with you tonight? There ain't that much for you to do, and you know it. *I* do all the real work, all the dangerous shit."

"Good. Then you get out there and flag one of them damn cars down by yourself, see if you can get Mr. John Q. Public to pull into the alley with *you*. And you can do the rest of it too, honey, all by yourself, go ahead, see if you can talk one of them white boys into showin' you they Johnson bar, see what they tell you."

"Diana . . ."

"Lenny . . ." LaMar mocked him. He crossed his arms and looked at Lenny. "Well? What's it gonna be? I ain't got all night. There's a guy been driving around wantin' me to perform, got a sticker on his windshield say he from Western Springs. One of your people, if you know what I mean."

Lenny went cold on him. What the hell was he doing, calling Lenny a fag? "What do you mean, my people, Diana?"

"Oh, lighten your ass up, would you, honeybunch? What do you think,

I'm scared of you? Go ahead, now, you put that hand right back down. You hit me, you bent-nose, ex-pug, gamblin'-addicted, drunken ugly motherfucker, you best plan on spending the rest of your entire life sleeping with both eyes open. That's right. Un*clench* that fist, baby, go ahead, you know better than that. I'll sneak into your house and cut your thing off whilst you sleep, you ever lay a hand on me." LaMar giggled. "In anger, I mean."

"Diana . . ."

"What you doing tonight, baby, pretending you Paul Anka? 'Di-an-a, Di-an-a.' Shit, I know my name. And to answer your question, I meant, when I said your people? An Eye-*tal*-ian-American, that's what I meant. Young guy, too, wouldn't remember who you used to be. Done drove around the block four, five times now. I go up to him, bastard want me to suck him, but without no rubber, he insist on that, say he don't like the way it make him *feel*. I told him to go suck his own self off, get one of the other girls, but he wants *me*. Offered me a full hundred, too, showed me cash. Got a roll stuck down his cute little shorts besides." LaMar smiled. "Now baby, do I get half?"

It came down, in Lenny's mind, to a choice: Give up the half without any argument, or punch this hooker out, right here on the spot. If he chose the latter he'd have to put a burglar alarm in his apartment. LaMar wasn't the type to make idle threats. He thought about Gerardi, about the Eagle, and old man Alleo.

"All right, Diana. You win. Half, split right down the middle."

"Ooh, I just love it when you talks dirty."

"Let's go." Lenny began to walk away from LaMar, then turned and threw a parting shot, wanting to hurt him just a little for extorting him out of the money.

He said, "Diana, you ever get pinched hard, take a serious fall? I'm gonna surrender myself in, confess to all the shit I ever done in my life. I want you in my cell, baby. We'll see who gets half then."

LaMar didn't even have to give his comeback as much as a second's thought. He shouted, "And that's the last place you want to be, honey: I put my mind to it, I can pitch just as good as I catch. Strong white boy like you, I get a full pack of smokes, easy, each time I turn you ass out onto the tier." LaMar turned his back on Lenny and walked away, strutting it, and Lenny had to walk all the way to the corner with the sound of the other hookers' laughter burning in his ears.

• • •

The car turned carefully into the alley, and Lenny pushed himself deeper into the shadows of the recessed doorway of the gray stone apartment building that had seen much better days. He smelled fried food, and grease. It almost made him sick, coupled as it was with the strong stench of human waste in the air. Lenny began to breathe through his mouth.

He felt the steel of the burglar bars on the door behind him digging into his back, felt the heavy padlock sticking into his side. Of all times to be doing this, when he was wearing a yellow shirt over light colored pants. But he hadn't planned on doing this sort of stuff tonight, he'd planned on winning big at the game. Ah, God, what a life he led.

The car passed Lenny and he saw that it really wasn't a car at all, it was one of those four-wheel-drive, half-a-truck things, a Wagoneer or a Bronco or whatever the hell they were called. The vehicle rode high, having pumped-up super shocks and tall wide wheels. Lenny could barely make out the shoulders and head of the guy driving. He wondered if LaMar had been kidding him, or if the guy was really an Italian.

The Jeep thing parked in what had one time been somebody's back yard, pulling in off the alley, the driver cutting the wheels hard. Lenny saw the brakelights flash bright red, then turn off. This must be what they meant in the commercials when they advertised these things as being off-road vehicles. He gave LaMar a couple of minutes to get the guy's joint out from his underwear, then slowly began to move along the shadows toward the lot. Lenny was bent way over, sneaking up on the driver's side of the car, thinking he had finally gotten this down to a science, when his beeper went off.

The John jumped, Lenny saw him jump, and he was halfway out of the truck by the time Lenny managed to fumble his beeper off. Lenny standing tall, with the guy still damn near sitting down, and Lenny had to look up to him. Jesus, what had LaMar picked this time? He was Italian all right. From a Roman Piazza, having just stepped off a pedestal.

A weightlifter's arm stuffed into a white T-shirt was what Lenny was looking at now, seeing the arm move toward him as the guy turned, getting out of the truck. Then a large, muscular chest began to emerge from the cab, then long heavy legs in biker shorts that were pulled halfway down his ass stepped down from the vehicle, the man turning, off balance, looking toward Lenny, scared but cocky.

Lenny did the only thing he could think of to do at the moment; he charged, then decked the guy, right-left, right-left, hard in the gut, punishing body shots. The guy was a weightlifter, but he wasn't much of a brawler. He bent at the waist as Lenny's punches landed, doubled over, then fell forward, face first, onto hard-packed dirt, next to his truck, sucking wind.

Lenny was breathing hard, excited, looked up and saw LaMar running around the side of the truck toward him. He smiled sheepishly, noticed the horror on LaMar's face, LaMar not looking at Lenny, but at the John lying in the dirt. Lenny looked down, saw that the man wasn't lying in the dirt anymore. The John had somehow managed to crawl over a few feet, was now fumbling with a pistol that had been hidden under the truck's front seat.

The John was pulling the gun up out of its holster when Lenny dropped down onto his chest, both knees together. The shock of the blow took whatever fight was left in the guy right out of him. He lay prostrate, his arms out at his sides, dago Jesus with blood coming out of his mouth. Lenny, still on top of the guy, leaned over and took the gun all the way out of the holster, aware on some level that LaMar was digging at the John's tight biker shorts. Lenny quickly checked the load, put the gun back in its holster, and stuffed it down the back of his pants.

"I *knew* it!" LaMar said.

"What?" Lenny stood, fighting for breath, while LaMar waved a wad of bills at him.

"He had this stuck in his pants, told me to close my eyes while he was wriggling out of his shorts." LaMar flashed through the bills. "Got to be over a thousand dollars in here, easy."

Less than Lenny had hoped for, and he had to give LaMar half, but still, it was five hundred more in his pocket than he had in it right now. He felt quickly under the seat to see what else might be under there, maybe some credit cards, anything negotiable that he could keep for himself, wouldn't have to mention to LaMar. His fingers touched something, and he pulled at it; it was something metal, metal and seemingly sharp. Instinctively, he pulled his hand away from it. He and LaMar watched as the Sheriff's badge fell to the ground, rolled around twice then stopped, face up.

LaMar said, "Shit."

Lenny said, "Hurry up," fumbling for the handcuffs, pulling them out of his belt. "Count the money, La—*shit*—Diana." He pulled the cop over and up, holding him under the arms, sweating from fear as much as from the heavy nighttime humidity. He hefted the man up partway into the truck, let him drop there, reaching out and grabbing one wrist as the man's lower body weight tried to drag the rest of him back out onto the dirt. Lenny hung onto the hand, twisted as he held on, heard a sickening crack, and winced. Weightlifters must have brittle bones. Had to be from all the steroids they took. Lenny cuffed the John's wrist, snapped the other cuff around the steering wheel.

Lenny said, "Diana?" Then, louder, a little frantically: "*Diana?*"

Lenny looked up and saw that LaMar was gone. Before he could re-act, as his mind was still registering the fact that he had skipped out on him with all the money for himself, Lenny's beeper went off again. He absently reached to his side and shut it down, wondering if the cop was working a sting, or was just out hunting. If it was a sting, it wouldn't matter, the cops would be on him in a matter of seconds. They'd get LaMar, too, put them in a cell together down at Twenty-sixth and Cal-ifornia. Lenny almost looked forward to that happening. If it wasn't a sting, Lenny vowed, he would hunt LaMar down and choke him till he died.

He waited, in the alley, hearing the rats scurrying all around him. The cop cuffed to the steering wheel began to groan, the groans growing louder and louder, until the pain brought him fully alert and awake, and then the cop couldn't help himself, he began to scream in anguish.

Lenny began to walk out of the alley. If it was a sting, the other cop-pers would have swooped down on him by now. Lenny came out of the alley, turned right, went up to the corner and turned onto the stroll.

It was empty. The brazen hookers were gone, their cruising Johns gone, too. The first sight of LaMar running terrified down the street would have been the signal: something bad was going down, get the fuck out, right now.

He couldn't catch a cab here, the drivers were afraid of this street at night. They couldn't, by law, refuse a ride to the hookers, and any cop with an inkling to do so could take their cabs away from them the sec-ond they picked one up. Shake them down worse than Lenny had been planning to shake down the John who had turned out to be a copper.

Christ.

Lenny walked unhurriedly down the street, knowing that the copper's screams would bring the curious to their storefront windows, drive them to push their newspaper and tin-foil curtains aside, look out and try to get a glimpse at whatever might be going on. Two blocks away, Lenny waved down a trolling cab, a Checker driven by a foreigner who didn't care about engaging his customer in some friendly conversation.

It was only then, after he was safe, that Lenny looked down at the numbers floating around on his beeper. He had to bring the beeper up and turn it toward the window so that he could make out the number of whoever'd called him, and the second he saw the number there, he knew that if he needed more evidence that it wasn't going to be his night, this was it in spades. The evidence was right there, floating in crystal, tiny black numbers denoting the telephone exchange of the Man himself, Thomas Gerardi.

Lenny said, "Jesus Christ."

The cabdriver said, "Pardon, pardon? Were you speaking to me, sir?"

"Look, Sahib, save the charm for the spitting cobras. Pull over to that phone over there on the corner and let me out of this shitbox."

CHAPTER

26

THEY PICKED HIM UP ON A CORNER DOWNTOWN, THREE OF THEM along with Gerardi, Thomas not taking any chances tonight. Lenny got scared when the Lincoln pulled up, but he didn't show it to these guys, because he knew that they would feed upon it like sharks smelling blood and then seek out its source.

Gerardi was in the front seat with the driver, leaning over the seat and giving Lenny a benign, welcoming smile. One of the goons in the back got out so that Lenny would have to sit in the middle, in the back seat. Lenny didn't like that, but he was in no position to argue.

He got in and nodded to the other guy in the back, held out his hand to Gerardi, and was relieved when Gerardi took it, gave it a manly shake.

"Mr. G. How you been?"

"Had better days, Len," Thomas said.

"Sorry to hear that."

It was hard for Lenny not to ask if Gerardi's bad day was in any way connected to himself. He knew that if it was, he would find out soon enough.

"Nice car."

"I like cars," Gerardi said. Lenny looked at him, shrugged, looked around at the other men. Their faces told him nothing, and he knew that they'd wear the same expression if they were drinking together or working him over. It would all be the same to them. Guys like this, they didn't have feelings.

Lenny sat back in the seat, crushed between the two muscular goons, and looked out the window toward the lake, as the driver took his time going down Lake Shore Drive, heading north. He wasn't surprised when they turned off on Sheridan Road. They were heading to the Eagle's house, something had gone wrong. Maybe Harris had insulted them somehow, refused to perform a service, and they were going to kill Lenny as a warning to Harris.

He tightened his muscles, made fists on his lap, felt the fear come in waves off the men on either side of him. One of them reached into his sportcoat pocket. Good. They were intimidated by him, knew that he took the occasional job busting somebody's head just to do somebody else a favor. They weren't taking Lenny lightly. For him, it was an epitaph.

He said, "I got this stupid fake radio on my belt, it's digging into me. Can I take it off?"

"Sure," Gerardi said. Lenny unhooked the radio, dropped it on the floor. Nobody moved, neither man would ever suspect that Lenny was carrying a piece. Everyone knew that he was a killer with his hands, why would he need a gun?

"I'll remind you it's there, when we take you home. So you don't forget about it," the goon on his right said to him, and Lenny knew that it was a calculated lie, that they were taking him to his death.

The house was bigger than Lenny had imagined, with the kind of roof that looked to be made up of red pipes that had been cut in half. As they drove up a winding driveway, Lenny, strangely detached, had time to admire it. The back of the house would face the lake, the Eagle would have his own private beach where his grandchildren could swim and splash around, make sandcastles while men like Lenny were being tortured and mutilated in a soundproofed basement.

How many rooms would a joint like this have? Lenny had to know, so he asked, making conversation, and Gerardi told him: twenty-one. Twenty-one rooms. He wondered if that included the bathrooms and the kitchens, the utility room and the basement. It had to.

Lenny himself had never in his entire life lived in a place that had more than five rooms, counting the kitchen and john. Even in his best day, he'd never lived real high. And today he was far removed from his peak earning years. He lived in a small furnished North Side flat, with a Murphy bed and a dresser in one room, a stove and small icebox in what passed for a kitchen; a ratty couch in front of a color TV in a small and dirty living room. The only things he'd brought with him on moving day were his clothing, and the picture of his father, the one taken years ago, in Dino's Den at the Riviera, which was now hung over the couch, thumb-tacked to the off-white wall.

Twenty-one rooms, Jesus.

The car pulled to a stop in the circular drive, and Lenny got out, his first time ever to a suburban mansion. The only suburbs he'd ever been in were Calumet City for dice and card games, and the ones the race-tracks were located in. He stood listening to crickets, for Christ's sake, instead of buses, cab horns, the loud booming bass of stereos worth more money than the cars they were installed in. A good way to live. Maybe not too bad a place to die in, either.

He'd noticed that the driver had left the keys in the car. Lenny fig-ured that you could get away with that up here in Winnetka. Especially if the car belonged to the Eagle. Nobody touched him, nudged him to-ward the house. He just naturally followed them, in the center of the four.

"What's up?" he finally asked, and Gerardi shook his head as if he'd been waiting for the question.

"The Man wants to talk to you."

Lenny stopped on the bottom of several concrete steps that led to heavy double oak doors with brass doorknobs and knockers. Everyone stopped when he did, except Gerardi, who kept going up the stairs be-fore he stopped, turned, stood looking down at Lenny.

"Come on, we wanted to kill you, you think we'd bring you up here?"

Made sense. If you weren't smart enough to figure out that the Eagle didn't know who the Collector was. Gerardi had always underestimated Lenny. It had been a good thing for him, having the boss think he was stupid. It could work in his favor tonight, too, if he played it right, like a good poker hand. And so Lenny smiled, acting relieved, and nodded his head in feigned relief.

"It's just, you know," he said, swaggering up the last few steps, "up here and all, it seems strange."

"Get used to it, Lenny. The people you know, before you know it, you'll *own* a place up here." Only one of the muscleboys was dumb enough to grunt a laugh, and Lenny watched Gerardi glare at him, then the doors were being opened and Lenny stepped into heaven.

Once, when he'd been in New York, he'd walked through the lobby of the Plaza Hotel, looking for the toilet as much as wanting to see what the joint was like. The Eagle's house gave him the same feeling he'd had back then, it reminded him of that lobby, all high-class and expensive, large and airy, at least the foyer was. Lenny felt that long-ago resentment too, knowing that he could view but he could never touch; it was all out of his league.

Guys were hanging out everywhere. Lenny wondered where they'd parked their cars. There had only been one other car out in the drive-way, a long stretch limo that he assumed belonged to the Eagle. Maybe the cars were parked in one of the many garages.

Gerardi walked him past the living room, where a bunch of guys play-ing cards didn't even bother to look up. The table they were playing on looked real old, refinished. An antique. The Eagle had class. The three guys who'd been in the car gravitated toward the card game. Lenny fol-lowed Gerardi, who walked up to a set of very dark, very tall, very wide, old-looking brown doors, stopped, knocked once, then went in after he'd gotten the okay: a feeble half-heard command from somewhere inside the room.

Lenny felt pretty good, considering. Fact was, he was in a state of high excitement. Murder didn't get committed inside the walls of houses like these. No more than it was committed in the plush gambling casi-nos in Vegas, even though everyone knew that if you fucked around too much it could happen.

It was the same thing here, the sense of danger was real and turning him on, but he felt that he had it all in the palm of his hand, that he was about to hit a lucky streak, Lenny playing for the highest stakes of his life. As he walked into the room, Lenny Roman appeared calm and collected.

The Eagle was sitting in a tall black leather chair that was all cracked and shiny. The back of it on either side seemed to come out toward him, as if they were huge bat wings about to crush him. It was the sort of chair that Ming the Merciless used to sit in on "Flash Gordon." He didn't rise when Lenny came into the room, which wasn't a good sign. Gerardi went and stood behind the chair, leaned his forearms across the top, rested his body on them. Lenny stopped a good ten feet from the chair. There was no point in going closer, the Eagle wouldn't be shaking his hand.

The old man looked at Lenny. Lenny stood there trying to act confi-dently, and raised his eyebrows in inquiry, the high-roller about to play his hand. Gerardi had a slight, cruel smile on his lips. He would be thinking that Lenny was in way over his head. Lenny thought, fuck him, what does he know? What did he ever know?

The room they were in was huge, and Lenny looked around casually, sizing the place up. Double glass doors led out on to some kind of patio. He guessed that they were on the side of the house; Lenny couldn't see the lake or the driveway through the glass. The doors were closed. Lenny heard the quiet *whoosh* of the air-conditioning system. There was a gigantic but now empty fireplace built into one wall. Over it hung a crucifix large enough to have been stolen out of a church. Bookshelves had been built into another wall, were filled with volumes whose spines were all turned outward. On another wall were paintings that looked real old to Lenny. One of them he recognized. It was a painting of The Last Supper.

Lenny looked back over at the Eagle, who appeared to be half the man he used to be. A man who'd once been tall and strong now seemed shriveled and old. Heavily wrinkled, his skin gone sallow. The only thing he had that looked alive were those flaming eyes, piercing Lenny. The nose that had given him his street name looked too large now, out of place on the old man's shriveled, sickly, skinny face.

Lenny said, "Mr. Venicie? Can I ask you a question?"

The Eagle's face showed surprise at Lenny's temerity; he'd been sitting there giving Lenny The Glare, and Lenny hadn't been intimidated. Fuck this guy, too.

Out of the side of his mouth, the Eagle said, "What."

"How much does it cost you every month to air-condition this castle?"

Gerardi straightened up, his face losing its smile and going hard, but the Eagle seemed to know that Gerardi had moved, and he waved a dismissive hand over his shoulder. Gerardi stood still. The Eagle folded his hands and rested them on his stomach, smiling.

He said, "I got an accountant gets paid to worry about that shit."

"Now, Mr. Venicie, I gotta hand it to you, that's class, that's real class."

"You know why I sent for you?"

"No, sir. If I did something wrong, insulted one of your people, I didn't mean it." Lenny paused for timing. Venicie was waiting patiently, a perfect sucker for Lenny's punch line. "They shouldn't'a been out on the Halsted Street stroll, buying pussy, or it wouldn't have happened."

This time the Eagle laughed. Even Gerardi cracked a smile.

"Thomas told me you were a simple man. Liked to kid around, didn't scare too easy."

If he only knew. Lenny was scared to death. But he'd be damned if he'd let it show. Besides, it felt good. The ultimate gamble. Lenny didn't know if he'd make it out of here alive, but if he did, he was sure that playing cards and rolling dice would never be the same.

"Says you were a good driver, that driving was your calling."

"Fighting, Mr. Venicie, I used to be good at that, too, at one time."

"I made some money off the fights you threw."

"I'd'a never lost one of them, I'd'a retired undefeated, if you guys hadn't paid me as good as you did."

"I got racehorses I put more money on, Lenny, didn't have the fix in with them, either. It wasn't much for us, a couple of dollars here and there. Same with our drivers, they come, they go. Small potatoes, guys like that. Less fuckin' important to me than the cooks or the butlers that been around this house. But Lenny, you sent a guy over to see me tonight. Him, now, Lenny, he's not small potatoes. He's a pretty tough guy, did right by me last year."

"Yes, sir, he sure did."

"You work for him. You're his driver or his valet, his butler, something like that."

"Mr. Venicie, there's no call for that, you ain't got to treat me like no dog. I never disrespected you."

"You didn't?" The old man sat up further in his chair, twisting his lips, working himself up for something.

"You come into my home, into a room with a crucifix and a picture of Jesus Christ Himself on the wall, and you curse, talk to me like we're equals, that's not disrespect?"

"I apologize." Lenny didn't point out to him that he himself had cursed.

The Eagle said, "But you're not sorry."

"I ain't nobody's driver no more, Mr. Venicie. Those days are over."

"That's right," the Eagle said, with a touch of mockery. "You're a shake-down artist, ain't you? Pretend you're a cop and shake down hookers and Johns over on the South Side. Small-time hustles. I understand you break a few heads now and again for Thomas, too, so you can get enough money to keep going back to the gambling."

it taste of brass. He remembered the ringing in his ears.

Once he'd hit blackjack. The other time, he'd pulled two kings and the dealer had seventeen.

The time he'd bet it all when he'd been losing, Lenny had busted out.

Was he winning or losing tonight? Lenny had no way of knowing. But that time in Vegas, when he'd been losing, he hadn't gotten the tingle, the erotic flutter through his body that he had gotten when he had been winning big, and had bet every chip in front of him, along with all of the cash in his pockets.

The thing was, he had that tingle now. Intensified, because Lenny had a lot more on the line than cash and chips. Lenny nearly swooned, standing there, and the old man chose to see his reaction as being one of fear. The Eagle raised his eyes skyward, then, looking up, spoke to Gerardi. "Didn't I tell you?" he said, as if the two of them had bet on whether Lenny would fold.

Lenny wasn't folding. He was building himself up for what he had to do.

He was breathing heavily, that sensation flowing through him, half a hard-on filling his pants, Lenny ready to go. He reached behind him and pulled the pistol that he'd taken from the John.

"Don't move, don't neither one of you son of a bitches move a muscle. YOU!" Lenny held the piece in both hands and pointed it at Gerardi, who'd opened his mouth, as if to shout out for help.

"You say a word, you son of a bitch, I swear to Christ, I'll kill the old man first, shoot him right through the heart I helped him get."

"Thomas, stand still." The Eagle's voice sounded filled with disgust. Contempt, too. He'd had higher hopes for Lenny. Lenny had better things to do than to try and figure this degenerate out.

"I'll give the orders around here now, old man." Lenny waved the pistol at Thomas. "Go over to those curtains, pull down those cords, go ahead. You're gonna tie and gag the old motherfucker, then I'm gonna do you, too."

"Why don't you just kill us, Lenny? Right now. Go ahead," the Eagle said.

"Don't tempt me, you wrinkled, ugly, shriveled up son of a bitch, or I might." Lenny stole a glance at him, saw the way the Eagle was glaring at him. If he were caught escaping from the grounds, he swore that he'd eat the pistol before he'd step foot back in this room.

"That's good," he said to Thomas. "Now step back while I check the knots."

Gerardi had tied the old man well, had shoved his own handkerchief into the Eagle's mouth, used part of the cord the old man was tied up with to hold it in place, tied around the old man's head.

Lenny said to Gerardi, "Turn around," and Gerardi did, holding his wrists out behind his back, expecting that Lenny was going to use the rest of the cord to tie him up. Lenny had other plans.

He slapped the barrel of the gun hard up under Gerardi's ear, grabbed him so he wouldn't make any noise as he fell to the carpet. Lenny let him down slowly, the feeling filling him now, Lenny on the verge of a spiritual orgasm, not knowing what to make of it.

He walked over to the French windows, unlocked them and stepped outside. The heat hit him like a fist, and he closed the door behind him, sweating hard from fear as much as the mugginess. From there it was a simple matter of walking around to the front of the house, getting into the Lincoln, and heading out of there fast, after he'd flattened both of the front tires on the limousine sitting in the Eagle's driveway.

CHAPTER 27

TULIO SAT ON HIS BED WITH HIS DEAD WIFE'S PILLOW IN HIS LAP, his hands on top of it, Tulio staring off at the cracked wall and listening to the messages that were coming in, left on the answering machine by people who were growing increasingly more angry as the sky grew brighter. The words came to Tulio but he paid them little attention; he was aware that voices were speaking, but he didn't much care who it was or what they wanted.

He wondered if he should just go out, find an all-night joint and get drunk, float away from all the pain. He had no family, no social life, no friends, really, not anymore. He had lost Marian. And now he had no job. He could have gotten through anything if he'd been able to keep his work, nothing could have destroyed him. Sooner or later he could have overcome anything, even the loss of Marian. But he knew that without his work, he couldn't hold on anymore.

Martie. Jess. Marian. The job. Jesus Christ almighty, he had nothing left.

The phone rang again, and Tulio figured that it was the eighth call he'd gotten. Maybe this time it was Marian. It would be nice to hear from her right about now. He heard the machine engage after the third ring, waited for the message.

"Tony, you there? Look, it's Royal. You got to come in here, man, right away, before all this shit gets any damn worse. You're on *call* for Christ's sake, and you got your beeper cut off! You know better than that. Now look, something bad happened. There's brass everywhere, tearing into your desk and your files. Moore's filing direct charges, signing *paper* on you, Tulio, you hear me? He says as long as you're on the street he feels threatened. There're IAD and OPS and the People's Law Office motherfuckers running around everywhere. What'd you say to those parents last night? Did you *promise* them you'd get the guy who killed their kid? And there's some gangbanger punk in here saying you broke into his house and threatened his life. *He's* filing charges, too."

The captain was going on like that, showing no sign of letting up. He could fill the tape, go on for an entire half hour and the machine would record it, with Tulio sitting there half-listening. Tulio reached over and took the phone off the hook. He debated as to whether he should just leave it off the hook, then decided not to. He lifted the phone to his ear.

"Royal."

"Tulio! Jesus Christ, man, get in here. Right now you're suspended, but if you don't get in here and start mollifying these motherfuckers, you're fired!"

"I'm fired already, Royal, all they want to do is go through the motions, make it all legal, but I'm out, and you know it."

"Look, it's worse than that. The feds are here—"

"Fuck 'em."

"Vic's family, man named Conners, called them in, said their kid was kidnapped out of their home, said *you* told them it hadn't happened. All hell's breaking loose, Tony. Come down. There's enough people owe you to take care of this."

"Bullshit. I stepped on too many toes last night, Royal."

"Mine, too, shit, asking me if I was with them."

"I know better."

"You ought to."

The FBI was there. Big-leaguers. Brass, OPS, and IAD, the People's Law Office. Someone with a lot of power—like Alleo—was after his ass, too, or the PLO wouldn't be sucking around, looking for blood to drink. It had to be Alleo. Or the young gangbanger's family. Whoever it was, they knew the right place to go. Those assholes from PLO never went anywhere without a camera crew in tow.

"Tulio? Tony? You still there?"

"Moore's signing paper?"

"Formal complaint, man. Wants your ass locked *up*. And Calhoun, too, he's down here with witnesses, a lawyer, every fucking thing. He's the one called in the goddamn PLO. They got reporters coming in at ten this morning, gonna hold a press conference on the steps right here at headquarters."

He placed the receiver back down, cutting Royal off in midstatement. To hell with it. He took the phone off the hook and set it down on the bedstand.

It wouldn't be long before one of these bigshots got the bright idea in their head to come over to the house and get him. The feds or Moore or even a member of his own squad, looking to kiss some ass.

They'd send someone they thought Tulio trusted, which would be their mistake. Tulio didn't trust anyone.

Well, there was still one person left, maybe. Marian. She might even still love him, would surely still have some feelings left for him, no matter that some handsome young stud might have tried to convince her to let them go. He'd see her.

If Marian stood behind him, he might even get his job back. He needed the job, but he needed something else more.

Someone who loved him. Was that too much to ask for? And was it too late to ask for it?

Tulio looked at the bedside clock. 7:11. Seven come eleven, how lucky was he today? The high-pitched whine of the phone was starting to get on his nerves. He put it back on the hook. Tulio stood and put his gun back where it belonged, grabbed his keys, and left.

Paul Harris was in the kitchen, leaning over the stove and prepping the bottom of a pan with lightly spiced butter, when he heard Marian's footsteps walking through the apartment. He smiled.

Should he tell her now? About himself? No, the timing wasn't right.

He'd almost told her everything last night, when he'd found her in his computer room. Almost, but he hadn't, and he hadn't because he loved her. News like this would have to wait until the weekend. She would need time to think it over, to comprehend what he was telling her. She would have to be watched, and carefully, after Harris revealed the truth. He loved her, and with all his heart. But if he thought for a second that she would go to the law with what he told her, then he would have no choice but to kill her. He'd hate to, but he'd do it. So he'd wait, at least until the weekend.

"Omelet?" he said.

She was wearing his white bathrobe. It hung to the floor, puddled at her feet and spread out behind her, like a queen's train. He could see the soft flesh of the top of her breasts in the V that the robe made. She'd belted it loosely around her. Her hair was wet and hanging down, her makeup washed off. In the morning, he understood, Marian looked her age. She was five years younger than he. Born on the same day. Was that some kind of an omen? Harris kept smiling.

"No, thank you," she said, sounding bashful. Marian wouldn't be used to waking up in a man's apartment. "I *will* take some of that coffee, though," then said, "if there's enough."

She walked past him and began looking through the cabinets, greatly relieving him by acting as if she belonged there.

Harris said, "Second cabinet, lower shelf."

"Thank you." Now she was acting shy. Damn!

He wanted her to feel at ease, had to make her feel welcome. How? He wasn't sure. It was a notion that hadn't even crossed his mind with Marian's predecessors.

He dropped the beaten eggs into the pan then whisked them around. He added more spices, sliced tomatoes, diced potatoes, and green peppers, holding the pan above the flame, shaking it with one hand while he briskly stirred the contents. When it was finished he carefully deposited the food onto a china plate, used the spatula to divide it into two relatively even pieces. He scooped one half onto a second plate, waved it alluringly beneath Marian's nose.

"You're sure?"

"All right." Marian giggled.

Harris set the plate down in front of her, leaned over and kissed her neck. She leaned into it, tilted her head so he could kiss a wider area. Is that the way to do it? With touches and kisses and what people saw as kindness? He could do that, he could act like that.

Tonight he'd bring home an aged wine and prepare a light dinner, perhaps a fish that he would broil. He'd stop at that new North Side specialty store he'd heard about and buy some unusual condoms this afternoon. Then later, tonight, after they had dinner, he'd make slow, passionate love to her. He'd drive Marian completely out of her mind, take her to heaven, then maybe she'd feel more at home with him. Maybe she'd even move in.

He was in a state of mind that was unusual for him, feeling confused.

But it wasn't a distracting confusion. In fact, it was sort of pleasant. He would enjoy finding out how a man was supposed to act. Marian could teach him. By trial and error, he'd learn.

"Paul?"

"Hm?" He looked up at her with a pleasant, benign expression on his face.

"Listen," she started out strongly, then lost her nerve. Marian lowered her eyes to her plate, pushed some of the food around with her fork.

Harris put his fork down on his plate, reached over and reassuringly patted her hand. "You're uneasy." She looked up at him. "Please don't be." He twisted his face into the most sincere expression that he was capable of, and knew from the look on Marian's face that he'd pulled it off quite well. The hours spent practicing in front of a mirror were always paying off.

He said, "Marian, I'm in love with you," and watched the tears fill her eyes. "I want you here. To stay, if you'd like. If you're uncomfortable, then so am I. If it's going to work, we have to be able to tell each other everything, without worrying that we might be hurting the other person's feelings."

"Please, was it something I said?" he asked.

Marian squeezed his hand.

"Paul, my God, you always know just the right thing to say." She flashed a relieved smile. "You should have been a mind reader." She took a deep breath, looked directly into his eyes.

"It's not you, Paul, it's me. Last night, with it being my thirty-fifth birthday, and after what happened between Tony and me, I don't know, maybe I rushed it, maybe we moved too fast."

She paused, and Harris jumped in before she could continue.

"Please don't say that, Marian. I've waited so long . . . "

"Paul, let me finish." Said firmly. Harris sat there looking at her, with his mouth open, feeling a heaviness in his chest. He watched her look quickly down at her plate, gathering strength, then once again she raised her eyes to his.

"Something's not right, and I think we both feel it. Last night, when you came up to me in your other room, you frightened me, and I'm not used to that. I don't like it. For a minute there I felt that you were treating me like some thief you'd caught in your art gallery."

"I'm sorry."

"Don't be, Paul, it's not your problem, it's mine, it really is. It's the way I *feel*, that doesn't make it the way it *is*."

"If I'd known it would upset you—"

"And you told me I could stay."

"Stay? You can keep the computer, if you want it. There's nothing that could ever be more important to me than you. I'd take an ax to it, destroy it, before I'd let it come between us."

"Thank you, Paul." She squeezed his hand again, then held it tight. He had to make her believe that he loved her.

"Then why did you lock the door when we left the room?"

That took him by surprise, and he knew it showed on his face. He let it work for him, made himself look even more confused, then said, "Did I?"

"Yes, Paul, you did . . . " Marian left it hanging there, as if she didn't believe him.

He had to be careful now, she was looking at him skeptically. He said, "Marian, I'm so used to locking things: my car, the doors and windows at the gallery, that I guess I've started doing it here." He ate a bite of his omelet, shook his head in surprise at his own silliness. Waited until he had swallowed before he continued speaking.

"Listen, sometimes I come home late and find that I've locked my own bedroom door."

"Why would you need to lock everything? With the security in this building. My God, cameras in every hallway, your own private elevator . . . "

"Second nature, I guess. I've lived alone too long."

Marian seemed to be buying it. She took a nibble of her breakfast, washed it down with coffee.

"Mmm, that's good."

"Thank you."

She said, "Do you usually get up this early?"

"I've got the Schommer etchings show coming up; an entire set needs to be hung. There are buyers who want to corner the market." He shrugged. "Teresa Schommer's hot right now."

He was sweating, talking too fast. He was feeling what she'd been talking about, some tension in the air between them. How could he change that? What could he do? There was only one way to do it, Harris knew.

Tell her the truth. Let her know what he was. Let her know, then tell her that he wasn't that man any longer. He'd do it, but not right now. She didn't have the time to digest what he'd be saying. Tonight, he would tell her. Tonight, their love would grow.

For now, he changed the subject, said lightly, "What do you have planned for today?"

"First I've got to get home and change clothes. Then I've got a hearing for a kid who confessed a murder to me last night. I showed off a little, went against established procedure, but we'll be before my father, so it should be all right. The assistant state's attorney won't like the way I did what I did, but she'll *love* the fact that I did it. I got a confession, and she can prosecute the older boys my kid was with.

"Then I've got a lunch with a different ASA, wants to bargain my sixteen-year-old out. Kid's been in Audy a year and a half on a drug ripoff that turned into double murder, and this guy thinks I'm gonna let him charge him as an adult if he offers me ten years flat."

"Isn't that a good deal, though? Wouldn't he get out in five years?"

"That's what he'll be out in if he's tried as a kid, max. And he'll do it in juvie. I take the ten, he's in Stateville."

"I see," Harris said, but really didn't. Was he losing her?

He said, "At the hearing this morning, will Tulio be there?"

"No, he shouldn't be. Unless he shows up just to give me a hard time. He gave the pinch to juvie, he has no business being there."

"I should be freed up for lunch, can you get out of yours?"

"I can't . . ."

"Pity."

"How about an early dinner? My treat."

"I've got Ed Paschke's showing to put together. It's not for a month, but I have to get the catalogue together, and then there's the Fitzpatrick thing that has to be hung . . . I can get someone to do it."

"Not that Lenny person."

"Lenny?" Harris laughed. "No, I don't think he'll be supervising Paschke's hanging. You know what Ed calls him? The Leech."

"I agree with him."

"Lenny has his uses," Harris said.

"I actively dislike that man."

"Look, I can break free about six, I want to cook you dinner. Can you come by and get me then, at six?"

"To the gallery?"

"Take my car with you today, I won't be needing it."

"Down to Harrison? You must want the insurance money."

"Go ahead and take it. It's well-insured and well-alarmed. The extra keys are over in the breakfront by the door, right-hand drawer." Again, he shrugged. "Then you can come back up here without having to have the doorman buzz for the elevator."

"You sure you don't mind?"

"I'm in River North, for heaven's sake, I can walk it from here. If I need a car, I'll get one from somewhere, there's always somebody around—" he gave her a self-deprecating smile—"trying to win my favor."

"I don't blame them. It's worth its weight in gold." She rose, kissed him on the cheek. "You're really too good to be true, you know that?"

"I know. Marian?" Paul Harris said, feeling shy now himself. Plus another new emotion; he was afraid. "Pack a bag when you're home, bring some things back, if you'd like."

"You really are a doll," she said, then hurried out of the room.

With Harris watching her, the smile now gone from his lips, replaced by the look of a man who was nowhere near as sure of himself as he liked to pretend.

CHAPTER 28

H E COULD GET IN ANYWHERE, ANYTIME, WITHIN MINUTES, WITH-out a problem. Tulio was well-known for his prowess with his picks. He carried them everywhere, had been known to stop on the street and offer his services when he'd seen someone who'd locked themselves out of their vehicles. Tulio would throw away their hangers with disdain, bend over the lock and have the door open in seconds, then get casually into his car and wave goodbye. His good deed all in a day's work for a faithful servant of the city. All of the people he'd helped over the years had thought he'd been doing them a favor. Only he himself knew that he'd really been showing off.

It was a gift, the ability to feel his way through a lock, a talent he had, in much the same manner that he could often offer quick resolutions to the toughest of crimes.

He'd gone through Marian's apartment earlier, but he hadn't had to use his picks to get in; he still had his keys. Marian lived in a nice Wrigleyville apartment, with her landlady living downstairs on the first floor. The landlady was a woman who had seen Tulio before. She smiled and nodded pleasantly, had gone back to the business of sweeping the sidewalk in front of her building. Tulio had calmly wished her a pleasant good morning.

Now he sat across the street in his car on a sweltering summer morning, with the air conditioner running and the police radio shut off, looking at the entrance to Marian's building and feeling depressed. He could smell himself, but he was afraid to go home and take a shower and clean up. He should have thought of that before he left, but he hadn't and now he was stuck. He was certain that the FBI or someone else had his house staked out by now. And Marian would have a heart attack if she came in and he was in her bathtub.

He wouldn't do that, unless she didn't come home at all this morning. He checked the clock, saw that it was now 8:12. He'd give her until 9:00. If she wasn't back by then, he'd go in again and use her shower, brush his teeth and shave. Maybe he even still had some underwear and a clean shirt lying around.

Where in the hell was she? He was starting to get worried. He calmed himself down. He'd been wrong, he thought now, there hadn't been another man, Marian couldn't do that to him. She loved him. She'd probably spent the night with a girlfriend, talked about him, telling her girlfriend all about him, about how much she cared for him. Celebrated her birthday with someone that she'd known since high school.

Tulio rubbed his face roughly, felt the two-day stubble of beard, shook his head to try and clear it but that didn't do any good.

Oh, Jesus, Marian, please come home.

Where the hell was she? Who the hell was she with? It had better be a girlfriend, it had just better be. He'd ask her and she'd answer him, she'd tell him where she'd spent the night. He would make her tell him the truth, the second he got her alone.

Tulio shook his head, knew he was grasping at straws.

There was no girlfriend. She'd spent the night fucking another man, giving some young good-looking club-hopping bastard the sex that she'd been withholding from him for the past few months. Probably some lawyer, someone she'd met through work. They would drink white wine on his patio, and laugh about the cop who'd been dumb enough to think that a woman of Marian's station and status could find it in her heart to love him.

What the hell did she think he was, some toy to be played around with? He'd given her his heart, and she had trifled with it until it broke. He'd been there to amuse her, to be used and then cast aside.

If he had any sense, he'd get the hell out of there, right away, before he did something that he might spend the rest of his life regretting. He was overly tired, incredibly depressed. And jealous. He shouldn't be here.

He'd given this city the most productive years of his life, willingly and without a second's hesitation. His devotion to his work was what had driven his wife into the arms of another man, and, at last, had even driven her to her death. And now they, too, his fellow officers, had coldly cast him aside.

As surely and as easily as Marian had last night.

He might have to accept it from the city, but he didn't have to take it from her. He'd demand that she talk to him, that she tell him the truth. Nothing else mattered to Tulio now, not Alleo, not the victim, not his dead wife and kid, nothing. Just Marian. And the Truth. For once, he'd like to hear it.

He sat there for an hour in his air-conditioned car, dozing. He opened his eyes, saw a jet black Jaguar sedan pull to the curb in front of Marian's building, painstakingly backing in to a spot that a red Mustang had vacated not ten minutes before. He watched as Marian stepped out of the car, casually set the alarm, nearly danced up her stoop and into the building.

She seemed so happy. So young and carefree and in love. She hadn't even glanced in Tulio's direction.

He felt his face tighten, felt his eyes squeeze shut. Felt a spasm of jealousy that crushed him. Tulio laid his head back on the rest, tossed it from side to side. His fists came up and pounded on the inner roof of the Cadillac, short, hard punches that left dents on the outer side. He punched at the dashboard, at the steering wheel, at the leather seat beside him, he punched at the door, stopping short of punching a hole through the window.

He stopped when he took notice of the pain in his hands.

Tulio bowed his head and took deep breaths, until he was sure that he could confront Marian without losing his temper. He couldn't leave now, not after she'd flaunted her affair right in his face like this.

Tulio got out of the car and walked over to the Jaguar, wrote its license plate number down on his notepad, then buttoned the pad back into his pocket. He managed to get away from the car without punching out its windshield or scratching its polish with his key.

Tulio slowly mounted the stairs that led to Marian's apartment.

Marian didn't bother to shower; she'd already done that over at Paul's. Paul. She thought of him as she quickly unbuttoned her blouse, smiling at his kindness, at the miracle she'd been granted. For so long it had been losers, and now she'd found the winner.

He wanted her to pack a bag and move in with him. She wondered if she should, if it was too soon in the relationship.

Marian hurriedly stepped out of her pants and pulled on a pair of pantyhose, then stepped into a gray skirt, and was pulling a yellow silk shirt off a hanger when she heard the sound of a key being turned in her lock. She started, then got control of herself. Was it a break-in? The locksmith rapist? Marian didn't have time to wonder; she barely had time to act.

She ran to her dresser, got the gun out of its hiding place, walked quickly out of her bedroom and had the pistol raised, in the firing position, with the hammer back and her finger on the trigger when Tony Tulio walked in, saw her, and froze.

"I'm happy to see you, too," Tony said, and Marian, as relieved as she was angry, dropped the pistol to her side and carefully lowered the hammer.

"What's *wrong* with you! I nearly shot you!"

Marian looked at him, at what was left of the man she had once thought she'd loved. What was in her doorway was a skeleton of that man, truly less than a shadow. Unshaven and filthy, Tulio was red-eyed, shaking. He looked like a man coming off a three-day drunk. But she knew that he couldn't have been, she'd been with him less than twelve hours ago. He might have gotten drunk since she'd turned him away though, since she'd told him it was over between them.

Marian didn't protest when Tony closed the door behind himself.

He said, "Go ahead, shoot. I lost you, now my job, what's left? Go ahead, shoot; it'd be a good career move for you, get you on the front page: 'Public Defender Shoots Maniac Cop.'"

"Tony, what are you doing here?"

"You forgot these." He held his keys up at shoulder level and shook them. He put the ring back in his pocket, moving carefuly, slowly.

"Leave them and get out."

"Whose Jag is that?"

"None of your business!"

"The hell it's not!" Tony shouted, but stayed where he was, did not move at her or give the impression that he was about to.

"Look, I'm sorry, all right? But you just can't leave me like this, Marian—"

"Leave you like this, *leave* you like this!" Marian felt her anger rising.

"I didn't leave you, you pushed me away! Now I'm gone, it's over, and it's your fault, Tony, not mine!"

Marian stopped, bit her lower lip, made a strong effort and was able to lower her voice. She was suddenly aware that she wasn't wearing a top. She was showing less than she would have in her bathing suit, but right now, with him standing there, she felt suddenly naked, far too vulnerable. She wanted him out of her apartment, right now.

"Let's get something straight, right here, right now. I am not about to be intimidated by you. I will not allow you to stalk me, to threaten me, or to break into my home or harass me where I work."

"Whose *Jaguar* is it!"

"It's my boyfriend's, that's whose!"

"I'll kill him, you bitch!"

Marian took a deep breath; she knew what she was dealing with. Knew, too, that she wasn't at all qualified to handle it.

There was a night-and-day difference between calming a violent youth in a controlled setting with a prosecutor and a couple of cops in the room, and standing here, trying to calm an irrational, armed man in her apartment. A man who thought he had some sort of proprietary right to her life.

She knew, too, that she'd made the wrong move, should not have mentioned a boyfriend. But she would not allow herself to be controlled by him. He had no power over her emotions; she had to think in a rational manner, with her head, instead of her heart. Most of all, of primary importance, she had to get him out of her apartment without either one of them getting hurt.

Marian calmly said, "Tony, it's over. You're hurt and confused and angry, and from what you said, you're in trouble at your job. You're—"

Tony took a step toward her. Without thinking about it, Marian raised the pistol and pointed it straight at his chest.

"Don't you take another goddamn step." She kept her voice soft, but firm. She saw the gun at the end of her hands, steady in her grip. If he tried to touch her, she was capable of shooting him.

Tulio stopped, looked at her with his mouth open, his jaw working back and forth, up and down, soundlessly.

"I will not live in terror of you. I will not, Tony. I'll kill you first. I'm deadly with this weapon. Believe it. I practice at the range, and I'm an expert with it. Now you listen to me very carefully, Tony, because I won't say it twice: If you come near me again, if you come near my home or my office, or near my friend's house or office, Tony, I swear to God, I'll shoot you if I have to."

"Please, Marian, don't do it like this, don't let it end this way . . . "

"It ended a long time ago, Tony, only you couldn't recognize it, you wouldn't let it die a natural death." The gun was getting heavy in Marian's hands. She had to make an effort to keep it pointed straight, to keep it from shaking. He would sense her weakness, and he would prey on it.

"This gun is unregistered, it's unlicensed. It was given to me by someone who thought my life might be in danger someday. He didn't know the half of it. If I use it on you, Tony, I'll get away with it, and you know it."

"I can't buy you a Jaguar!"

"That's not my car!"

"It will be!" He was glaring at her so intently she was certain he was about to make a run toward her, to try and grab the gun. "You're for sale!" Tony shouted. "*All* of you whores are for sale!"

"Get out, get out of my house, right now, goddamnit!" Marian shouted the words and they seemed to have their desired effect. He stepped back, shocked at her intensity. He reached into his pocket and Marian harshly, loudly pulled back the hammer of the pistol. It made its unique, distinctive sound, stopped him in his tracks.

"Don't make me shoot you, Tony."

He took his hand slowly out of his pocket, emerged with his ring of keys. He held it out in front of him, exaggerating his actions as he worked both of her apartment door keys around and off the ring.

"Let's find out how tough he is." Tony let the keys drop to the floor, turned, and walked out of Marian's apartment.

She ran to the door and slammed it behind him, then threw both locks and slid the brass chain into its grooved slot. She let the pistol's hammer down, turned her back to the door and leaned against it. She looked at the gun with disgust, threw it across the room, watched it bounce off the sofa and land on the carpet. She lowered her head, shook it slowly, back and forth.

After a minute she went over and picked up the pistol, took it with her into the bedroom. She put the gun back in her drawer, got into her yellow blouse and tucked it into her skirt. Her hands and breathing were both steady, which surprised her. She wasn't even particularly nervous. More than anything else, Marian felt proud of herself.

C H A P T E R

29

T ULIO WAS OUTSIDE MARIAN'S APARTMENT, SITTING IN THE CAR, devastated. Still, he would not leave, he would follow her. To her boyfriend's house. Tulio would confront the man. Confront the man and—what? He did not know yet what he would do. At the very least, he'd punch him, let him know what pain felt like.

He could relate what he was feeling now to how he'd felt when he'd first quit drinking; that itch in his bloodstream, one that could not be scratched, the blood *need* for poison. He had to do something. *He had to do something.*

Alcohol withdrawal had been a snap compared to this.

He saw motion out of the corner of his eye, looked over and saw Marian coming out of the building, and he felt the humiliation, down deep, in his balls. Felt it deepen as she spotted him and raced across the street, her lips curled back in disgust, Marian shouting in his face:

"Get out! Get out of here!"

Tulio couldn't let her do this to him. He sneered right back, said, "What are you going to do, call a cop?"

"That's *exactly* what I'm going to do, you bastard!"

He'd said the first thing that had come to mind, trying to show her that he wasn't anywhere near as hurt as she might think. They were the exact words he'd often spoken to his wife when they'd been fighting; cops didn't bust other cops over domestic disputes. Not unless there was a murder involved and the cop held a smoking gun.

But today, with Marian, it was the wrong thing to say; it only made her more angry.

He said, "I'm out of here," was about to say more, was about to curse her, Marian and her boyfriend both, but he was stopped by the look on her face, by the odd way she was staring at him.

No, not at him. Marian was staring at something beside him. Tulio looked over at the passenger seat. What the hell was she looking at? There were only files there.

"Who is that." Marian spoke flatly, no anger left in her tone.

"Who?"

"There, in that picture."

Carole Conners's death photo was lying face-up on the seat. Tulio's own anger was great enough that he had to decide whether to tell Marian the truth, or to say something flippant, toss her an insult. He decided—to keep up the façade of unhurt indignation—on the latter.

"Just some broad. Some dead broad. With blond hair and green eyes. Why? You think your boyfriend might like to fuck her, too?"

Marian looked away from the picture, looked at him with an expression so pained that even in the state he was in he backtracked. "Marian, I'm sorry."

She kept looking at him in a way that made him want to curl up and die. There was disgust in her expression, but a longing there, too, and startled incomprehension. She had the look he'd seen on women who'd been beaten for the first time by the man they loved. Women who had suddenly and harshly discovered that the world was a cruel, grotesque place.

He couldn't stand to look at that, not for another second. He threw the car into gear and tore away from the curb.

Marian stood watching him as he raced away, then turned and angrily turned off the Jaguar's alarm, got into the car and started it up, angled her way back and forth, trying to get out of the parking space, in the sort of pain she hadn't felt since the day her grandmother had died.

Her greatest anger, though, was leveled at herself. How could she have been so wrong about him? What had happened to the man who used to rub her back, take her to Grant Park and kid her until she worked her way out of a foul mood? Had this creature always been inside, ready to strike the moment it didn't get its own way? She couldn't have been that bad a judge of character. She couldn't have been.

No, because she'd chosen Paul.

A quick blast of a siren startled her as she started to pull away from the curb. She hit the brake and jerked to a stop, looking behind her in the rearview mirror and saw the squad car, with a young officer behind the wheel, speaking into his microphone. What had she done? Were Paul's plates expired? Dear Lord, she didn't need this shit, not this morning, not after what had just happened with Tony.

She put the car in Park as the officer came around her side of the car, one hand on his weapon, as if she constituted a threat. Cars drove around them, curious faces glancing at her from behind glass barriers. For some reason, Marian was ashamed. She powered down the window as the officer reached her door.

"How fast you think you can go on this block, hon?"

Hon? Had this boy just called her hon?

"Pardon me?"

"*Pardon* you? What are you, Caspar Weinberger?"

Marian had to think for a second before she got the joke. She didn't smile when she did.

She said, "Officer, why did you stop me?"

"I didn't. *You* stopped *me*." He gave her what he probably thought to be an irresistible grin. "Those green eyes of yours nearly stopped my heart."

Marian looked at him, at a kid who was at the most in his mid-twenties, his blond hair cut short, his uniform snug, his body muscular. There was a little bulge right above the waist of his dingy blue shirt, where his bulletproof vest ended. He was looking at her as if he believed all women had been biogenetically programmed to melt at his glance.

She said, again, "Pardon me?" conveying her exasperation, and the officer sighed heavily, as if deciding that she had to be a lesbian to refuse his charm.

"License and registration, please, ma'am."

"What did I do?"

"License and registration, please, I said." There was a firmness in his tone. Don't fuck with me, lady, it's hot out.

"Look, Officer, I just pulled out of that space there—"

"Pulled out like a maniac, I heard you all the way around the corner."

"But you didn't see me."

"What are you now, a lawyer?"

"Because I didn't squeal away, that was one of your fellow officers, Lieutenant Tony Tulio."

"Right. Tulio gets to this part of town about as often as he gets to Mars."

"Officer—"

"Lady, I'm not gonna be polite about it again: Give me your license and registration. *Please.*"

Marian reached into her purse and found her license. She opened the glove compartment, fished around until she found Paul's registration. She handed both over.

"You Paul Harris?"

"The car's his. The license's mine. Now listen to me, Officer. I did not pull out of that spot in a dangerous manner, nor did I race down the street. And I'm late for court."

"Traffic court, I'll bet. Why ain't I surprised?"

"You didn't see anything, there are no tire marks on this side of the street. We both know that if you give me a ticket, I'll beat it in court, you're just wasting both of our time."

"You think so?" He held up her license and smiled. "This license expired yesterday."

Damnit. "Look at it again. Yesterday, Sunday, was my birthday. I've got the rest of the day to renew this license, and you know that, too. If you don't know it, then you should be back in the academy, instead of out here practicing your pickup lines on citizens." He glared at her. Marian decided to tell him a lie.

She said, "I have to be in court in fifteen minutes. If I'm not, a rapist-killer will be cut loose to the street. Is that worth it to you? Giving me a ticket you know you can't win, and letting a killer loose because the prosecutor wasn't in court?"

"You a lawyer?"

"I'm not the judge, Officer, but I know him. I want your name and badge number. If I'm late, the judge'll want to know them, too."

The officer handed her back her license and Paul's registration.

"You get this license renewed before the end of the day, lady." She watched him strut back to his patrol car, then she put the registration back inside the glove compartment. She was about to put the driver's license back into her purse, too, when something about it caught her eye.

Marian looked down at the license, stared at it, puzzled. Tulio, the traffic cop, even Paul were erased from her mind as she stared at it, growing increasingly frightened and not altogether certain why. She stared at her driver's license, entranced by it. Her smiling picture, one that she hated. It had never looked anything like her.

Opposite her picture was her driver's license number and the date of expiration. Under that, her name, then her address. Under that was her sex, height, weight, date of birth, eye color, type of license, any restrictions . . .

What was grabbing at her? What the hell was wrong with her, niggling at her mind? She couldn't stop staring at the license.

Whatever it was, it was important. She had a sense of dread, a sense of impending danger so grave that she was afraid to look away from the picture, as if even that simple act would somehow cause her to die on the spot.

She turned the license over. On the back side was the anatomical gift section of the card, asking her if she wanted to donate, and if she did, which organs . . .

Marian had marked the little box that read: Entire Body.

Next to that was her blood type . . .

It hit her then, with the shock of a hard slap to her face. Marian put both hands on her cheeks; she gasped for breath. She felt herself flush, saw little clear dots swimming in front of her eyes. All her strength left her; her head was swimming madly. She was afraid that she would pass out. She sat there, her head on the steering wheel, taking deep breaths, thinking terrible thoughts and trying not to vomit onto the floor mat of a fifty-thousand-dollar car.

"Oh, Christ, oh dear Lord Jesus Christ in heaven."

She knew with a great and sudden clarity what it was about her driver's license that had caused this reaction. She had put it together with that picture on Tony's seat, the picture of the dead woman. She'd seen the picture, then her license. With her vital statistics right there on the front, the space for her blood type on back.

The picture of the girl on Tony's seat was the same as the picture of the woman she'd seen last night, on Paul's computer. Only on the computer image, the young woman had been alive and smiling. An awkward smile, with her vital statistics printed next to it.

As if they had been copied off a driver's license.

A siren sounded behind her, and Marian leaped in her seat. She looked in her rearview mirror, saw the cop sitting in his car, his flashers still on. She'd forgotten about him. He made a *move it* gesture with both hands, putting his shoulders into it.

Marian somehow managed to put the car into Drive, then drove slowly away from her building. She felt a strong sense of terror slithering steadily up her spine.

Trembling, not knowing what any of it was about, Marian turned the corner and began to drive away from there, away from the cop, away from Tony, away from Paul, away from everyone. She had to find a place where she could be alone, where she could think. She had to find a way to figure out what all this was about. How Tony and Paul were connected, and, if they were, what that connection was.

CHAPTER
30

Harris walked into his River North art gallery with a smile on his face, the smile and his debonair demeanor hiding his inner turmoil. Since he'd become an adult, life had always been so simple for him, and now there were unwelcome complications, things he had to think about, things he did not like.

Marian had brought things out in him that he'd thought were forever dead. With her kindness, with her love. With her sweetness and compassion. She would touch him, hold him, kiss his neck, and he felt reborn. She seemed so old-fashioned, the only woman he had ever known who loved him for what he was.

Marian never judged, Marian never demanded. She was just there, accepting. She'd take his hand in hers and he would feel things move inside him.

She was the sort of woman that Harris, given even half a chance, would have looked for twenty years ago. And now he'd found her, and if he were going to keep her, the Collector would have to die.

The last time he'd felt like this had been a long time—some twenty years—ago. Back at the beginning, after his first killing. When the overwhelming sorrow over what he'd done had almost driven him into the arms of the law, ready to make a full confession. He'd awakened the day after the first killing with a feeling of dread, of unreality, wishing that it was all a dream, wondering how he ever could have done such a thing.

Even in the state he'd been in, back in what he considered to be a "human" condition, he'd still somehow had the sense to know that there would be no forgiveness, that there was no judge on earth who would pat his head and understand, then set him free into the world. What had stopped Harris was the fact that he knew he would never get help if he turned himself in. He was in Louisiana, they would fry him in the chair. All the law would seek would be retribution, so he waited. And, after a time, the feeling of sorrow passed, replaced by one of superior, snickering joy; he'd beaten them, the law and everyone, he'd literally gotten away with murder.

It had taken him only a little while longer to truly understand what he'd been really feeling that first day; guilt, that's what it had been. That and nothing more. And the fear of being found out. He'd purged himself of it, he had no time or use for guilt, he would not allow himself to experience it.

Which was a wonderful thing. Harris had crawled into himself and pulled his mind over his emotions in the same manner that he would cover his body with a blanket on a cold winter night. He'd buried them so deeply that in time, they'd disappeared.

Which was when he'd felt himself transform, from a human into the Collector.

Without the trappings of emotion, each killing had been easier and easier for him to perform. He'd learned from that first one, and from all the ones that followed. He was not a psychotic, nor was he a serial killer. He killed for the art of it, and for the money that it brought him. His proficiency at his art had brought him great wealth. When he had enough money, or a different, better, incentive, he knew he'd be able to stop.

There'd been a shift inside him recently, just in the past couple of months. He didn't know what it was, had no idea what was happening to him. He'd always been so strong, so uninvolved, above the petty mundanities that seemed common to most other men. He would listen to them, study them, sometimes with a look of concern and understanding on his face, trying to comprehend what drove the species. At last, he'd given up. Had come to the conclusion that their existence would forever be unfathomable to him. That, he'd thought, was because he'd been so far above them. He didn't feel so superior anymore; now, he felt involved.

That morning, in his kitchen, a war had been waged within him, emotions he hadn't thought himself to have had been doing bitter battle. One part of him wanted to confess; the guilt and his need for her had nearly driven him to immediately tell Marian all there was to know. The other part of him wanted to take her into his arms and tell her every-thing would work out, it would all be fine. The other part of him wanted him to keep all his secrets, forever. The way she'd looked, so simple and yet so elegant, in his robe, not wearing makeup.

So, he'd felt guilt again, and love. He'd felt something else, too, some-thing he hadn't felt as an adult. When he'd thought that he might be losing her, Harris had felt fear.

When was the last time that he'd felt afraid?

When Daddy had been—

Stop!

Harris stood suddenly immobile, shocked into statue-stillness. What had he been thinking of? What was that memory? Even as he tried hard to remember, he was aware on a conscious level that he truly did not want to know. He was in dangerous territory, with things better left undis-turbed. It was nighttime stuff, dream stuff, not for the here and now, not for when he was awake and strong, with his strong thin muscles and his insurmountable confidence. His good looks and his strength and his money. They protected him from the past.

"Are you all right, Paul?"

It was Merri, who thought she was his assistant, instead of only his secretary. Merri, who also thought herself to be in love with Harris. Har-ris didn't try to disabuse her of the notion, he got more out of her that way. Merri was twenty-eight years old, with a short, mannish hairstyle. Merri, with her presentable appearance and her toned, slender body. She was in her own way attractive, and she dressed well enough. Harris paid her more than enough money to ensure that she did. There would be no old torn blue jeans or trendy T-shirts with sayings written on them ever allowed in here, inside the Paul Harris Gallery. Merri was articulate, ag-gressive, and extremely well-educated, yet at the proper moments she acted humbly enough so that the rich didn't avoid the gallery. She let them look down their noses at her, aware that Harris never would.

He looked at her, raised his eyebrows.

"Hmm? What's that, Merri?"

"Are you okay? You just stopped dead, Paul, you looked sick."

"I'm fine. I was just admiring the job you did hanging the show."

Her face lit up, and she smiled proudly.

"Really?"

"It's lovely. Every etching the exact same distance from the floor and ceiling—just perfect."

"Well—thank you." She would not be used to such praise from him. But he hadn't lied to her about one thing; he was fine, he thought. He was having slight lapses, but coming back from them with no trouble.

He said, "I'll be in my office, and I can't be disturbed for a while. Don't send any calls back. I'll buzz you when I'm clear."

"All right." She was glowing at him, smiling, and Harris had to move away from her quickly. What the hell was he feeling, what was wrong with him? He felt the urge to smile at her, to somehow show her that she was appreciated. One of the reasons that he paid her as handsomely as he did was so he wouldn't have to compliment her every other day. What was wrong with him? He had no use for words of praise. He heard her humming as he walked into the back of the gallery, to his private office.

He'd be just fine. It was a temporary thing. He wasn't the type to have ego-driven feelings, to have silly emotions bothering him; they only got in the way. Which was why the unusually harsh nightmare had awakened him last night, why he'd gone out to search for Marian when he'd discovered her gone from his bed. He'd been desperate for her, for closeness with her. Strange. Beyond strange. Bizarre.

It was also why he'd partially remembered the nightmare, why he'd felt a little bit afraid since awakening that morning.

He had to get a grip on himself; he could not go on like this. There was work to do, even if there were no more organs to be acquired, there was still money that had to be collected. Lots of money, too. Above and beyond what the Eagle had paid him, the double-payoff which Alleo had promised. He'd have to keep his wits about him, stay razor sharp, if he were to walk into that man's lair.

He'd have to get his mind off the half-remembered recollections of a time long ago, when he wasn't yet the Collector. Had to steadily remind himself that he was strong, a rock, that no one or nothing could ever hurt or break him.

But he felt so *weak* this morning. Here he was, in his office, alone, fighting a sense of fear that might be capable of destroying him. Frightened men made mistakes, they caved in. Gave in. Without a fight, as he had always done with his fath—

"*No!!*" Harris shouted the word, then covered his mouth with both hands. Had Merri heard him? She had better not have. His eyes were wide and panic-stricken, and he looked around his office, terrified.

Don't think about it, you mustn't, you mustn't you mustn't! Paulie don't!

He could picture the man in his mind, hulking and huge, coming for Paulie in the night, making Paulie do things. Then later, immediately afterward, brutally whipping Paulie for what he'd made his father do. Beating him senseless, which Paulie could have taken.

It was what his father had said while he'd done it that had stayed with Harris throughout the years.

Harris realized that he was making whining noises, that he was sweating heavily, right through his suit. He forced his mind to stop working, managed to take control of himself. He sat in his chair and stared at the wall and imagined himself in front of his mirror, thought of his naked body, of what it looked like. Strong and powerful, coiled danger.

In a moment, he was almost fine.

Midlife crisis, that's what it had to be. Last night the thought of turning forty had been a joke to Harris. Today, this morning, it was getting to him. That had to be it. Even he had some feelings. The thought of which made him smile.

Of course he had feelings; in fact, he was in love. With Marian. And love must make you crazy. It was why all the sad songs were on the radio. Why men were driven to smuggle weapons into court, shoot down their wife's divorce lawyers and the judges in cold blood. Love had to do that to men. Harris had no frame of reference from his life experience, no data from which to draw. Maybe loving Marian made him feel what others felt. No wonder humans were so weak. Pathetic little sheep waiting for men like Harris to come along and lead them. But now he felt what they felt, now he understood.

He loved her. He loved her.

Harris sat back in his chair and laughed like a happy child. He knew what had been wrong with him, what it was that had been bothering him.

He had *felt*, which was what in turn had made him feel fear.

That was it.

Paul Harris sat in his chair, smiling, glad that he'd figured things out. Glad that he was in love with Marian. Glad that Marian loved him, too.

He felt a lightness, as if invisible weights he hadn't known he'd been carrying had somehow been dropped from his shoulders. He felt stronger, too. But a good strength, not a bad one. He had walked out of a void. All right. He was in love. And now he had to make some plans.

First, he had to rid himself of his past, wipe out every trace. It could not be allowed to ever return. And she could not find out! He must not weaken and tell her. Someone as good as Marian must never be allowed to know the truth. He would settle with Alleo this morning, right now. Get it out of his way, put the money with the rest of it, inside his wall safe here in the office. This afternoon he'd start depositing it, $9,900 at a time.

The computer would have to be wiped clean. He'd destroy its memory, allow the virus he'd installed when he'd first gotten it to do its work. Once a week, the internal date had to be changed, the computer set back to the Fourth of July. If it ever got to the eleventh, the virus would infect the computer.

He'd installed it in case the authorities ever found it, in case someone like Tulio had ever caught on to his work. They would, he knew, put the computer into an evidence room, unplugged, but there was an internal battery, one which would keep the clock working whether the machine was plugged in or not. They wouldn't have much evidence, once Mr. Virus kicked in.

Harris felt bliss. Something as unfamiliar to him as a sunset is to the blind. Forty years he'd waited, forty years he'd wasted. But he'd waste no more time. That was all behind him. He would show Marian how he felt, prove his love to her, and she'd never disappoint him. She'd only thought that she'd loved Tulio. A man like that, what a joke!

She'd love him, though. For the rest of her life. Because once he proclaimed his love for her, he could never let her go.

Paul Harris took deep breaths, tried to get back his inner emptiness, the void, just for a few more hours. It was like trying to change the course of the tide. Once it was gone, it could never come back. But he could fake it well enough to fool a man like Mr. Alleo. Men like that looked no further than their own selfishness, never saw anything that they didn't expect to see. He could fool that little man, one last time.

And then he'd be through. The Collector would be done. He had enough money to last them for the rest of their lives, had had it for a long time; he'd never really worked for the money, anyway. It was an idea whose time was past. Someone else could pick up the slack. Lenny, maybe, if he had the strength inside him, but Harris didn't think that he did.

Lenny had been allowed to live due simply to his loyalty. The Eagle's men had threatened to kill him last year if he didn't give them Harris's name, and he hadn't. Harris had rewarded the fat ex-fighter well financially, and at the time that had been enough, had in fact been all that he was capable of giving.

But not now. Now, Harris knew a way to reward Lenny for his loyalty. Call it a bonus. A going-away present. He'd give Lenny what he'd built up, all of it, as a gift.

Then he'd spend the rest of his life with Marian. It was frightening, in fact terrifying, but it also felt so wonderful.

C H A P T E R
31

TULIO TOOK A RISK, CALLED IN THE JAGUAR'S LICENSE PLATE, USING his own radio number. He was in luck, and it surprised him. No one had bothered to warn the dispatchers that he was no longer a city employee.

He looked at his notepad, where he'd written down the name and address he'd been given. Paul Harris. Whitebread motherfucker. With an address on the Gold Coast. Didn't that figure? She'd gone for the bucks. Mr. High-rise, Mr. Jaguar. Mr. Rich. Richie Rich. Mr. Asshole, is who he was. Let's see how he acted when Tulio broke one of his knees for him. He wanted to steal Marian? He'd do it from a fucking wheelchair.

Harris would be like all the rest of the rich civilians Tulio had ever dealt with; in love with themselves, thinking themselves safe and above being victims of crime. Until it happened. Then they became whining little sheep, blamed the cops for not protecting them. In their pre-victim life, they belonged to groups that were dedicated to destroying the powers of the law. After they became victimized, they wanted to bestow precognition on the cops. Somehow give them the power to divine who was going to commit crimes, then get them off the streets before they did. This man would be like that. He'd be easy. Easier than Marian.

"Mr. Alleo? Do you recognize my voice." Harris did not make this a question, he knew that Alleo would.

"Yes."

"I'm calling to set up a meeting, in order to collect what is mine."

"You said last night that you set things up in advance. You found my number. Do you know where I live?"

"I do."

"Then come here. I'll give you what I promised. I'll stick to my end of the bargain."

"I never for a moment doubted that you would."

"I'll be waiting," Mr. Alleo said, and hung up without another word.

They were inarticulate, they were scum. They were stupid, low-class fools. But they kept their word. Honor was big to them, showing respect as important as getting it, as long as it was to the right person.

Harris was such a person. Or, rather, had been, until today.

It had been easy, slipping just a mask of the man he had been back on. Fun, too, knowing that he was no longer that man. Like taking part in a play, or being the artist he'd once wanted to be more than he'd wanted anything else in his life. Those days were over, too.

Should he call Marian at work? Beep her, perhaps? She'd said she had a big morning, some killer to represent. He'd leave her alone. Have Merri tend to the gallery business, spend the day wiping out any traces of his past.

There was a frightened knock at his door, and he stared at it, growing angry. Hadn't he told her that he wasn't to be disturbed? Merri stuck her head in the door, and he glared at her, disapprovingly.

"I'm sorry, Paul, but I didn't know what to do."

"What?"

She was uncomfortable, frightened. "Your friend Lenny's on line one . . ." *Lenny?* "and he says he has to talk to you, he says that it's life and death."

Lenny. That was interesting. He'd told this man, many times, not to mingle what they did together with Harris's gallery business. Still, sometimes, there was no way around it. Everyone who worked for him, even some of the temporary help he hired to tend bar at openings, knew who Lenny was. He'd even introduced him to Marian. Lenny had spoken to her with his eyes glued to her cleavage. At the time, Harris had thought it amusing, almost funny, but now, remembering, he felt anger.

Harris lifted the phone to his ear, stabbed at line one.

"Yes, Lenny?" He didn't have to act to make himself sound exasperated.

"Sorry to bother you, Paul—"

"I'm sure you are. What do you want?"

"I have to talk to you right away."

"I'm afraid that's not possible."

"Look, you don't get it, it's urgent."

"Maybe tomorrow, Lenny, but I can't meet you today."

"Paul—"

"What did you do, lose your life savings last night? You need money? I'll leave some for you in an envelope with Merri, you can come and get it."

"That's what I want to talk to you about."

"Then talk."

"Not over the phone." There was an edge to his tone that made Harris hesitate.

"What's wrong, Lenny?" Harris said, and thought that he already knew.

"You got to meet me, right now, Paul, before you do anything else. They might already have you figured out, they might have had somebody follow you."

Harris made up his mind. He said, "All right. Meet me at Eleventh and State. I'll pick you up in front of Police Headquarters."

"Police Headquarters? What are you—" Lenny paused. Harris knew he'd been about to ask if Harris were nuts. "Anywhere but there, Paul, come on, I can't go there."

Harris knew that; he'd given Lenny that address on purpose. He wanted Lenny thinking that they would meet where he'd be safe. He wanted the man to trust him for a little while more. Because if what he suspected was true, Lenny wasn't long for this world.

Harris felt the thing that he truly was slip back upon him like a fresh layer of skin. As if it had never left. His reality. His actuality. Everything else was fiction. The weight was back, and heavy, but it replaced the fear, the uneasiness he'd felt, what had come with his sense of happiness.

That, too, was gone. Maybe it wouldn't come back. Because Lenny was proving to him that you couldn't trust anyone, that the world was filled with liars and thieves, with those who would prey on any weakness that you showed.

Love was the most mortal of weaknesses, he knew. He'd only been deluding himself by believing otherwise. Love was a cancer. He'd once loved his fath—

"Lenny," he realized that he was breathing heavily. He could not let Lenny hear it.

"Yeah, Paul? Are you okay?"

Was Lenny daring to ask this question of him? See what happened when you were weak? When you were a sniveling *weak faggot motherfucker!*

It took him a few seconds before he could speak again.

"Meet me at Eleventh and Wabash, then. That's a block away. I'll be driving—a van."

"Eleventh and Wabash. How long?"

"Better give me half an hour, maybe even an hour. There are a number of things that need to be attended to first."

"Paul, take my word for it, there ain't *nothing* needs tending to except this—"

Harris hung up on him. There was something more important, but Lenny couldn't ever be allowed to figure out what it was.

C H A P T E R

32

TULIO PARKED IN THE CIRCULAR DRIVE, LEFT THE CAR RIGHT THERE and flashed his badge at the angry young Mexican valet who was running toward him, waving him off. The kid backed off when Tulio flashed his badge, then took on a skeptical expression after he'd looked Tulio over. But he kept his mouth shut. Tulio walked past him, entered the building without so much as a word passing between them. He could feel the kid's eyes on his back. Tulio thought: Fuck you. He was tired, he was incredibly depressed. His life, as he'd known it, was about to change forever. He wasn't even sure what he was doing in this place, but he knew that he wanted Harris more than he'd ever wanted Alleo. Wanted him lying at his feet, bloody.

Everything he'd ever had had been taken away from Tulio. This Harris guy was the one thing he was able to do something about.

There wasn't much doubt that the guy sitting behind the security desk was a retired city policeman. He assumed the typical and pathetic style of such men the second he looked at Tulio's badge, the old guy wanting to be a part of it still, but his new uniform, his demeanor, what he was in his life today was now only cause for embarrassment. His age now separated him from ever being a part of the real action again, no matter what his past accomplishments might have been, and that caused him resentment as strong as his desire to once more be a part of it all. Tulio had seen it before, many, many times. A man like this would think that time had betrayed him, and would blame Tulio's relative youth on how far down he'd come in his world. Tulio knew that he'd have to step carefully if he were going to get what he wanted from the guy.

"Got something important going on with one of your penthouse tenants, Sarge."

"There's only one," the old guy said, leaning over the desk and talking out of the side of his mouth. He'd probably retired a patrolman, working North Side traffic. Calling him Sarge had gone a long way, Tulio could tell that from the look on his face.

"Paul Harris?"

"That's him. Ain't no other tenant up there; they want too much fuckin' money for the other apartment. Even the rich assholes that want to live in this building just for the address balk at the kind of dough they're asking, and the building, shit, they think they should raise the price even higher. Harris, he got the best view in town. Besides, you could afford that kind of price, you'd buy an estate in Lake Forest, watch the Bears practice from your rooftop and never get closer to a nigger than the ones that tend your lawn."

He was being one of the boys. The talkative bastard smiled when Tulio grunted what he hoped the old guy would see as assent.

The guard said, "What did you say your name was again?"

"Tulio, want my badge number?"

"Nah. I know who you are." Damn. The guy would take it personally that he had never been important enough for Tulio to recognize in return.

"He in? Harris?" Tulio asked, and watched the old man decide whether he should give him the information.

At last, the guard said, "Saw him leave through the lobby a while ago, I ain't sure if he come back. He comes, he goes. He's rich. Don't have to keep regular hours. Besides, he can go right to the parking garage from his elevator if he wants to. You turn the penthouse key, it bypasses the lobby. One of the perks of bein' dumb enough to pay millions for an apartment; the elevator don't make no stops when you get in it." He shrugged. "He could be up there right now if he came back in a vehicle."

"Even if he left on foot?"

The guy shrugged, a little embarrassed. "You never can tell, can you?"

Tulio looked at him, saw the anger on the man's face. The top of his balding head was bright red. He'd put on a few pounds in his golden years, but he still carried himself well, with the unmistakable bearing and arrogance of a proud twenty-year copper.

Tulio also saw fear in the man's expression, and wondered why it was there. He hadn't made any threats, had in fact been overly friendly. Then he got it, knew why the rent-a-cop was afraid. Harris must be a big tipper, going out of his way to try and buy the loyalty of the people who worked in the building.

Tulio knew how to play the guy now. He had to work on his true loyalty. His allegiance would be with the department, first and always. He leaned into the counter a little more, man to man; cop to cop. He even looked over his shoulder a little to make sure that none of the building tenants had come into the lobby while they'd been talking. If he was going to get what he wanted, he had to make the man think that they were partners in a police conspiracy. He would remember other such occasions, when they had to bend the law a little, do away with the idiotic, handcuffing pretensions of the judiciary system.

Tulio said, "Listen, I got to get in there, you know what I mean, Sarge?"

"Black bag, or you got a warrant?" The guy was keenly interested. Probably had a hard-on under his fancy security uniform. Back in action, peripherally.

Tulio whispered, "Black bag."

"Jesus." The security guy was whispering, too.

"Can you help me out here?"

"How bad is it?"

"Murder, double."

Tulio said it low but hard, and saw the man make up his mind. He even nodded a little as he did so. There were some things that Harris's money still couldn't buy.

"Don't surprise me, there's something about him. Like ice water comes to him for lessons in how to be cold. He could kill someone. He could do a double."

"You think so?" Tulio acted as if he were enthusiastic. "That's good to hear. He's been a strong suspect, but hearing that, he just moved up a notch."

The old guy's chest filled his uniform.

He said, "Listen, I'll call down the elevator, it'll take you right up to the penthouse."

The guy stopped talking and smiled over Tulio's shoulder. Tulio straight-ened, and waited as a well-dressed older couple walked past them, the wife with her nose in the air and the husband glaring suspiciously at Tulio. They had just come in from the street; how could they not be sweating?

"Folks," the security guy said, and nodded cordially. They ignored him, walked over to the elevator.

Tulio said, "Gotta be a bitch, putting up with snooty assholes like that."

"But if their TVs disappear, they come running down to me with their assholes puckered, begging me for help."

"So what else is new?"

"I hear you. Spent twenty-five years of my life with the same bullshit. Listen, Tulio, go ahead, as soon as it's clear. But when you come down, you do me one favor. Take the penthouse elevator all the way down to the basement. Our garage is down there. There's a big red button to push there just inside the corrugated door, you can't miss it. It'll open the doorway and you can walk right out to the street. You got a car?" He looked over Tulio's shoulder, toward the driveway.

"That your Cadillac? All right. Give me the keys. I'll have Nunzio take it around the corner, park it next to the hydrant. The keys'll be on the floor, under the mat. It'll be unlocked. Don't worry, he'll keep his mouth shut. He's illegal, been sent back four times. He'll do whatever I tell him."

"Harris got an alarm?"

"In this building? Who needs one?"

"Thanks, brother," Tulio said, and saw the man's quick look of pride. He nodded curtly at Tulio, as if he somehow had seniority on him, was doing a rookie a favor. Tulio let him think that way, he'd gotten what he was looking for. Tulio turned and walked over to the elevator banks, waited for a car, then got in as if he lived there, folded his hands in front of him, and stood waiting for it to rise.

The elevator rose rapidly, nonstop, shaking slightly from side to side, and in seconds it started to slow down, glided to a stop. The doors hissed open, and Tulio stepped out on to the penthouse floor, looked down the hall until the elevator doors closed behind him.

He'd never seen anything quite like this setup before. There were two doors, on either side of the wide, heavily carpeted hallway. The doors were large, double sets, made of thick, dark, highly polished wood. At the far end of the hallway was a window that looked out over the city. Tulio could see the very tip of the antenna of the Hancock Building. He decided that he had to be a minimum eighty floors above the city, probably even more.

He walked down the hallway, glad that the other penthouse apartment was empty. He wouldn't have to worry about being quiet as he worked the locks. There were two small antique-looking tables on either side of Harris's door. One held a telephone, the other a crystal bowl of mints. It must be where deliveries could be left. It would be nice to live in a place where you could leave money on a table outside your door and not have to worry about it.

He took out his lockpicks, knelt down in front of Harris's door, and within a minute it was open. He pushed it wide, stepped in, and closed the door behind him, relocked it from within, and then could only just stand there for a minute, looking around in awe.

The last time he'd seen this much interior space, he had been in a warehouse, as a kid, doing a B&E, stealing coils of painted aluminum that they sold for a dime a pound. The apartment took up half the top of the entire building, and it was no small building to begin with; it covered the entire city block.

This place had to have run Harris millions.

A large portion of the three walls in front and to the sides of Tulio were made of glass. He could see the lake and part of the city spread out before him, as breathtaking to him now as it had been the first time he'd seen it from this height: through the window of a state airplane, transporting a prisoner, coming in for a tight landing at Meigs Field. From the hallway, he could see the tiny boats out on the lake. He looked over and down, saw the top of high-rise penthouse roofs. Jesus.

There was a small hallway, and he walked down it, saw that the parts of the walls that weren't made of glass had three doors set into it, the doors widely spaced, guaranteeing familial privacy. A large kitchen filled one corner over by the northern window. Half a wall wrapped around it. Tulio looked past the stove, at a wide expanse of lake. It would be like cooking in mid-air, a thousand feet above the Gold Coast.

There was a living area set up near the window, the furniture facing what looked like a small painting on the wall. The area was made up of a leather couch, and two leather chairs, all black, all cracked, all old and well-used. Harris must have bought them that way. There was a sense of loneliness in the apartment; there would not have been many parties up here.

There was no TV, and Tulio could not see any stereo equipment. But there were speakers built into the parts of the walls that weren't made out of glass. It could be an intercom, or a sound system. The rug felt lively under his feet, as if its padding had been made of super-thick rubber. Tulio moved silently toward the door that was nearest to him, turned the knob, found that the door was locked.

The other two were open.

The first one opened onto a large, windowless bedroom, with a bed bigger than any that Tulio had ever seen in any furniture store. There was no clock in the room that he could see. On one end was a bathroom, with a huge shower-tub. The stall had a great many small shower nozzles, running from head to ankle. Tulio thought of Marian in there, with Harris, both of them naked, laughing and playing as they soaped each other down. He cringed.

The second open room held a fully equipped home gym, with a Nautilus machine that was stacked with chrome weights. There was a TV hanging from the wall in front of the treadmill, a good stereo system with large speakers in one corner. Tulio had seen cheaper setups in exclusive health clubs. The guy had taste, all right.

On to the locked room. Tulio took a fast look at the painting as he walked toward the locked doors, stopped dead in his tracks, and stared at it with his mouth open.

It was Marian. She must have posed for this, she'd have *had* to have posed for this. It was a perfect likeness of her, in miniature, a tiny Marian in old-time clothing, but without a doubt, it was Marian. Had Harris had this commissioned? The paint was cracked and aged. Tulio knew nothing about art. A name in the corner would mean nothing to him if it wasn't Picasso or Chagall or one of the others common to a layman. He shook his head and turned from the painting, toward the locked door.

He opened it easily, stepped in and saw a computer setup, the machine atop a desk, still quietly humming. Across the room was another desk, set closer to the floor, one with four different telephones, each one hooked up to a separate answering machine. One of the machines had a blinking message light, signifying that there were three messages for

Harris. Tulio walked over, pressed the proper button.

"Paul? Paul, you there?" A somehow familiar, tinny voice came out of the speaker, high and desperate. There was an angry, muttered, "Christ almighty," then: "All right, listen to me, Paul, I got to talk to you, right away, the second you check this message. But you got to wait for my call, don't call my place, there's people there by now, if you get me. This is urgent, Paul, this is fucking life and death. We're in serious shit. Don't go *any*where to see *any*one until you talk to me, all right?"

Tulio waited, heard the beep, then the same voice came back over the tape, sounding even more desperate than it had.

"Paul, it's Lenny again."

Lenny. That was it. The caller was Lenny Roman, the stiff who used to throw fights at the Aragon back when Tulio was in uniform. Tulio knew the name, as did all downtown and South Side policemen. They were under strict orders to never try and bring the man in by themselves. Lenny Roman was a walking time bomb, and he loved to drink and pick fights with cops. How could he be hooked up with a yuppie Richie Rich motherfucker like Harris?

The rest of the message was just a variation of the first, and the third message was nearly the same, but even more despairing. Whatever Lenny wanted, it was of the utmost importance. At least to him.

He probably did Harris's legbreaking for him. A man with this much money had to make some powerful enemies on the way up. Even if he'd inherited the dough, there'd always be those who'd want to take it away from him.

Still, an ex-fighter. A guy with known mob connections.

Lenny had whined over the telephone, though, the guy was obviously terrified of something. Something the two of them were involved in. Wouldn't that be sweet, to learn that the guy was a crook. It wouldn't get Tulio his job back, but it would definitely be the end of the romance between Harris and Marian. She wouldn't be able to live with that.

Tulio couldn't remember the last time he'd felt so alive. Everything was crystal clear to him now, all the depression lifted. His ass was tight, his muscles strong, his will powerful. He was in control.

He turned away from the telephone banks, looked over at the computer, curiously. He turned on the monitor, saw a little green light go on in the corner, heard the electronic *click* as it came alive and began to warm up. A picture swam into view, the image grainy at first, as the monitor brought it to life. In seconds it was clear and distinct, and Tulio looked at it, instantly shocked. He had to grab on to the back of the computer chair in order to stay on his feet. His head swam, his legs lost their strength. Tulio managed to fall into the chair, never taking his eyes off the image.

Carole Conners's picture smiled back at him with delight.

C H A P T E R
33

W HAT THE HELL WAS THIS HARRIS GUY DOING WITH A PICTURE OF
Carole Conners on his computer? Tulio wasn't feeling so wonderful anymore. He reached out a shaking hand and touched the page-down button. Another picture took Carole's place. He did it again, over and over,
saw image after image of healthy smiling faces. He paged back to Carole's picture, sat looking at her, then sat straight up in the chair.

It all came to him then, what had been happening, what was going
on. It was so brilliant it was staggering.

Harris was his killer. There *was* a killer. It wasn't some far-flung paranoid fantasy. Harris was the man he'd spent the last two years hunting.
And oh dear sweet Jesus, Harris had somehow manipulated Marian into
falling in love with him.

What could Tulio do about it? The feds were at the station, wanting
to talk to him. He couldn't turn to the department. Who could he trust?
He couldn't go to them, not even if he wasn't in trouble. He'd broken in
here; done a black-bag job, an illegal entry. Even if he found a typed confession on the desk, it couldn't be used against Harris in any court in the
land.

And even if he was in good standing in the department, there wouldn't
be anything he could do right now. By the time he *did* get a warrant to
search the place, Harris could have destroyed all the evidence, hell, the
security guy might tell him about Tulio, having doubts about what Tulio
wanted or else looking for a payday from Harris.

He had no choice but to stay here, to wait. To wait and hope that

Marian wasn't with him when Harris came home. Because Tulio only had one option, and he knew it.

He would have to kill Paul Harris.

A man like this would have no feelings. Would not know the meaning of fear. He'd be more animal than human. Tulio could take no chances.

What had the ex-cop said to him downstairs? Something about ice water coming to this guy, to get lessons in being cold.

This ruthless, cold-blooded, miserable bastard had seduced Marian just to find out where Tulio's investigation was heading. If for no other reason, he would have to die for that.

All Tulio could do was wait for him. With his back turned to the panoramic view. Because there was no doubt in his mind that if Harris got even the ghost of a chance he would kill Tulio as quickly and as ruthlessly as he'd killed Carole Conners and God knew how many others.

Tulio pulled his pistol, walked out of the room, leaving the door open. He walked over to the picture of Marian, took it off the wall, placed his pistol down on the glass end table, and smashed the picture frame, pulled the canvas from it, and had to bite into it to get it to rip. He tore it into tiny pieces, until there wasn't one recognizable shred of the painting left. Tulio picked up the pistol and walked back into the computer room, sat down, and began to scroll through it. They'd all be in there somewhere, all of Tulio's special victims.

He sensed something different in the room, felt the *air* move somewhere behind him. Gun in hand, Tulio leaped from the chair, spun, and felt an incredible red flash of pain as his wrist snapped before he even saw the man standing there in front of him. The gun flew out of his shattered hand, Tulio in pain so intense that it sapped all his strength. He fell to the floor, stifling a scream. He rolled over, testing his arm. The wrist was broken. Where was the man? Where was the gun? There it was, leaning against the wall. Tulio used his left arm and his legs, began crawling toward his weapon.

A pair of leather-shod feet stepped in front of him. He saw one rise, saw it come down on his shattered wrist. He screamed. Tulio buried his head in the carpet and retched, then he felt his head lifted up by the hair. He looked up, saw the skinny guy glaring at him, and knew that he was meeting Paul Harris. He knew, too, that he was about to die at Harris's hand.

"You're in my *house?!*" The man hissed at him like a snake. "*In my house?! How dare you, how fucking* dare *you enter here!*"

The sweat was pouring down Tulio's face, he felt it stinging his eyes. From a distance of a few inches, Harris spat into his face. He jerked Tulio's head further back. Tulio was in agony. Harris rose, dragging Tulio out of the room by his hair, like a caveman with a conquest.

How could he be so strong? What had Harris used to disarm him? Tulio hadn't seen a weapon; the man had to be some sort of karate freak. Consciousness tried to fade, his body trying to ease his torment. Tulio bit his tongue hard so he could stay awake. The man might think he was totally out of it and leave him an opening, one chance for Tulio to kick him in his balls or get at the gun.

Tulio felt his toes bang the threshold, felt himself being dropped to the floor, felt the blessed relief when Harris released his hair. There was blood flowing down into his face now, burning his eyes. Harris had pulled out entire chunks of his hair. Harris's hand strength would have to be inhuman. Where was he? Tulio tried to rise. He managed to only get to his knees before he heard a door slam hard, felt something smash into the side of his head. He fell face forward onto the carpet. He opened his eyes, saw the man's legs in front of him again.

It would do no good to beg. To a man like this, begging would have all the effect of chalk on a board. Dusted off easily, leaving no impression. Tulio worked his mouth, felt it slapped shut.

"You don't say a word unless I tell you to." There was still anger in the man's voice, but Tulio could tell that he was trying to control himself. This man would pride himself on never losing his temper. Anger was a sign of weakness, and weakness would be less desirable to him than small-cell stomach cancer. Could he use this against him? Tulio didn't know how he could. He was so weak, so weak . . .

"She told you, didn't she."

See? The man was calm. Speaking as if he were in his country club with his cronies.

"Wh—who—" Tulio managed. He was dizzy and incredibly weak, the pain in his arm intense.

"Oh, you know who." There was a crazed irony in his voice, a deep and stunning disappointment.

Tulio's head was lifted again by the hair. Harris held Tulio's head in one hand, had Tulio's gun held loosely in the other. He tapped Tulio on the wrist with the piece, and Tulio screamed.

"That's a symphony to me, do you understand?"

"Stop. *Please!*"

Harris's smile grew broader. He was relaxed, calm, curious. A child discovering ants.

"I saw you on television, heard you question my manhood. Would you like to question it now?" Harris shook his head, winked at Tulio, man to man. "Ask Marian about my virility; she didn't leave you for nothing."

"Fuck—you—" It was hard to speak. Hard even to breathe. When he did, Tulio could smell himself; vomit, sweat, fear.

Harris made a slight gesture with the gun toward Tulio's wrist, and Tulio tried to pull away, then gasped in agony as bone fragments rubbed against each other.

Harris laughed. "See? See how puny you are?"

Tulio opened his eyes, saw Harris's laughing face. The pain in his wrist was nearly offset by the pain in the top of his head. He couldn't help himself. He simply couldn't stop himself.

He begged.

"Please . . . "

"I love it when they beg." Harris was dryly joking. He made a face, mocked Tulio in a terrifying voice.

"Please! Please!" Then he smiled again, the life of the party. Tulio began to shiver, felt his bladder weaken.

"Look what you're doing to my rug. My God, blood, vomit, now piss." He laughed. "I'll have to clean it up myself, the maid would get suspicious." Then his voice lost its humor. "I'll have Marian lick it up. Maybe I'll hold her upside down and use her hair as my mop."

"Told—"

"What, what's that? Speak up, Tony, I can't understand you. Don't be shy, you can even scream; this place is virtually bombproof, your squad couldn't hear you if they were standing outside the door."

"Are. Squad—knows about you."

"I doubt it, or they'd be here. I'll bet you didn't tell anyone about me, did you? Not Tony Tulio. Not the lone wolf."

The top of his head was on fire, the blood no longer dripping, now it was literally pouring down into his eyes. There was sudden pressure then great pain in his mouth, and Tulio realized that Harris had slapped him in the teeth with his gun. He swallowed blood. He swallowed teeth.

"Did you see your file on the computer? It's in there, several pages' worth. I know all about you, Tony. Everything there is to know. I know about your wife, too. I wish she hadn't died. It would have been a lot more fun for me, fucking her, with you away at work trying to see if I existed. I might have taken a shot at your daughter, too, or maybe the both of them together. Word was, she fucked around, your wife. Martina, wasn't it? And Jessica. Car crash, wasn't it? Or maybe something else . . . ?"

Tulio made a feeble attempt to bite at Harris. Harris released his grip on Tulio's hair, and Tulio's face smashed down into the carpet.

"You're going to die, you know."

In Tulio's mind, there was no doubt.

"The only question is, do you die fast, or do I amuse myself with you? I can put you in the tub and skin you alive, keep you alert and awake while I do it. We could wait for Marian to come by. She loves me, you know. I could tear your eyelids off and make you watch while I skin her. You'd be amazed at what I know about the human anatomy. I studied it very closely, for years. Part of my training as a boxer and an art connoisseur. It's a truly fascinating subject."

He grabbed Tulio's hair again, lifted him up until they were face to face.

"Open your eyes, Tony. Come on, I can't trust a man who doesn't look me in the eye when we're talking. That's better. Now, Tony, I'm going to leave it up to you. I'm a man of my word, too, remember that before you open your mouth. Tell me the truth, and you'll both die fast and easy. Lie, and dying takes hours. Maybe even days. Lie, and we wait for Marian, and I'll bite her to death, bit by bit, while you watch. Tony, pay attention, this is important. Do you believe what I just said?"

"Yuh—"

"Good. I have only have four questions for you. Easy enough, right? You don't even have to try to speak until the last two. Most of your front teeth are missing, it won't be easy for you to speak. Oh, and your tongue's cut to ribbons, too, I don't know if you can feel it. When you try to speak, it'll burn. If I suspect you're lying, I'll pour pepper on it to loosen it. Just blink once for yes, twice for no, all right?"

Through the numbness, Tulio recognized the devil himself there, looking at him through the eyes of Paul Harris.

Tulio blinked his eyes once, obedient and anxious to please.

"Okay. Did Marian know all along? Did she set me up?"

Tulio blinked twice.

"I'm not sure I believe you. Who else knows about me, did you tell anyone else, anyone at all?"

Two blinks, rapidly.

"You sure?" Harris teased him, and Tulio blinked once, vehemently. Harris laughed.

"How did you get into my apartment? How did you get up in a private elevator?"

Tulio tried to speak, fragments of words coming out of his mouth along with parts of his teeth.

"—ahd—"

"What? I can't understand what you're saying."

"'ecutey ahd—" This was tough, but he had to somehow make the man understand him. "*ecutey* ahd, owntair—"

"Security guard! Is that what you're trying to say? You expect me to believe that?"

Tulio blinked once.

"Here's the kicker, Tony. The sixty-four-thousand-dollar question. Think carefully before you speak, this will truly decide your fate: How did you find me?"

Tulio was relieved. This was not a trick question. It hurt to talk, but he had to make the devil understand that it had been easy.

He spoke very slowly. "I—ense p—ate."

"My *license* plate?"

Tulio blinked once.

"Off the Jaguar?"

Once again.

"If you're telling the truth, it shows you what happens when you're a gentleman." He stopped laughing and patted Tulio on the head, as he would a dog who'd brought him his slippers.

"That's good, Tony, you did fine. Now, I have something to take care of. And you're coming with me to help. But I have to change my clothes and get ready first, all right?"

Tulio blinked once.

"By the way, I saw what you did to my Vermeer, Tony. The painting of Marian." Harris paused, and when he spoke, he was angry again. "That *was* a Vermeer, Tony. That was also a painting of Marian. It was over three hundred years old. Just so you know, Tony, and listen very closely; I want you to take this to your grave. She's going to die hard and slow, Tony. So hard. So slow. What you did to that painting? It's passionate love compared to what I'm going to do to that cow."

Tulio tried to scream as he saw the gun barrel coming toward his head, but there was no time, Harris moved too fast, and Tulio was immediately swept into a world of blessed, painless night.

CHAPTER

34

Lᴇɴɴʏ ʜᴀᴅ ᴋɴᴏᴡɴ ᴛʜᴀᴛ ᴛʜᴇʏ'ᴅ ʙᴇ ᴀꜰᴛᴇʀ ʜɪᴍ ɪɴ ᴀ ʜᴜʀʀʏ, ѕᴏ ʜᴇ'ᴅ stopped at his apartment only long enough to grab one thing, which he now carried under his arm, wrapped in a paper grocery bag that he'd gotten from the Jewel. He'd had to dump his garbage out of it.

He'd called Harris three times in less than two hours. Had, at last, reached him. And what did the man want to do? Meet outside the police station. *That* was smart of him.

Harris was slipping. He had treated Lenny like shit, too, while he was at it. After all that Lenny was going through for the son of a bitch. Harris was losing it. Lenny had seen such behavior before in men who had risen so high they'd forgotten that there was even a down. They would start to make mistakes, and before you knew it, they'd be in a federal penitentiary, three levels below the ground and wondering where they'd gone wrong. Harris was starting to get like that, starting to think that he was God.

Not a very pleasant conclusion for Lenny to reach, especially when he needed Harris more than he ever had. Needed that quick mind to find him a way out of the mess he was in. The mess *they* were in. It wasn't Lenny alone. Harris was in the shit, too. The Eagle needed his blood to calm down Mr. Alleo. Lenny knew that Mr. Alleo would take a life today, somebody's, anybody's, whoever was involved with the deal would be all right with Mr. Alleo.

Lenny shivered at the thought. He'd hold Harris up for some money so he could escape the city, and warn him to lay low. Nobody knew who the Collector was except Lenny, and Lenny wasn't talking. If Harris did what Lenny told him to do, he'd wind up being all right.

But Lenny wouldn't be, not ever again. He'd been on national television a great many times in his career; there was no place for him to hide where he wouldn't risk being recognized. He'd spend the rest of his life looking over his shoulder, wondering if some stud who'd just glanced at him had made him. Every faggot who looked at him a little too long would be a source of suspicion.

He could shave his head and grow a beard, but even then he'd have to change twenty-year lifestyle patterns. He could never even go to a race track again, let alone think about vacationing in Atlantic City or Vegas. Undercover card games, dice games, they were out. Lenny knew that for the rest of his entire life he was through with any type of action. The thought broke his heart.

But he'd stood up, that was what counted. When you stood up, there was often a price to pay. Lenny's would be living a life that would be in many ways worse than death.

He'd have to get a straight-John job, couldn't even be a hustler or even the lowest kind of thief. He could not afford to ever get pinched again, cause when they pinched you they ran your prints as part of the deal, and someone, somewhere, would recognize him, would know who he was and who it was that was looking for him. A corrupt copper could make one phone call, and bang, that would be it for Lenny.

He knew there would be no more chances for him with the mob. If they caught up with him, he was dead, and they wouldn't take him out fast.

He knew what the Eagle would do to him, too, knew that it would not be pleasant. Gerardi and his boys would do the work, but the Eagle would be a part of it. Would be right there cheering them on, giving them pointers from the old days on how to make Lenny's death more painful. That old wrinkled-up, half-dead, eagle-beaked prick, he'd have the old Sicilian potions sitting on shelves in his kitchen, the poisons to rub into Lenny's wounds and make them burn and fester.

See what happened when you stood up for people? It cost you. And now Lenny had no choice, it would have to cost Harris, too. There was a price to loyalty, and Harris would have to come up with the bucks. Lenny had signed his own death warrant in order to protect the guy, Harris owed him for that, and Harris would just have to come across, one way or another. Knowing the guy the way Lenny did, he thought that Harris might even understand.

If Harris freaked out, Lenny decided, he would shoot him. Not to kill, just in the leg or arm, enough of a wound to get the guy's total and complete attention. Then he'd persuade Harris to give up the number to the hidden office safe. Lenny knew about that all right, even though Harris probably thought he didn't. Lenny would take what was in there, take Harris's van, and split.

There was no way that Lenny could lose. He couldn't afford to. One way or another, before the afternoon was over, he'd be scoring big off Harris.

Lenny looked closely at every van that passed, peered through the driver's window but Harris was never behind the wheel. He watched as a guy in a rusted-out piece of shit van stared back at him, and started to pull to the curb. Lenny quickly looked away, avoided the man's eyes. He did not need any trouble this morning, would let the guy stare at him.

He looked over at the van out of the corner of his eye. Shit, the guy was rolling down the window.

"Lenny, come on!" He heard the voice come from the van and did a double take, looked closely. The guy resembled Harris a little.

"Lenny, it's Paul, what the fuck are you waiting for?"

Lenny walked slowly, cautiously toward the van. The driver was the right size, had the same build, but the face was somehow different, in a strange, subtle way. This guy was wearing aviator glasses that didn't have a tint to them. It was almost scary. The driver didn't look much like Paul, but the guy, he had Paul's voice.

"Lenny, get *in*." It was Paul all right. Talking down to Lenny, as usual. Well, screw him.

Lenny got into the van, biting down his resentment. He couldn't afford the luxury of anger right now. There were other things that had to be discussed, serious matters that could get them both killed if they played the wrong card. Paul pulled away from the curb, and Lenny snapped on his seat belt, wanting to avoid any bullshit small-time pinch from some overzealous rookie traffic cop. Did this van stink, or what? What did Harris do, shit in his pants while he was stealing it? He looked around, trying to find the source of the smell, as he began to question Paul.

"What the hell you got on, makeup? I didn't even know it was—*Jesus!*"

There was a guy in the back of the van, a battered pulp lying there, blood bubbles forming on his lips each time he breathed.

"Who the fuck is that?"

"Tulio." Harris was speaking calmly enough, as if it were an everyday occurrence to have a bloody, beaten copper in the back seat of your vehicle.

"Paul, hey, Paul, this shit is getting too heavy for me, man."

"You're in it, Lenny, both of us are in it all the way."

"Paul, you don't know what's happening, what I went through last night. I got the Eagle's people after me, and Alleo's, by now. I can't have the law after me too, I'll never make it out of town."

"What did you tell them?"

"Who?"

"Did you set me up for them, Lenny?"

"Goddamnit, you know better than that." This guy was pissing him off. "They were gonna torture your name outta me, Paul. I pulled a gun on them to get away."

"Sure you did. You never carry guns."

Lenny pulled his pistol and stuck it right under Harris's nose.

"This look like a chocolate bar to you, motherfucker?" He stuck the gun down his waistband in front. Lenny kept his hand close to it, in case he had to get at it in a hurry.

"Look, I don't need all of this bullshit. I got five thousand guys want to shoot me on sight, the Eagle wants to cut off my balls, feed them to me one at a time, and you're gonna sit there and question my honesty with a dying cop laying in the back of the car? Fuck this, let me out."

"Calm down, Lenny."

"Fuck you, too, Harris. This shit ain't funny. I almost got killed for you."

"All right, all right. I'm sorry I questioned your loyalty."

"You fucking well better be."

Lenny was still angry, but he felt himself calming down. Harris had been braced by this cop or something, Lenny didn't know what had happened. It was normal for him to be anxious, worried. He was used to doing what he did under severely controlled situations.

Besides, Harris had money, and right now Lenny needed some of it.

He said, "Alleo's kid died under the knife," and looked over to see Harris's reaction. He didn't even blink. "He wants you, Paul."

Funny. The guy didn't seem at all concerned. He just sat there with one arm hanging out his window, the hot breeze from the open window messing up his hair.

"Lenny, you have to listen carefully. This is more important even than Alleo's kid. You owe people, you're into bookies and loansharks and you deal with hookers. I'm not questioning your courage, your integrity, your loyalty or your character, I just need you to think very carefully.

"In all the time we've worked together, Lenny, have you told *anyone* my name? Not even to brag, but just in passing, shooting the shit in the bar or at some card game, telling your buddies about the art dealer you're friends with?"

This guy was even more paranoid than Lenny. "Paul, I swear before God, I never told *any*one about you. The guys I run with? Shit. They'd come to you in a minute, tell you to blow me off and use them instead. Want to get in on the gravy train themselves. I never said your name to anyone, ever."

"I believe you," Harris said, and Lenny got resentful all over again.

"Well thank you all to fuckin' hell."

"Don't be that way, Lenny, you're so ugly when you're angry."

The son of a bitch, was he cold, or what? There was a cop back there who was obviously dying, the mob wanted them dead, cops were zipping down the street in squad cars every few yards, and here was this guy, making his voice sound like a fag while he made cute jokes.

Lenny said, "No offense, Paul, but I ain't a part of this thing with the cop. I just wanted to warn you, let you know what was going on. And then I want some money, I gotta get out of town, and you have to help me out."

"You offering to sell me your loyalty?"

"Now you're way out of line, Paul, there ain't no call to talk to me like that. I could'a give you up last night and gotten paid for it, and I kept my mouth shut, so don't lay that shit on me."

"Sorry."

He said it lightly, as if he wasn't really sorry at all. Lenny thought about pulling the piece and shoving it into Harris's throat, but he didn't. It was broad daylight, there were cars everywhere, pedestrians walking across the streets, cops, it seemed, everywhere. He'd wait. Get the money, *then* shoot the prick.

"How much do you think you need?"

"Gimme a number, Paul, you tell me: How much you think your life is worth?"

"My life?" There he went again, acting cute. Like he was in some fancy college discussing *theories*. "*My* life? Millions, at least."

Lenny said, "Well, I ain't gonna need that much. I'm lettin' you off the hook real cheap."

Two could play that cute game. Lenny saw Harris look over at him, the man's face blank. Lenny said, "I figure a hundred grand. That ought'a about do it."

"The Eagle gave me a quarter million last night, to perform the acquisition. Half of it's yours. I see how you could have that coming, particularly as I didn't perform my work properly; the girl, after all, died."

"Really?" Lenny couldn't hide his glee. "That's great, Paul, thanks. I appreciate it."

"But you have to help me with this problem."

"Which problem is that?"

"Tulio. You have to help me take care of Tulio."

Lenny had wanted fifty grand, so he'd said a hundred, planning to negotiate. Paul had given right in, though, had even upped the ante to a hundred and a quarter. The way Lenny saw the deal, he was getting an extra seventy-five, just to help dump a body. Paul was no dummy, either. He'd only fucked up this one time. He would know what to do with this Tulio guy, do it and get away clean. Paul had too much going for him in the city to ever make the kind of mistakes that Lenny seemed to make as easily as he walked and breathed.

Besides, what did he have to lose? Even if Paul brought the whole department down on his head, he wouldn't give up Lenny. Loyalty was a two-way street. And Lenny himself would be long gone.

He said, "That ain't a problem, that's a pleasure." He sat back in the van, decided to fuck with Paul a little bit.

He said, "Tulio. I know this copper pretty good. He's the guy keeps going on TV and shit, calling you a fag in front of God and everybody." Lenny smiled inside. See? He could dish it out, too.

But Paul didn't think it was very funny. When he spoke his voice was frigid. It made Lenny sorry he'd brought the subject up.

"Yes. That's him. What's left of him, Lenny."

"Where we taking the guy?"

"Home, Lenny. We're taking our friend Tony here home."

Lenny sat back after that and kept his mouth shut. There was no figuring this guy out, no sense in even trying. He had to save his strength, had to think this through. Because right now he was stuck with a hard question, one that until this moment he never thought he'd have to ask himself: After he got the money from this madman, should he leave him alone or should he kill him?

C H A P T E R
35

TULIO LIVED IN A TWO-STORY SHINGLE-SIDED HOUSE THAT WAS JUST a couple of blocks away from the new ballpark. That wasn't good news for Harris. It was an older house, and Harris knew from Marian that Tulio had grown up there, had inherited the place after his parents died. The neighbors would all know him, would be longtime friends, sucking up to the cop down the block who could get them out of traffic tickets, get their kids out of childhood brushes with the law.

Harris had no choice but to do it the way he'd planned. He couldn't see any other way to get this wrapped up in a pretty little ribbon. With Lenny playing the part of the ribbon. He had to plan every detail, and do it on the fly. There could be no repercussions; this could never be allowed to come back to haunt Harris. He knew what happened when a cop was killed in this city. He couldn't let an investigation even get off the ground, so he'd stop it before it began, make Tulio's death an airtight, open-and-shut investigation.

He'd leave Tulio at his own house, with Lenny dead beside him. Stupid, pathetic little Lenny, who thought that loyalty would be more important to Harris than an alibi.

If he could get in and out, without any witnesses seeing or hearing him, he'd be home free.

Unless either of these dead men in the van with him had lied.

That thought terrified him, because he knew that was always a possibility. The two of them had spent their lives being masters of deception. Lenny lied as easily as most people breathed, and Tulio, by the nature of his work, would be well-practiced at the art of deception.

If either of them had lied, though, it spelled the end of the road for Harris. If Lenny was being dishonest, Harris would be dead before the moon rose in the sky. And he couldn't question Lenny any further than he already had, he had to leave the man alone and let him think that he was safe. Lenny was out of shape, but he still knew how to hit, and he had a pistol sticking out of the waistband of his pants that he wouldn't be afraid to use if he felt that he absolutely had to.

As for the cop, if he had indeed been lying, if Marian had been working undercover for him, then the law would be on to him as soon as they found Tulio's corpse. It was almost inconceivable to him that Marian could be that good an actress.

But it wasn't a risk he was willing to take with his life.

He wondered about that, wondered how he felt. He took a quick inventory, scanned his emotions.

Harris only felt a professional sense of sorrow over the death of the Alleo girl. And for the arrogant manner in which he had underestimated and misjudged Alleo. The man was deeper than Harris had given him credit for being; he'd had Harris totally fooled. "Then come here. I'll give you what I promised. I'll stick to my end of the bargain," the man had said.

He hadn't been lying. He'd warned Harris in advance as to what the price of his failure would be. Harris could have learned much from the man, but now it was too late.

It was too late for a lot of things.

Harris kept his face straight, his breathing slow and regular, but inside he was nowhere near as calm as he pretended. He was used to thinking things out far in advance, knowing every move he would make, allowing for every single possible mischance and mistake, any action of his victims, or, later, of their families. Now, he felt like a cowboy. No longer a chess master, Harris was now playing checkers.

Last night it had been fun, seeking out the Carole Conners acquisition without a detailed plan. It was a once-in-a-lifetime thrill, with a pot of gold waiting for him if he were able to pull it off. It had been a challenge, but he no longer felt challenged.

What he felt was hunted.

It was another new and unpleasant sensation for him. No matter what happened this afternoon, how successfully it went, he would always wonder, have his doubts. Were they planning, plotting against him? He would tear this apart in his mind a thousand, a million times, go over every detail and remember the mistakes he'd made. They would glare at him, haunt him. Maybe someday, if he were lucky, they'd go away and leave him alone. But Harris didn't think so; it wasn't the way his mind worked.

He'd have a whole new set of nightmares to contend with.

Harris circled the block a couple of times, to make sure there were no police cars out cruising the area. He would do what had to be done here and now, and then there would be only two more slender pieces of thread that would need to be tied together before he could once again rest easy.

Number one: Marian. The irony of the situation was not lost on him. If the cop hadn't been lying, then his predicament was indeed all his own fault. If he'd never seduced Marian, to discover the depth of Tulio's investigation into one of Harris's killings, then Tulio would not have been at his house that morning. He'd said he'd taken Harris's license plate number from the Jag, Tulio had admitted that. Harris's own overzealous precautions had almost been his downfall. If Tulio hadn't been so preoccupied with the computer screen he might have turned in time to see Harris, might have been able to shoot him.

It was that, or she was working with Tulio. Had led Harris on from the beginning. He wouldn't put it past her, cursed himself for ever believing that he could fit in with normal society.

Who did he think he was? What did he think he was? He had no fucking *right* pretending he was a normal man, that option had been taken away from him when he'd been just a child.

It was really something, the way things sometimes worked out. The fates had always been kind to Harris, who was unused to relying on any power greater than himself. But now they seemed to be turning on him. Because he'd weakened, because he'd tried to love somebody.

It wasn't a mistake he would ever make again.

He thought about the second thread, the one that was truly unraveling.

The security man who'd let Tulio into his apartment. The guard was someone who could be left dead in an alley somewhere on the South or West Sides. Harris hoped that he hadn't told anyone about Tulio. Harris knew that he would have to ask the man in detail exactly whom he had spoken with. The guard would not be allowed the blessing of a quick and painless death.

And no cops would come to question him. Harris lived in the most exclusive building in the entire city; the death of a security guard–door-man would not be tied to its tenants, especially if the corpse was found miles away from the building, with his pockets turned inside out and his watch torn from his wrist. It would be just another junkie murder, done to get enough money to catch a high.

All right. Enough was enough. He had to get this over with and get on with everything else.

Harris pulled the van into Tulio's driveway, got out, and, without look-ing either way, casually used Tulio's keys to unlock the door to the garage. He stepped in, hit the button, and the garage door began to open. He waited for it to rise, walked out of the garage, still not looking either way, then he got back into the van. Harris pulled into the garage, got out and closed the door. The garage was attached. He would draw no more ex-posure until he left.

He opened the back door of the van, told Lenny to come and help him. Lenny came around and started to lift Tulio out of the van, as Har-ris, using the keys, unlocked the connecting door. He tossed the keys to Lenny, told him to make sure that he put them back in Tulio's right front pocket.

Harris stepped into the house, flipped on the kitchen light. Good. Just as he'd expected, the house was stifling hot. Tulio would not turn on the air conditioner unless he was home. And he was going to catch Harris? No one who thought and lived on such a scale would ever have a hope of pulling a stunt of that magnitude off, not without a lot of help. Harris knew that he was brilliant. Too smart for any of them. The thought of his superiority made Harris, inwardly, smile.

"Right in here, just lay him down on the floor, as if he fell there."

Lenny was puffing hard, out of shape and feeling it. He looked up at Harris angrily.

"Thanks for all your fuckin' help, Paul."

"You're doing just fine on your own. That's it, just leave him right there."

Lenny dropped Tulio and turned to close the door, turned back, and froze. Harris knew that something was wrong, was about to turn and look, then felt what could only be a pistol barrel shoved roughly into the back of his neck.

"All right, you skinny, no-ass, four-eyed motherfucker, don't you move one inch." The voice was low and filled with hate, without even a hint of fear; whoever he was, this man had done this sort of thing before.

"You!" the voice shouted, and Lenny raised his hands high in the air. "Stop right there, lardass. Look at you. Mutt and Jeff." Then, "Hey, I know you, you're that fuckin' Lenny, Lenny Roman—oh, shit. Oh, goddamn."

The man was indecisive, now he sounded afraid. The gun was abruptly taken away from the back of Harris's neck.

Harris took a shot in the dark, said, "That's better. Now, Officer, do you know who we are?"

"I think I know who sent you."

"And you're not here to arrest us, are you?"

"No, no. But, shit, couldn't Alleo wait?"

Alleo. Lenny flinched when he heard the name. He was looking at the man behind Harris with what could only be called a hangdog expression. The two of them knew each other. Then Harris got it. The cop knew that Lenny was connected to the mob.

Harris said, "Mr. Alleo, Officer, if you're going to say his name. And if you know who he is, then you know what we're doing here, don't you."

"You can turn around if you want," the cop said. He became contrite. "I didn't know who you were, I been in here all day, waiting for Tulio to come home."

Harris turned and looked at the man, wondering how he had the nerve to call Lenny fat. He was definitely frightened, and he thought that Lenny and Harris worked for Alleo. Which was fine. But what the hell was he doing here? And what could he be thinking, putting his gun away like that?

"Listen," the fat cop said, "I know I got no right to ask, but you got to help me out here, fellas. You got to make things right for me with the Man. I was here, doing what the Man told me to do. I been waiting here for Tulio, I wasn't disobeying orders. If I'd'a known where he was, I'd'a taken care of him the same way you did." He looked down at Tulio. "Ain't he dead?"

"Not yet."

The fat cop quickly pulled his weapon, pointed it at Tulio and fired, once. The top of Tulio's head exploded against the far wall of the kitchen. Lenny jumped, shouted something. Harris just stood there watching the man, half-smiling. He heard Lenny behind him, sucking in his breath. Harris put his hands into the deep wide pockets of his jumpsuit. He shook his head as if in wonder, smiling at the cop.

"Beautiful."

The cop put his gun away, again looked over at Harris.

"Hey, no offense, but I got a vested interest here. I was told to do this a long time ago. Mr. A was pissed, too."

Harris pulled the trigger of the gun in his pocket and shot the fat cop through his heart, the force tearing the pocket out of his jumpsuit, causing the pantleg to start on fire. He patted at it with his free hand, had it out before the fat cop's body was through rolling around on the kitchen tile.

Lenny said, "Jesus, oh Jesus, oh dear Jesus Christ . . . " in a shaky voice, hyperventilating. Harris heard a chair scrape back, heard Lenny's fat ass plop down in it. "Oh, dear sweet fucking Jesus Christ," he heard Lenny say.

The fire was out, but smoke still rose from the pantleg. There was nothing Harris could do about it; he wasn't about to douse it with water from the faucet. He hadn't touched anything in this house yet. Only Lenny had. Lenny and the dead fat cop.

Harris looked over at Lenny. So far, things couldn't be going any better.

He smiled at Lenny, said, "Well."

Lenny looked up, shaking his head in disbelief. He held his hands out to Harris, in some ancient, foolish gesture of Italian supplication.

"Do you know who that *was?*" Lenny said.

"Friend of yours?"

"That was fucking Jerry *Moore,* for Christ's sake. He's locked into the mob even worse than I am. Does their drug pickups, the dirty work. The guy's maybe the richest cop on the entire department, and you just killed his ass. Jesus Christ, Paul, did you just fuck up."

"Say hello to him for me."

"What?"

"When you get to hell."

Lenny understood what was happening a second too late. He leaped to his feet, reaching for his waistband, and Harris shot him, wasting only one bullet because he wanted to hold back on the noise. The bullet went through Lenny's chest; a fine spray of red mist shot out of his back, settled slowly onto Lenny's corpse.

Harris quickly wiped down the weapon, went over and shoved it into Tulio's hand. He dropped the hand and kicked the gun a few feet from the body. The hero cop would have fired his last shot at the same moment that a bullet from the rogue cop's gun had entered his own brain and killed him. Good scenario. It would make Tulio a dead legend within his clan. See how they'd beaten him? He'd been tortured, but he'd still had the balls to get his hands on his gun and kill them both.

Lenny Roman was thrown in for good measure. The entire police department knew that Lenny had a longtime history of sufferance to the mob. His death would only sweeten the pot, serve to further intrigue the cops and reporters and lead them away from Harris.

Harris went into the garage, hit the button to raise the door, backed the van slowly out of the garage and into Tulio's driveway. He got out, closed the garage door, relocked it, then got back into the van, backed it out into the street, and drove slowly away from the scene.

There was no one out on Tulio's street; it was too hot for anyone in their right mind to be outside. The thick old walls of Tulio's house would have absorbed most of the noise, and what had escaped would have been further muffled by the walls of the neighbors' houses. Their air conditioners would have covered any sound that had gotten through. He saw no curtains pulled back, no curious faces peeking out at him.

The fates were now being kind to him, and he hoped that they'd forgive him his earlier, temporary loss of strength. Because he'd be needing them again, with all their power, before the day was done.

He'd decided that he didn't trust his building's security guard to keep his mouth shut for long. The guard wouldn't say anything to the other workers in the building; he would be shrewd enough to know that one of them would smile and nod, then rat him out to Harris for a chance at a twenty-dollar bill.

But he would talk, later, at home or in some bar. Feel the need to brag about what he'd done and what he knew. So Harris would have to wait for the man to get off work.

After that, his only unfinished business would be something called Marian Hannerty, and he knew that it was in love with him. It would pose no real problem. He just had to do what had to be done in a way where its death would not even be investigated, and he knew just how to do that. It would have to commit suicide.

His mind made up, Harris drove slowly and carefully away from the neighborhood. He stopped at a light while it was still turning yellow, looked at the shopping bag that Lenny had left in the van. He pulled it toward him, looked inside.

There was an old picture in there, with tiny holes in the top from being pinned to various walls. The picture was of a bunch of middle-aged men, seated at a table with drinks in front of them, trying to look tough for the camera. In a bar somewhere in Las Vegas.

Harris would dispose of it at the first garbage can that he passed. The last tie that bound him to Lenny Roman, to be picked up at dawn and taken to a landfill.

CHAPTER
36

Jake Phillips sat stunned, dizzy and uncomprehending, out-side of Captain Royal's office, while the brass inside made decisions that didn't involve him in any way. He'd been awakened and brought in, ques-tioned at length about his whereabouts before leaving the building that morning, what Tulio had said to him, the way the man had acted. They'd made sure up front that he knew how much weight his answers carried, told him that except for the killer, he was probably the last person to have seen Tulio alive.

They didn't know for sure how long Tulio had been inside his house. With Moore. And some guy who used to be some kind of fighter. Jake certainly hadn't been able to shed much light on the subject for them. At least he had been able to tell them the approximate time that Tulio had left the headquarters building.

At first they'd treated Phillips almost as a suspect, but they'd backed off that right away, there was no way he'd killed Tulio and Moore. Even if he'd been tempted to kill his ex-partner, he wouldn't have killed Tulio as well, there'd have been no reason for that. Or the fighter. He hadn't even known who the guy was until they'd told him.

So now he sat, feeling useless and abandoned, on the hard wooden bench across the hall from the captain's door. From time to time one of the guys from the squad would come over and ask him a question, and he would tell them that they'd have to ask the captain, he didn't know shit. Except that his career as a Homicide bull was now sadly, but un-doubtedly, over.

Still, he didn't regret being short with the bulls. Jake didn't have the time for speculation or gossip, hadn't yet learned that these were two of a homicide investigator's most valuable assets. So he sat, staring straight ahead, exposed, naked, wondering if they'd forgotten about him. He was starting to work up a pretty good resentment when Tulio's girlfriend stepped out of the elevator.

Marian saw the young man sitting there and couldn't remember his name, even though she remembered meeting him briefly, just last night. He was Moore's partner. Jerry Moore. She remembered that much only because Jerry Moore was such a pig, and she figured that anyone who hung out with him had to be cut from the same pig mold.

But the kid was respectful, didn't eye her up and down, rather he stood and put out his hand, as he mumbled some sort of apology. She shook his hand, looking at him quizzically, then suddenly she got it, and felt her knees go weak.

Tony must have committed suicide. What else could this kid be so sorry about? Phillips! That was his name. With a biblical first name; Moses, Aaron, Adam? Jacob! Jake, they'd called him. Short for Jack, though, rather then Jacob. Somebody had told her last night when she'd met him that his father had once been a pretty heavy hitter.

"Jake?" Marian tried to smile, worried about the look on his face. "Jake, the captain called my boss, demanded I get over here right away." She paused, not really wanting an answer, before she said, "What's going on?"

She saw the kid's face fall, saw his disappointment over the fact that she hadn't been informed. He was upset because he was going to have to be the one to break the news to her.

"Is he—dead?" Marian was determined not to make a scene. She would not cry, no matter what.

Until she saw the tears in Jake's eyes. That somehow gave her permission. As soon as he nodded his head, she felt the tears start to flow. But she still managed to cut them off though, when the door to the captain's office came flying open . . .

Three hours later Marian was in her apartment, and she did not recognize the number on her beeper, although she suspected she knew who was calling. The beeper went off again as she walked out of her apartment, and she ignored it; she wanted to be alone for just a little while longer. She walked in a trance down to Racine, turned left and kept walking. The beeper went off again. The thing was starting to get on her nerves.

Marian returned the call from a pay phone on the corner, punched in the unfamiliar number, and she recognized his voice the second he picked up the phone.

"Paul? Thank God it was you trying to reach me. I've been trying to call you at home and at the gallery for almost an hour."

"Marian?" He sounded concerned. "Marian, what's wrong? Darling, you sound terrible." Then the worry turned to anger. "Did he bother you? Did Tulio come to court?"

"I only wish he had." Marian paused, took a deep breath, then said, "He's dead."

"Who? Marian, *who's* dead!"

"Tony. He was killed sometime after he left my apartment this morning. They don't know what time for sure, because of the heat—the problem with calculating the decomposition . . . "

"My God!" Paul said.

"I have to see you, Paul. Can you come get me? Please? I don't trust myself to drive."

"Oh, Marian, I'm so sorry. Can you tell me what happened?"

"They're not sure yet, they're still investigating, as far as I know. They spent hours questioning me, I was with them until just a little while ago. They wouldn't tell me anything."

"Where are you now?"

She looked up at the street sign on the corner, then told him. Told him that his car was in a lot, a block away from Police Headquarters. Told him that the attendant had the keys. He said he could cab to his car and be there in twenty minutes, told her he was in a place he kept on the near South Side. They could go there and be alone, where no phones would ring, and they could talk in a place where nothing or no one could bother them. Marian thanked him, hung up the phone, then went to the corner to wait for Paul.

His mind was racing, Harris wondering how much she might have figured out, what she might have told the police. Too many people around him had suddenly disappeared, and a lot of people knew about him and Lenny Roman. Had she told them about their relationship? Had they told her about Lenny being found with the dead cops? My God, the cops, the mob, could he get through this? Could he make it?

Harris was, for the first time in his adult life, totally out of control. He had to fight down the panic. He kept telling himself that panic solved nothing, that using logic and keeping a cool head were the only ways for him to survive.

If they knew about it he would somehow have to bluff his way out of it, and hope that no one made the connection between him and the dead doorman that they'd find pretty soon in an alley on the far South Side.

What they would have to do is deal with his lawyer, because he would tell them nothing. If they came and told him that Marian was dead, he would break down, he would cry, because there were other doormen who could put her with him. But that would be it. He would not allow them to question him without having a lawyer present. With his looks, his reputation, his money, and his gallery, he could turn this into a media circus, get his face on every news show, demanding that his name be cleared.

Harris gripped the steering wheel tightly as he drove toward Racine. He took deep breaths and expelled them through puffed out lips. It was all his fault. All his own fault. Exactly the way his father had always said that it was.

He was nothing but a fucking bastard.

He was a filthy, fucking pervert.

Harris felt a great sadness, a sudden longing for his childhood, a shot at another chance . . .

No!

He wiped at his tears and sniffed hard as he saw her, standing on the corner looking forlorn and shaken. The heat had matted her hair; her silk blouse clung to her, seductively. She looked like a peasant girl who'd been out in the field all morning. Her eyes, her posture, made her seem like a living dead woman. A zombie in Haiti. That's what she looked like. She wouldn't have to carry the angst for very much longer.

"Oh, Paul, I'm so glad to see you." She threw her arms around his neck and kissed his cheek. Harris wiped at his tears with the arm of his sport jacket, shook his head to clear it. He drove away from the corner quickly. The tears would work to his advantage; she would think that they had only fallen because of his pain over her upset.

He said, "Marian, Marian, oh, God, Marian, are you all right?"

"I don't know. I don't know, Paul. I wish I did, but I'm not sure."

"How did it happen? Did they tell you anything?"

"Tell me anything? If I wasn't a judge's daughter, I think they might have read me my rights before they questioned me. They asked me a lot of questions, but they didn't tell me anything. What I know I found out from a new detective, and he didn't even know anything."

"How did he die? Was it suicide?"

"No, I think I told you. He was killed, somebody tortured him, then shot him. They don't know who yet."

"Dear God," Harris said. "This miserable fucking city."

"Twenty-two years he was a cop, Paul. How could someone get away with this? He didn't trust anyone enough to let them into his house. How could it have happened? He told me himself that I was the first person besides himself to step foot into the house since his wife died."

"Marian, God knows what he was into, who he might have been doing business with, or had under investigation."

"He wasn't alone, Paul, there were two other men with him."

"Do you know who?"

"They wouldn't tell me, and the other one, the cop, didn't know. All the captain told me was that he spoke to Tony around seven-fifteen this morning. That would have been an hour or so before he came into my apartment. They were shocked to find that out, they thought he'd been home the entire time. I think it narrowed down the time he was killed for them."

Marian was weeping as she spoke. She wiped at her eyes frequently with the back of her hand. Harris handed her his handkerchief, kept his eyes on the road.

"Did you tell them that you were with me last night? Did you tell them that you weren't with him? They must be aware that you were dating him, dear God, Marian, please tell me that you told them you were with me, what time you left my place. I can vouch for your whereabouts." The concern in his voice was nearly overwhelming.

Marian said, "I didn't mention you. They didn't even ask me where I was last night, they just wanted to know what happened this morning, what Tulio said and did. I told them the truth, that I was getting ready for work when he came into my apartment, and I asked him to leave."

"Marian, you should have told them." There was just the slightest hint of reproach in his voice.

"I couldn't." She shook her head. "I didn't want to complicate it. I didn't want them knowing about us, everyone in there thought that Tony and I were dating. Exclusively."

He pulled the car over to the curb outside a brick building on the near South Side. There was a beauty salon at the corner. Above it was a bright hand-painted sign declaring part of the building to be the headquarters for something called STREETSMART; then in smaller letters, HELPING THE HOMELESS HELP THEMSELVES. A huge painted finger pointed around the corner. Black men and women walked up and down the block, openly eyeing the Jaguar.

The other side of the street was more crowded, with beat-up cars lining the curb. There was a welfare hotel in the middle of the block. Young black children were playing in the street, dodging cars that were going too fast. Young men, some of them with crutches or canes, one of them in a wheelchair, stood or sat around the curb in the afternoon heat, passing around brown paper bags, talking loudly.

Wet cars were pulling into the street out of a carwash driveway at the end of the block; men and women with rags waved at the cars, willing to dry them off for a dollar.

Harris got out of the car.

He walked around to Marian's side, opened the door and held out his hand. She took it, and he pushed the button on his key ring that set the car alarm, led her to what looked like a vacant building, a place with a huge, windowless steel door for an entrance. Harris unlocked it, pushed it open with his shoulder, and led Marian inside. He locked the door behind them.

He led her up a dark staircase. The place smelled musty. The stairway was winding. The building might have once been elegant, a long time ago. Harris stopped on the third floor, felt around in the darkness and screwed in a bulb, and there was soft light that showed what years of neglect can do to tile, to walls that might have been green.

They faced another steel door, a fire door, but it would also keep out thieves. Harris opened it. He locked this door behind them, too. Beyond it was a corridor. He led Marian down the corridor, stopped at a wooden door that was protected by three deadbolts. He opened the door, stepped inside, flipped on a light, and turned toward Marian with just a hint of a smile.

"We can get all the privacy we want in here," he said.

CHAPTER
37

I<small>T WAS A STRANGE ROOM, WITH HARDLY ANY FURNISHINGS. S</small>HE
couldn't tell if it had once been a rented sleeping room, or maybe it had
been an office. There was a toilet without a cover in a small room without a door, over in one corner. A bank of four phones sat on a low table
in the opposite corner, away from the single large, filthy window. Under
the window was an Army cot. Paul's? A previous tenant's, perhaps.

"Aren't you curious about this?" he asked.

There were two chairs in the room. One covered with dirty green vinyl,
the second a chair that had obviously been taken from an ancient kitchen
set. It had a flowery pattern on the seat and back. Four cracked rubber
grommets protected its legs from scratching the wooden floor. Now that
she was in here, Marian dropped her pretense. Let the deadness that she
felt inside come out into her expression, into her tone of voice.

"What is this place, Paul?"

"You know, you're the only person I've ever brought in here who wasn't
kicking and screaming." He flashed that small smile again, as if only
partly kidding. "Not literally, of course. I mean, they came in—reluctantly. You must trust me implicitly."

"Shouldn't I?"

It was a strange question, one he obviously hadn't been expecting.
Harris looked at her, shook his head slightly, walked over to the vinyl-
covered chair and sat down. Marian went to the other chair and sat down
herself, not bothering to brush at the dust that covered the flowery seat.

"You're not afraid?"

There was a tone in his voice, something about it that was bothersome. As if he were being playful. Marian put her purse on her lap, leaned back in the chair and stared at him.

He broke the silence first.

"Who knows about us." His voice was robotic. Nothing human about it. Marian shivered but smiled.

"I'm not sure."

"Be sure, Marian. You *will* tell me, you know, one way or another."

So. He knew, too.

"Those phones, they look like the ones I saw in your office last night," Marian said, and Harris seemed to admire the deft way she'd changed the subject. Stalling for time, as if it mattered.

"This is where those lines originate. I send the signals over there. Five phone lines, counting the one in the apartment, and maybe ten, fifteen people have any of the numbers."

"Does anyone have them all?"

"No one. You would have been the first."

"You were going to give them to me?"

Harris's face twisted suddenly, and he leaned over and grabbed at his stomach like a man who'd been punched hard in the belly. Marian made no move to comfort him. His lips moved, as if he were speaking, though no sound came out.

She waited, watched the herculean effort he made, wondered what it took for him to get himself together. Wondered, too, if the pain was a constant thing in his life. Self-directed pain. Reaching out to no one else unless it was to hurt them. Slowly, he somehow managed to clear his face of the pain. When he straightened up and spoke, it was through clenched teeth, and his voice, always so strong and confident, was now weak and strained.

"I loved you!" It was a low, quiet shout.

Marian did not respond.

She watched the look on his face, knew when he truly, fully understood.

"So you know." There was no strain in his voice now, no weakness there, either, anymore, or evidence of pain. Marian nodded. "I thought as much, when you didn't balk at coming up here. Why did you? Is life so empty, Marian? Or do you think I won't hurt you?" He smiled, broadly.

"That's it, isn't it. You thought that you were so special to me that I wouldn't be able to harm you."

She said, softly and dryly, "You're going to kill me, aren't you, Paul."

Before he could speak a faint banging noise came to them, through the walls of the building, a steady, metronomic pounding from somewhere out on the street. It was nothing, really, just another city noise, but it made him pause and hold up his hand, his face turned, listening, Harris wary and puzzled.

At last he looked toward her again. His face was now blank, giving her nothing. For a moment he didn't blink, and it became almost frightening; he looked like a men's store mannequin.

"How many know?"

"You figure it out."

"You know he's dead. You know I tortured him first. He's dead, and I killed two others and left them with him. And you're going to sit there and try to play games with me now? You can't be that stupid. Or that suicidal."

There was louder banging now, the same steady beating as before, but closer, emanating from somewhere inside the building. Marian saw panic in Paul's eyes, although his face remained expressionless.

"Police."

"That's right."

"You're wired."

"That's right." Now Marian half-smiled. "And you admitted to killing Tony Tulio, you rotten son of a bitch."

He rose and took a step toward her.

Marian kicked the chair away and screamed, "Paul, please, *no!*" at the same time that she pulled her pistol out of her purse and shot Paul Harris in the center of his stomach.

Harris looked at her, in shock and pain. He slowly crumpled to the filthy floor, collapsing in degrees, as if being beaten down by steady blows from a hammer rather than from a single shot from a .38-caliber revolver. He did not want to go down, did not want to show weakness. Maybe he didn't even want to die. The pounding sound came more quickly, the police now outside the third-floor steel door and wanting in, bad. She knew how angry they would be with her. She'd accelerated the agenda on her own, and she'd have to answer to them.

Marian walked over to Harris, stood outside of his armspan and looked down at him until she was sure, without any doubt, that he was watching her and was aware. She ripped open her silk blouse and tore the wire from between her breasts. It came away from the recording device. She winced as the battery pack pulled at the skin of her thighs. She heard the buttons from her blouse rolling across the floor. She held the wire out toward him.

"You confessed, you son of a bitch." She pointed the gun at his head.

"Marian—" his voice was an urgent whisper. "Marian, don't, I love you!"

She stood there, pointing the pistol at his head, knowing that she wouldn't have to pull the trigger. She could see that Harris was dying.

Marian walked over to the telephone table and kicked it over, then tore at her blouse even harder, ripped it from the neckline down. She dropped the wire next to his outstretched hand. His fingers opened and closed, as if trying to reach for her, trying to squeeze her to death.

She watched him writhe for only a second, seeing a six-foot rattlesnake instead of a man she had loved.

She took a breath, let it out slow, did it again. She felt herself being held; the gun lifted from her fingers.

"It's all right, you're okay." That wasn't Paul's voice.

She turned her head and recognized Jake. The room was swarming with cops. She heard someone say, "He's gone."

"He pulled the gun, grabbed me, tore the wire . . . "

"Just relax, Ms. Hannerty, you can tell us all about it later."

His voice was flat. She would say this once, then, with luck, not have to speak of it again.

"I somehow got the gun away from him, I shouted for him to stop . . . " she sobbed. "He kept on coming, I didn't have any choice."

She could hear other cops making encouraging noises behind her, heard voices saying not to worry about a thing, this jagoff had it coming, no problem. There seemed to be a lot of people in the room. More than had been upstairs at Police Headquarters, when they'd put the plan together.

"Why?" Phillips whispered the word, with a curious expression on his face.

He'd figured it out. She was only supposed to stall Harris, try and get him to confess. No matter where he'd take her, they'd said, they'd be right there, in position anywhere with ten minutes, they'd told her. She was supposed to hold him off that long, and she hadn't, and Jake Phillips wanted to know why. Wanted to know why she'd killed Paul Harris.

This Phillips, he was no dummy. A Tony Tulio in training. Would he understand? Should she tell him? No, she didn't trust him. He couldn't be expected to understand.

One of Tulio's lines ran through her mind, what he'd said to her just last night, in an Interrogation Room at police headquarters: "What is he, psychotic? They never worry about shit except themselves."

Tony hadn't lived long enough to find out how right he'd been.

Tony would have understand what she'd done, but this man was no Tony.

Still, he *had* whispered the question.

She shook her head at Jake, as if she didn't understand his question. Then, for some reason, maybe wanting to explain, or maybe even to show off, she whispered one of Tulio's favorite lines.

"Sometimes you have to do bad things in order to get a good thing done."